"Admit it, you like me just a little."

Inwardly Katrina gasped. She couldn't believe she'd just said that. But what really shook her was how much Boyd's answer meant to her. *Maybe blurting that out wasn't such a bad thing,* she reasoned. *He'll say no, and that will put an end to this attraction I keep experiencing.*

"If I liked you just a little, this would be easy," Boyd said curtly.

She smiled at the implication in his words. "You like me a lot."

"It's only lust, and I don't plan to give in to it."

She liked the idea that he was lusting after her....

Dear Reader,

You'll be glad the kids are going back to school, leaving you time to read every one of this month's fabulous Silhouette Intimate Moments novels. And you'll want to start with *One Moment Past Midnight,* by multiaward-winning Emilie Richards. You'll be on the edge of your seat as Hannah Blackstone and her gorgeous neighbor, Quinn McDermott, go in search of Hannah's kidnapped daughter.

Elizabeth August makes a welcome return with *Logan's Bride,* a cop-meets-cop romance to make your heart beat just a little faster. With *The Marriage Protection Program,* Margaret Watson completes her CAMERON, UTAH miniseries, and a memorable finale it is. Historical author Lyn Stone has written her first contemporary romance, *Beauty and the Badge,* and you'll be glad to know she intends to keep setting stories in the present day. *Remembering Jake* is a twisty story of secrets and hidden identities from talented Cheryl Biggs. And finally, welcome Bonnie K. Winn, with *The Hijacked Wife,* a FAMILIES ARE FOREVER title.

And once you've finished these terrific novels, mark October on your calendar, because next month Rachel Lee is back, with the next installment of her top-selling CONARD COUNTY miniseries.

Enjoy!

Leslie Wainger
Executive Senior Editor

Please address questions and book requests to:
Silhouette Reader Service
U.S.: 3010 Walden Ave., P.O. Box 1325, Buffalo, NY 14269
Canadian: P.O. Box 609, Fort Erie, Ont. L2A 5X3

LOGAN'S BRIDE

ELIZABETH AUGUST

Silhouette®
INTIMATE™MOMENTS®
Published by Silhouette Books
America's Publisher of Contemporary Romance

SILHOUETTE BOOKS

ISBN 0-373-07950-8

LOGAN'S BRIDE

Visit us at www.romance.net

Printed in U.S.A.

ELIZABETH AUGUST

lives in western North Carolina with her husband and three sons.

Elizabeth does counted cross-stitching to keep from eating at night. It doesn't always work. "I love to bowl, but I'm not very good. I keep my team's handicap high. I like hiking in the Shenandoahs, as long as we start up the mountain so the return trip is down rather than vice versa." She loves to go to Cape Hatteras to watch the sun rise over the ocean. Elizabeth August has also published under the pseudonym Betsy Page.

Chapter 1

"**L**ooks like we've got a new face." FBI Agent Boyd Logan began snapping pictures of the woman who'd driven up to the tall wrought iron gates barring the entrance to the Garduchi compound. Using a powerful zoom lens, he could see her fairly clearly from his vantage point on the wooded hillside across from the entrance to the estate, as she gave her name to the guard and waited to be admitted. He got the impression the guard, Joey Green, knew her and found her presence there amusing. She didn't look amused.

"What's she look like?" Lewis Hamond, Boyd's partner, asked.

"Late twenties. Brown hair. Short. Can't tell the color of the eyes from here. Pretty. Not a knockout. But pretty. Looks confident."

"You think Garduchi's bringing her in to take out Leona Serrenito?"

"Could be." He focused on the license plate. "She's

driving a local vehicle. Run the number.'' He recited the digits while Lewis jotted them down.

The gates opened and the car pulled through. The FBI had a long running file on Garduchi. They knew he was head of organized crime in St. Louis and involved in all the dark avenues of illegal trade—prostitution, drugs, numbers, loan-sharking, protection—but they'd never been able to come up with the evidence to put him behind bars.

Then two days ago word had hit the streets that a woman by the name of Leona Serrenito had been caught skimming and a contract had been put out on her life. Until that news had surfaced, the FBI had been keeping a file on a man by the name of Norbert Snider, figuring he was Garduchi's chief accountant. But all along Snider had been merely a red herring. Leona had been Garduchi's chief bookkeeper. For the umpteenth time Boyd cursed the lack of knowledge they had about the woman. She'd been considered so unimportant that until she disappeared they didn't even have a folder on her.

Now the race was on to see who found her first...the authorities or Garduchi. Boyd and his fellow agents were hoping she'd contact the FBI and ask for protection in exchange for information, but so far, she remained in hiding.

"The license plate belongs to Katrina Polenari.'' Lewis said, cutting into Boyd's thought. "Twenty-eight years old. Brown eyes in case you're interested. Five feet, six inches. Single. Address in one of the older municipalities in north county just outside the St. Louis city limits.'' Lewis punched in the name for more information, then gave a low whistle. "Interesting.''

"What?'' Boyd asked, his curiosity piqued.

"She's a cop.''

"A cop?''

"Five years on the St. Louis police force."

"Think she's on his payroll?" Boyd scowled. "Call her captain and find out if they've got a lead on Serrenito. Maybe she's here to collect the reward."

Lewis placed the call. "They've got nothing," he reported.

Boyd continued to look curiously toward the gate. "I wonder what our lady cop is up to."

Katrina had seen the car that had been behind her since she'd left her home. As she waited to be admitted through the gate, a flicker of a wave from the driver to the guard confirmed what she already suspected. Garduchi had had a tail on her.

Inside the Garduchi compound, she followed the tree-lined drive past two stylish homes. Those, she knew, housed Vince Garduchi's daughters and their families. Ahead, she saw the main house. It was Italian in design, resembling the estate homes of the wealthy in the old country.

Vince Garduchi, himself, came out to greet her. He was sixty-seven but looked ten years younger. His once playboy handsome face had grown distinguished with age. She noted that he continued to look fit. And he was as charming as ever. *Like a cobra just before it strikes.*

"It's been a long time, Katrina." Garduchi extended his hand.

Not long enough to suit me. She forced a smile. "A long time," she confirmed.

"How do you like my home?" He waved toward the palatial structure surrounded by gardens with fountains in their centers.

Her forced smile felt plastic. "It's nice." *If you like things built with blood money,* she added silently.

"It's a taste of the old country." He took her arm and led her inside. "A person should never forget his or her roots."

She was well aware this was an admonishment aimed at her. She wanted to tell him what he could do with her roots, but bit back the sarcastic response. She was here on a mission of mercy and making him angry would serve no purpose.

He noted her silence with a frown and she could tell that he knew what she was thinking. He shrugged as if to say he'd tried to talk sense to her and if she refused to listen then her fate was in her hands.

Releasing her arm, he motioned for a maid standing nearby to approach. "Considering your rebellious nature, I'm sure your father, were he still alive, would forgive me. I must ask that you be subjected to a search for listening or recording devices."

"Yes, of course," she replied, her tone letting him know that she'd expected this.

The maid led her to a small room off the hall. The search was respectful but thorough. When it was over the woman escorted Katrina to the living room where Garduchi was waiting.

He motioned for her to be seated. "Can I offer you some refreshment?"

"No, thank you." She fought to hide her nervousness. On the drive here, she'd reasoned that he wouldn't dare take a policeperson hostage even as bait. But now, inside his fortress, she wasn't so certain.

"To what do I owe this honor?" he asked, his charming smile once again in place.

"I've come about my aunt."

"Ah, yes. Leona." Garduchi shook his head slowly, his expression one of sadness. "She has disappointed me greatly. I trusted her like a sister." He studied Katrina suspiciously. "I was under the impression that you had severed all ties with her years ago."

"She has asked for my help. I didn't feel I could turn my back on her."

Garduchi nodded his understanding. "Go on."

"She called me last night and asked me to speak to you for her. She told me that after she lost her husband, she had a religious experience. An angel came to her and told her that she must do good deeds for the sake of his soul. That was when she began skimming money. Everything she took, she gave to charity or people in need."

"And you believe her?"

"Yes." She'd practiced this response in the mirror until it came out with innocent honesty. It had taken a lot of practice. Although her aunt had sounded sincere, Katrina was having a hard time picturing Leona as the pious, giving type.

Garduchi smiled. "Of course you do or you wouldn't be so foolish as to involve yourself in this matter. However, Leona should not have brought you into this." There was an underlying threat in his voice, letting Katrina know that he wanted her to get uninvolved. "I will assume that your aunt will contact you again. If she does, you tell her that I understand how her loss could have affected her judgment and that if she will come see me, I'm sure we can work something out."

Katrina was watching his eyes. There was an iciness in their depths that chilled her to the bone. "If anything happens to my aunt, I'll spend the rest of my life trying to put you behind bars."

"I had assumed that was why you joined the police in the first place." He raised an arm and motioned to someone.

Katrina looked over her shoulder to see Dominic Ruzito coming toward them. He was married to Garduchi's eldest daughter and functioned as Garduchi's right-hand man. It was generally accepted that he was being trained to take over when the old man died.

"Please see that Miss Polenari has safe passage to the gate," Garduchi instructed.

The implication that after that, she was on her own was not lost on Katrina. As she rose, he rose also.

"You will pass my message on to your aunt?" he said.

"I'll pass it on," she replied. She'd also warn her aunt to stay away from Vince Garduchi.

Retracing her route to the gate, she breathed a sigh of relief as she left the compound. A part of her had been afraid Garduchi might suddenly change his mind about letting her leave and try to use her to get to her aunt. Mentally she chided herself. He was smarter than that. He'd put a tail on her and wait for her to lead him to Leona. Well, she had no intention of doing that.

Back at her house, she checked her phones for bugs. She was certain Garduchi had been surprised that she had gone to see him on behalf of her aunt...he'd had a tail put on her as a precaution, but he hadn't really expected Leona to contact her. Still, she didn't want to take any chances. She found no bugs. For the next couple of hours, while she waited for her aunt to call, she kept a constant eye on the pole at the corner of her backyard for any activity that would suggest Garduchi had sent someone to tap into her line. She'd told Leona she was on the evening shift and Leona had promised to call before Katrina had to leave for work. When the phone finally rang, her nerves were so taut, it startled her.

"Is it safe to talk?" Leona asked before Katrina could even say hello.

"Yes," Katrina replied.

"It won't be by the time you get back from work," Leona cautioned.

"I know."

"What did Vince say?"

"He said that he wanted you to come talk to him and together, you'd work things out. But if I were you I wouldn't consider doing that. I was watching his eyes. They were unforgiving."

Leona sighed. "I know exactly what he'd say to me. He'd tell me that if he let his employees start spending his money in any way they saw fit, he'd lose control and once he lost control, his business would fall apart. Then he'd smile real sweet and tell Dominic to have Louey and Victor drive me home, but I'd never get there."

"That's the way I see it." Time to make her plea. "I did what I could. Now the only way for you to be safe is to go to the authorities and help put Garduchi behind bars."

"I would if you could guarantee my safety, but you can't. I'm safer on my own."

"The word on the street is that he's put a price on your head…a hundred thousand dollars. And he can have your picture Faxed to any city in the world in minutes."

"I hate modern technology," Leona grumbled. "All right. I'll give you two days to make arrangements, then I'll contact you again."

"You won't be able to by phone."

"I'll find a way. I hope you haven't blocked out all memories of the old days."

"Some remain very vivid," Katrina assured her.

"Remember the good times you and I had," Leona said, her voice holding a command. Then a click sounded on the other end of the line.

Katrina was congratulating herself on getting her aunt to come in when the phone rang again.

It was Leona. "There is one stipulation. You have to be one of my guardian angels and I refuse to have more than two of you. The bigger the crowd, the easier for Vince to spot us." Again, before Katrina could respond the line went dead.

Katrina frowned at the receiver in her hand. She knew Garduchi would have men following her every move. The smart thing to do would be for her to stay in town and lead them on a wild-goose chase. But she could tell from her aunt's voice that Leona's mind was set. "So when the time comes, I'll just have to get rid of my tail."

Boyd Logan had tailed Katrina Polenari from Garduchi's place. When it became evident she was heading home, he passed her street, then circled back. She lived in a quiet neighborhood of eclectic older homes. Hers, a single story, white frame, was among the smallest and was dwarfed by the huge two-story sprawling edifices on either side of it. Still she kept her home well maintained. Even the flower garden was weeded. Guessing that any strange car on the block would be noticed, he parked near the corner about three houses from hers and popped the hood. Pretending to be engrossed in the workings of his engine, he kept an eye on the street.

A car passed him with two men inside. He recognized the passenger as Dominic Ruzito. It rounded the corner at the far end of the street and parked near another car that had been following Officer Polenari since she left the Garduchi compound. The driver of the first car had quickly exited his vehicle to speak to Dominic. Boyd was too far away to see his face but his deferential manner suggested he was one of Garduchi's men. He kept nodding as if accepting orders. Then he returned to his car and drove off, leaving Dominic and his driver where they had a clear view of Katrina Polenari's house.

He loosened a wire and tried his engine. Pleased with the disabled sound it made, he retightened the wire, then continued to pretend to try to fix the engine. He was wondering just how long this charade would have to go on when movement at the house caught his attention.

Katrina had changed into her uniform and was heading toward her car. Suddenly two men came around the house from the far side. Each grabbed one of her arms. She let out a scream for help, then started kicking like a mule.

Boyd drew his gun on the run. "Let her go," he ordered.

Both men pulled out guns of their own. One aimed at him and the other turned his gun to Katrina's head.

"You drop your gun and no one gets hurt," the skinnier of the two men instructed.

"I don't think dropping my weapon would be such a good idea," Boyd returned in an easy drawl, assuming these men wouldn't want to leave any witnesses.

"We got here first. She's ours," the skinnier man growled.

A car had pulled up in front of the house. "Hurry up and get in. One of the neighbors is sure to have called the police," the driver yelled.

"Just shoot him and get it over with," the bigger of the two men holding on to Katrina told his partner.

Katrina had stopped struggling and was sizing up the situation. She recognized the two men holding her and the driver of the car as local hoods…minor fish. The driver was Frank Granelo, the smaller one holding her was Pauly something and the bigger one was Bruno Valpreo. But the black-haired man in the faded jeans, oversized T-shirt, cowboy boots and western drawl who was trying to take her away from them was a stranger. She looked into the stranger's eyes. Her father used to say you could tell if a man was bluffing by his eyes. The stranger's were the darkest she'd ever seen, nearly black. And there was no fear there, only cold purpose in those dark depths. She stiffened for action. He definitely wasn't bluffing. If he shot Pauly, Bruno was sure to turn his gun on the stranger and give her a chance to break free. While the two of them decided who would be left standing, she'd get behind her car and draw her own gun. No one was going to take her captive!

"I'll drop you before I go down," Boyd warned.

"Now, now, boys," a new voice entered the fray. "Vince won't take kindly to you spilling blood in this nice quiet neighborhood."

The bigger of the abductors looked over his shoulder. The car in which Dominic Ruzito had been sitting had pulled up in front of Katrina's house, and Dominic had gotten out.

"Dominic." The edge of fear in Bruno's voice was quickly replaced by belligerence. "No one's going to get shot. We just wanted to have a private chat with Katrina. Find out if she knows where her aunt is."

Quickly getting over the shock that his lady cop was Leona Serrenito's niece, Boyd noticed that Dominic had drawn no gun. But then no one would be stupid enough to take out Vince Garduchi's son-in-law.

"Vince has already spoken to her. She knows nothing. As everyone already knows, she severed her ties with her aunt a long time ago," Dominic said with calm assurance.

He's a good liar, Katrina thought.

"She's on the outside and a cop to boot," Dominic continued, his tone taking on a warning quality. "Harming her could cause some unpleasantness. Vince says I should pass the word that he'll take it real personal if even one hair on her head is mussed."

Catching movement out of the corner of his eye, Boyd saw Dominic's driver taking a position that gave him an easy shot at any of them. He was armed with a machine gun.

The skinny man released his hold on Katrina and pocketed his gun before turning to face Dominic. "We didn't know she was under Vince's protection. We were just trying to find Leona."

The larger man also released his hold on Katrina and put away his gun.

She stepped away, rubbing her arms and glaring at her would-be captors.

"I think it would be smart if you two left before the police arrive," Vince said. "And pass the word along about Katrina."

"Sure, Dominic," both men replied in unison, then hurried to their waiting car.

Uncertain of what would happen next, Boyd had changed his aim to Dominic's driver.

Dominic waved his driver away. The man slipped the machine gun back into its holster under his suit coat and climbed back in the car.

Boyd holstered his gun.

The sound of sirens filled the air.

"You owe Vince," Dominic said to Katrina, then quickly returned to his car. The moment he was inside, the driver took off.

Not wanting to identify himself, Boyd returned to his car, slammed down the hood, climbed inside and slid low into the seat before the two police cars rounded the corner. They passed him and came to a screeching halt in front of Katrina's house.

"It was just some goons looking for my aunt," he heard her telling them. "Everything's okay."

Sitting up as the police cars left, Boyd frowned at the thin manila envelope on the seat beside him with its photocopies of everything the local FBI office knew about Leona. The information inside stated that she had no close living relatives. But then according to Dominic Ruzito, Katrina Polenari had totally severed her ties with her aunt a long time ago. Boyd smirked. He wasn't buying into Dominic's claim that his father-in-law wasn't interested in Katrina other than to insure her protection. He was sure Garduchi was hoping Leona would contact her and lead him to her. And the old man didn't want any interference.

Boyd saw Katrina looking his way and noted that her hand was on the butt of her gun. Apparently she, like her two would-be-abductors, thought he was another goon hoping to cash in on the reward. Her gaze never leaving him, she rounded her car and climbed in. He waited until she'd pulled out of her driveway and started down the street, then followed. He didn't make any effort to pretend he wasn't tailing her.

Katrina scowled at her rearview mirror. The tall, black-haired man didn't seem to care if she knew he was following her. Recalling his eyes, a chill ran through her.

She smiled to herself as she turned into the police parking lot, sure even he wouldn't have the nerve to follow her into here.

Chapter 2

Boyd pulled into one of the visitor's spots in front of the station house. He would follow protocol, playing it straight until he knew the game. Inside, he headed toward the captain's office.

The captain's secretary eyed him suspiciously when he approached her desk. When he identified himself as an FBI agent and requested to see the captain, she continued to regard him skeptically. "I thought you guys always dressed in suits," she said, taking a close look at his badge.

"I've been doing some undercover work," he explained in an easy drawl.

She punched the button on her intercom. "Captain, there's a man here who says he's from the FBI," she said, her tone indicating she still wasn't convinced.

"Send him in," came the barked response.

"Martin Drake." The captain introduced himself, standing and leaning over his desk to shake Boyd's hand.

"Boyd Logan." Boyd said, accepting the handshake.

"You got some identification?"

Boyd produced his badge.

"Thought you guys always wore suits," Drake said, handing back the badge.

"Figured this was more appropriate for the work I've been doing." Boyd eased himself into a chair.

Drake grinned. "Staked out in the woods across from Garduchi's estate?"

Boyd nodded.

"You might as well park right in front and be comfortable. You've got to know he expects you to be there. If you want my opinion, it's a waste of your time. He'd never have Leona Serrenito brought there."

Drake's amused attitude was getting on Boyd's nerves but he didn't let it show. "We're keeping track of who comes and goes. Thought it might give us a lead." Boyd paused then added, "Saw one of your officers go into the compound today."

Drake's grin disappeared. "That what prompted that call I got earlier?"

"Yeah. That was my partner, Lewis Hamond."

"Which of my officers did you see?"

"Katrina Polenari."

Drake's jaw hardened. "She told me she didn't know anything about her aunt's whereabouts and if she did learn anything, she'd bring her in for safe keeping." Suspicion entered his voice. "Don't know why she'd be visiting Garduchi."

"You knew she was Leona Serrenito's niece?"

Drake gave him a dry look. "Of course. But she claims she broke ties with the family over ten years ago...the day following her father and brother's funerals. And, just yesterday she swore she hadn't spoken to her aunt since then."

"So what was she doing at Garduchi's estate?"

"Guess we ought to ask her." Drake punched his intercom and ordered his secretary to have Officer Polenari report to him as soon as the evening roll call and briefing was over.

As he and Drake settled in to wait, Boyd noticed that Drake remained tense. Clearly, he didn't like this turn of events.

Coming out of the evening briefing, Katrina was met by Drake's secretary, Rebecca Brown. "The captain wants to see you," the woman informed her. As they started down the hall together, Rebecca lowered her voice and added, "There's an FBI agent in his office. Guess they think you might know where your aunt is."

"Who doesn't?" Katrina muttered, recalling the grilling Drake had put her through the day they'd learned of Leona's disappearance and his daily questioning since then.

Entering Drake's office, she froze. The dark-eyed stranger was there.

Boyd rose, closed the door, then extended his hand. "I'm Boyd Logan."

"He's FBI," Drake said.

His eyes were actually dark brown, not black, Katrina noted. Her gaze traveled to the overly large black T-shirt she knew was covering a holstered pistol, then on to his faded jeans and western-cut boots. Identifications could be forged. She wasn't ready to believe this man was a good guy. "I thought you Feds always wore suits and ties."

Realizing she wasn't going to shake his hand, Boyd lowered it. "I've been doing some undercover work. A suit would have stuck out like a sore thumb."

Katrina continued to regard him suspiciously. "How do we know you're who you say you are?"

"Call Washington," he replied.

"Officer Polenari, you're overstepping your bounds," Drake warned.

Katrina squared her shoulders. "There's a very large reward out for my aunt, big enough to make someone consider impersonating an FBI agent."

For a long moment, they all stood silent.

"You could be right," Drake finally said. He punched his intercom. "Rebecca, get me whoever's in charge of the Garduchi task force at the FBI in Washington," Drake ordered.

"Gerald Eldridge." Boyd supplied the name.

"Get me Gerald Eldridge," Drake amended.

Settling back into his chair, Boyd noted that although Drake also seated himself, Officer Polenari remained standing. She did shift her position a little so that she'd have a cleaner shot at him in case he wasn't who he said he was. A distrusting soul, he mused. Well, he wasn't one to trust anyone on face value either. And he didn't trust her. Garduchi was protecting her. That could be because he wanted her to lead him to her aunt or it could be because she was too valuable an ally to lose.

His gaze traveled over her. Up close, her face had a sensual quality. It was the blend of her features but mostly it was her dark brown eyes and full lips. Nice figure, too. But then some of nature's most alluring creatures were her most deadly.

Katrina was acutely aware of his examination. She saw the spark of masculine interest in his eyes, then the quick return of cool indifference.

The buzz of Drake's intercom broke the heavy silence in the room. "The man you wanted to speak to is out, but I have his secretary on the line."

"Ask her if she knows Boyd Logan," Drake instructed.

"She says she does," Rebecca replied a few seconds later.

"Then I'll talk to her." Drake picked up the phone and identified himself. "I've got a man here claiming to be your Agent Logan. Can you describe him for me?" Drake listened for a minute, then looked to Katrina. "A Texan, half Apache, six foot one inch tall, thick black hair, luscious brown eyes, broad shoulders, a real hunk," he repeated the description, amusement in his voice at the secretary's choice of adjectives.

"I suppose that fits him," Katrina conceded. He did have broad shoulders, his face was handsome in a rugged sort of way and his Native American heritage was evident in his high cheekbones.

"She says that if we want further proof, he has a scar from a bullet wound on his chest and one from a knife on his back. She says my secretary or any lady cop on the force might enjoy making that inspection." Drake nodded at Boyd. "Let's have a look."

Katrina couldn't deny a feminine appreciation of the hard, well-defined muscles and flat abdomen as Boyd stood and raised his T-shirt to expose his chest. The scar was there too. When he turned to show the one on his back, she felt a heat building. Well, she was only human, and he was a nice specimen.

Drake nodded his satisfaction.

"It appears you know your boss's secretary very well," Katrina commented while Drake thanked the woman on the phone and hung up.

"The wounds are on my record," he returned with casual nonchalance.

She continued to regard him dryly. Either he and the secretary hadn't had a fling or he considered women nothing more than notches on his belt. That she wondered how many notches he had, irritated her. She didn't have time for that kind of speculation. Right now, all of her thoughts needed to be focused on keeping her aunt alive and bringing her in so that they could put Garduchi behind bars where he belonged.

"Well, now that you're satisfied I am who I claim I am," Boyd said, continuing to stand, his gaze hard on Katrina, "how about telling me why you paid Garduchi a visit this morning?"

Katrina looked to her superior and saw the suspicion in his eyes. It hurt. Even though her father's family had been a part of the Garduchi organization for generations, she thought she'd proved herself to Captain Drake. "My aunt contacted me this morning and asked me to help her."

"You should have called me immediately," Drake growled.

"Calling you wouldn't have helped, I owe Leona. After my mother died, she practically raised me."

"Did she ask you to go see Garduchi or was that your idea?" Boyd asked, wondering just how strong her family ties were.

"She asked me to speak to him for her. She said she'd had a religious conversion after her husband died and had been donating all of the skimmed money to the church and other charities. She wanted me to tell Garduchi that and ask him to forgive her."

"And did he?" Drake demanded, his displeasure with her actions clearly evident.

"No." She faced him defiantly. "I knew he wouldn't. I just needed to be able to swear to my aunt that that was the case. When she called back this afternoon, I convinced her that she should turn herself in to the authorities and let them protect her."

"That'd be me," Boyd said. "We want to get Garduchi

under federal indictment. And we can provide better protection for your aunt than any local police organization.'' He glanced at Drake. ''No offense.''

Drake reluctantly nodded his agreement. ''I'd like to be the one to bring her in and bring Garduchi down but, as much as I hate admitting it, I couldn't guarantee her safety. With that price on her head, we'd have shooters trying to break into our jail.''

From his less-than-hospitable manner toward her, Katrina guessed Agent Logan wasn't going to like what she had to say next. She wasn't interested in spending more time in his company either, but she didn't have a choice. ''There is one small catch. She won't come in unless I'm assigned to help guard her.''

''Consider yourself on loan to the FBI,'' Drake said without hesitation.

The suspicion she'd seen in his eyes coupled with the fact that he was so clearly glad to be getting rid of her cut deep. Katrina's chin stiffened with pride. ''Yes, sir,'' she replied briskly.

Boyd watched the exchange with interest. Her visit to Garduchi had shaken any faith Drake had in her. If she was straight, he felt sorry for her. If she wasn't, he didn't want her pawned off on him. ''Officer Polenari is known by Garduchi's associates to be a relative of Leona Serrenito. And since Garduchi knows she's been contacted, he's sure to keep a close watch on her. In fact, he's had a tail on her all day. I think it would be best if she stayed as far away from her aunt as possible.''

They were making her feel like unwanted garbage. ''I would agree with you,'' she said tersely, ''but my aunt won't come in unless I'm there.''

''From what I've heard, Mrs. Serrenito is a stubborn,

hardheaded woman," Drake confirmed. "My guess is that she's not going to come in unless you play by her rules."

Boyd realized he had no choice. "All right. Officer Polenari is in, but we'll have to be certain to get rid of any tails before we meet with her aunt."

She gave him a haughty glance. "I'd already figured that part out." Her expression once again businesslike, she added, "And one other thing. She refuses to have more than two of us guarding her." Having delivered all of her aunt's instructions, she turned her attention to her captain. "She's not going to contact me for a couple of days. Since I have to stick around, I think I should go on with my regular duties as if nothing is happening."

"She's right," Boyd said, then had second thoughts about sending her out into the streets. She could be nabbed by some thug who hadn't heard that she was under Garduchi's protection. The strength of the sharp wave of protectiveness he experienced, irritated him. He told himself that his concern was because she was his only lead to Leona. Aloud, he said, "However, it would probably be best if you found some paperwork for her that would keep her off the streets."

Drake nodded his agreement, then turned his attention back to Katrina. "Contact me the minute you hear from your aunt."

"I'll call in sick."

"Good. And for today you can help Shroder in the squad room with the paperwork on the Clemming's case," he said with dismissal.

Katrina had been sharply aware of his wariness. Performing a snappy salute, she turned and exited. Her stomach was in a knot. She was tired of having to prove herself. Putting her life on the line for five years should have been enough.

Wanting to keep his connection with officer Polenari as inconspicuous as possible for the moment, Boyd remained behind in Drake's office watching her through the windowed door. "You don't trust Officer Polenari?" he asked.

"I want to. She's been more scrutinized than any of my other people and as far as I can tell, she's squeaky clean. But all of her father's family was tied to Garduchi."

"I didn't see the name Polenari on my list of known associates."

"She and Leona are the last of the line. Her father and brother were taken out in a territorial war when she was seventeen."

"What about her mother's family?"

"They were never part of Garduchi's organization. They live out in California but, as far as I know, she doesn't have any contact with them."

"You ever ask her why she joined the force?" Boyd asked.

"She said she wanted to help right the wrongs her family had inflicted and in the process, maybe find evidence that would put Garduchi behind bars. She seemed sincere. She actually asked to be assigned to this precinct. It's one of the toughest in the city and she spends a lot of time talking to the kids, trying to keep them off drugs or getting them to go into rehab if they're already hooked."

Boyd was aware of the continuing underlying uncertainty in Drake's voice. "But you're still not certain where her loyalty lies."

"If she is a plant by Garduchi, she'd have to play her role perfectly or we'd know."

"So, if you don't trust her, why not get rid of her? Or, better still, why'd you hire her in the first place?"

"Didn't have a choice. She didn't have a record or anything that would prevent her from applying. Her scores on all tests and field maneuvers gave her a top ranking and we needed women recruits. If I'd turned her down, she could have sued for sex discrimination.''

Boyd didn't like what he was hearing. If Officer Polenari was working for Garduchi, then there were two possibilities. Either she was bringing her aunt in to set her up to be murdered or she had chosen to side with her aunt in which case Garduchi would be after both of them. Either way, anyone in their company could be caught in the cross fire. ''I'd like a copy of her personnel file.''

''Figured you would.'' Drake buzzed his secretary and requested Katrina's file.

While they were waiting, Boyd gave Drake his cellular phone number. ''For now, I'm going to stay in the background. I'll let her contact you when she hears from her aunt, then you contact me. Because my cell phone isn't a secure line, ask me out to dinner like we're old friends. That will be my signal to contact with officer Polinari.

''You're not going to tap her phone and try to trace Leona's call when it comes in?'' Drake asked.

''No. I figure Garduchi will already have her place wired by now and I don't want him to know we know she's been contacted. I want him to think she's keeping her aunt's call in the family, so to speak.''

''Good idea.''

Entering with the file, Rebecca eyed Boyd with open curiosity.

''Have you told anybody about the FBI visiting me?'' Drake asked as he accepted the file.

''Just Katrina,'' she replied, her gaze shifted to the file. ''You think she's involved somehow?''

''She's Leona's niece. She might be contacted.''

Good. Drake was playing this one close to the belt, Boyd

noted. The fewer people who knew what was going on, the better.

"I don't want you to say anything about the FBI being here or about them talking to Katrina or taking a look at her file," Drake ordered. "You got that?"

"I wouldn't have been your secretary for ten years if I couldn't keep my mouth shut," she snapped back, clearly upset about being accused of possibly gossiping.

Boyd also noted that the secretary didn't say anything in support of Katrina. In fact, there had been an edge in her voice that suggested she thought the lady cop could be right in the middle of whatever was going on.

And she'd be right. He just wished he knew which side Officer Polenari was really on. Thanking Drake for his help, he headed back to the hillside.

Lewis had seniority but Boyd wanted this assignment. He'd always thought of Lewis as being somewhat naive where women were concerned, and that could prove dangerous in this situation. By the time he joined his partner, he'd planned out his argument for being the one to pick up Leona.

"They've already verified my identity," he said when he finished filling Lewis in on the details. "Besides, as senior officer, you should be here to coordinate the teams keeping an eye on Garduchi."

Lewis grinned. "She even prettier up close?"

Boyd scowled. "Pretty as a copperhead basking in the sun."

Approval showed on Lewis's face. "Ever the cynic. Good. That'll keep you alive." His expression darkened. "But I don't like the idea of you going alone."

"That's one of Leona's stipulations. We don't want her to balk."

"All right," Lewis agreed grudgingly. "But watch your back."

"I always do."

Lewis still didn't look happy. "I'm counting on your mother's Apache blood to give you an edge."

"I'll be fine," Boyd assured him.

Chapter 3

Although Boyd's original plan was to stay away from Officer Polenari until contact with her aunt was made, the more he thought about this, the less he liked it. Not only was there the possibility that Garduchi's protection wasn't enough to keep money-hungry bounty hunters away from her or that outside talent might not even get the word that Garduchi didn't want her touched, but Garduchi might decide that he should keep her by his side.

Or, Katrina Polenari could have a plan of her own. When she discovered he was on to her, she could have made up the story about her aunt wanting to come in. She could be planning to disappear just like her aunt and join up with Leona so the two of them could enjoy the money Leona had skimmed from Garduchi.

Or, maybe inside she was cold as ice like her father and brother had been and was planning to turn Leona over to Garduchi for the reward.

Or, there was even the possibility that Drake could be bought. A hundred thousand was a lot of dough.

Deciding that there were too many ways this situation could play out to allow Ms. Polenari to be out from under his watchful eye, Boyd cruised Katrina's neighborhood. Garduchi had men watching both her front and back doors. He parked out of their view and waited for her to return home. Her shift ended at midnight. That was five minutes ago.

He frowned at the small white frame house in which she lived. After making arrangements for getting Leona to a safe house, he'd spent some time checking up on Katrina's family. The Polenaris' ties to Garduchi ran deep. Beginning with her grandfather, they had been trusted enforcers. Boyd had also read through Katrina's file. She'd received several commendations. But it was the personal information that interested him. It appeared to verify her aloneness in the world. She'd listed only her parish priest to be contacted in case of injury or death.

A little after twelve-thirty Katrina pulled into her driveway. Boyd waited until she'd been inside a few minutes, then drove around and parked in front of her house. In an attempt not to be recognized by Garduchi's men as the T-shirt-wearing stranger who had tailed her for a short time earlier in the day, he'd switched cars and changed into a button-down shirt and slacks with a sports coat hiding his shoulder holster. Carrying a large bouquet of flowers in a way that hid his face, he mounted the steps and rang the bell.

Katrina had just taken off her utility belt and laid it across the back of the couch. Wondering who would be calling at this time of night, she extracted her gun and approached the door. Looking through the peephole, she frowned. It was the FBI agent. She laid the gun on a nearby table and opened the door.

"Pretend I'm your boyfriend," he said leaning low enough that with the flowers between them and the on-lookers, he appeared to be kissing her.

His nearness caused her blood to race. Unused to having so strong a reaction to a man, she stepped back quickly. Well, like the secretary said, he was a hunk...a very mas-culine hunk.

Turning his back to the onlookers, Boyd extended the flowers in her direction causing her to step back further, allowing him to enter and close the door.

For one brief moment, Katrina was flattered by his gift, then she looked up and saw the ice in his eyes and knew they were merely part of his ruse. Her pleasure along with the attraction she'd experienced died a quick death.

"I know you're angry with me, sweetheart," he said, slipping her a note informing her that Garduchi's men were watching the house and had a clear view through her living room window. It also added that he suspected the house was bugged. "But I'm truly sorry about our little spat."

"You call it a 'little' spat?" she returned, playing along and having no trouble sounding irritated. Did he think she was an idiot? Of course Garduchi was watching her and she knew he'd probably bugged her house as well as her phone.

"I want to make it up to you." Boyd paced the room like a worried lover, this subterfuge giving him the oppor-tunity to check it out with the small bug detector in his hand. It indicated one device on a lamp, one on the back of a picture frame and one in the phone. Placing an arm around her waist, he began to guide her toward the back of the house, continuing to look for bugs as they went.

"You look tired. Why don't I give you a massage while we work out our differences?"

"I'm not sure if I want you back in my bedroom. We'll use the guest room. Since you refuse to learn any new tricks, at least the environment will be different," she said, insinuating their argument had been over his lack of adequate lovemaking. Inwardly, she smiled. He deserved the jab for underestimating her. In the next instant, her breath caught in her lungs. His hand had moved to her hip and tightened its grip. The imprint burned through the fabric of her slacks sparking a fire deep inside.

"I've decided that you're right. A little experimentation could be fun," he said, low and husky. She felt good beneath his touch and the desire to prove to her that he could satisfy a woman was strong. Letting lust and his male ego rule would be really stupid, he mocked himself. Still, he wondered if she would try to seduce him in an effort to gain his help in any plan she and her aunt may have cooked up. If she did, he'd be tempted to play along. But apparently that wasn't her kind of game, he mused regretfully, as they entered a room to their right and she immediately jerked free from his hold.

Katrina hated the way her legs felt shaky and the fire still flamed inside of her. She prided herself on her control but with no effort whatsoever, Boyd Logan had made her feel like a teenager in heat. Crossing to the window, she pulled down the shade, insuring their privacy, then switched on the lamp on the bedside table.

Boyd closed the door, then scanned the room. Like the hall, it was free from bugs.

"There's a phone in my bedroom and one in the kitchen. I've checked them. Like the one in the living room, they're bugged. I'd also spotted the bug on the lamp and the picture frame. So, I figure any room with a telephone will have at least one extra bug in case the bug they put in the phones didn't work,'' she said, letting him know she'd already thought through any moves Garduchi might make. She also made certain she had the bed between her and him. ''So now that we can talk, to what do I owe this late-night call?''

Choosing not to mention that his suspicious nature had caused him to wonder about her or Drake being on the level, he said, ''It occurred to me that Garduchi might decide that having you in his care would be better than letting you roam free or some of the bounty hunters might not get the word he doesn't want you touched. Then there's the possibility your aunt might need immediate assistance. Going through Drake to get to me would take time. So I've decided to be your constant companion. Now which side of the bed do you want?''

Katrina had been studying him closely. His expression had remained cool and distant, with no trace of friendliness. ''You don't trust me, do you?''

''Why should I? Your own captain doesn't trust you.''

Anger flashed in her eyes. ''I'm sick and tired of spending my life proving that I'm not following in my father's footsteps.''

''Your father's, your grandfather's, your brother's, your uncles', etc.,'' Boyd elaborated.

Katrina knew no amount of talk would convince him. ''Have it your way.'' She sank down in a chair. ''I want to take a shower before I go to sleep.'' She looked at her watch. ''How long do you want me to give you for your lovemaking. Five minutes enough?''

Boyd grinned wryly. ''I'd take at least an hour.''

She cast him a skeptical glance to insinuate she doubted that very much, propped her feet up on the trunk at the foot of the bed and made herself comfortable.

Boyd dropped his jacket on the trunk, kicked off his

shoes, switched off the lamp and stretched out on top of the bedspread. Katrina Polenari was not going to be easy to get along with. With any luck he'd be able to control himself and not shoot her before this was over. A sudden complication occurred to him. "Is there a real boyfriend who might show up on your doorstep?"

"No."

Now why didn't that surprise him? "I didn't think so but I wanted to be sure."

She heard the smugness in his voice suggesting that she was much too difficult a person for anyone to put up with and the hairs on the back of her neck bristled. "What about you? Is there a jealous girlfriend or a wife who might suddenly show up?"

"No."

"I didn't think so," she tossed back with the same smugness he'd used on her.

He'd set himself up for that one, Boyd admitted, and ordered himself to sleep with one ear open.

As her eyes grew accustomed to the dark, Katrina could vaguely see his long outline on the bed. The man was a bore, she told herself curtly. Still, she found herself wondering just what he would do with the hour he claimed he'd take with a woman. The remembered feel of his hand on her hip reawakened the fire inside. She jerked her gaze away. She'd never been the one-night-stand type and she most certainly wasn't going to break her code for the likes of Boyd Logan. Irritated with the path her mind had taken, she looked at her watch. Barely half an hour had passed. "He gets fifteen more minutes," she grumbled under her breath. "Not a second longer."

"I thought we'd agreed on an hour."

Startled that he was still awake, she frowned at the bed. "I thought you were asleep."

"I sleep lightly." The truth was he'd been aware of her scrutiny and couldn't help wondering what she was thinking. The hostile edge in her voice convinced him not to ask. "Now what about the hour we agreed on?"

"We're being watched by macho thugs. For them five minutes is probably the norm. Twenty minutes would make you their hero. I'm giving you forty-five. That'll put you in their record books."

He grinned. "What more can a man ask for?" Closing his eyes, he returned to his state of semislumber. When Katrina rose from the chair, he woke immediately. "I'll scan the rest of the hall and the bathroom."

Both were clear. Satisfied Garduchi wasn't a problem for the moment, he turned his attention to the window above the tub. He tried opening it. It stuck five inches up and there was a screen on the other side.

"I really doubt anyone would try to get to me through that," Katrina said, watching him with amusement.

"I wasn't worried about someone trying to get to you."

Her amusement vanished. "You think I might try to escape by way of that window? I'll admit, I find you a bore but if I want to leave, I'll do it by the front door."

"I'm merely making certain you don't use the sound of the running water to cover your leaving for a late-night rendezvous. You weren't expecting me to show up before I was summoned. Until I know what the game is, I intend to call all of the shots."

As the full impact of his words hit her, she stared at him dumbly, her anger so intense she couldn't speak. When she did find her voice, she said, "You think I might be setting up my own aunt for Garduchi."

"A hundred thousand is a lot of money."

Her temper raged out of control. She'd had about all of

this arrogant cowboy she could stand. She swung her hand to slap him.

Boyd caught her by the wrist before she could make contact. "So I'm a cynic. I've also considered the possibility that you and your aunt might be playing some game…using me to help get away from Garduchi. And, I've cut Drake out of the loop. Before I came over here, I dropped by and told him I was going to take over as your permanent bodyguard and you wouldn't be back until this business was over. Tomorrow morning you'll call in sick."

She jerked her wrist free as her irate glare turned to one of surprise. "You don't trust him either?"

"Like I said, a hundred thousand dollars is a lot of money."

Feeling the need to have the last word and also give him some warning, she said, "If you think you're going to be calling all the shots, you'd better think again. You haven't met Aunt Leona."

The sincerity in her voice gave him a jolt of uneasiness. It suggested that her aunt was even more difficult than she was. What kind of mess had he gotten himself into? Boyd wondered. Before she could head into the bathroom, he caught her by the arm and with a twist of his head, motioned for her to follow him into the living room.

Wondering what he was up to, she did. Once they were in range of the bugs, he said, "My apartment's being painted. Mind if I move in here with you for a couple of days?"

"I suppose I can't have you sleeping on the street," she replied.

"I'll get my bag while you take your shower." Lowering his voice to a whisper, he added in her ear, "Don't lock the bathroom door."

His breath heated the sensitive skin of her neck and embers sparked to life. Furious with herself for feeling any attraction toward him, she asked through clenched teeth, "Would you like for me to hum the whole time so you can be certain I'm in there?"

She looked kind of cute when she was angry, Boyd thought. Unable to stop himself from doing a little teasing, he said, "That's a good idea."

"Ridiculous!" she seethed under her breath and turned and stalked down the hall.

She was a handful, he thought and his palms itched to test how she would feel in them. In the next instant he was cursing himself. *You keep letting yourself think things like that and you could end up dead.*

As soon as she was in the bathroom, Boyd made a quick trip to his car and got his suitcase from the trunk. When he returned to the house, he opened the bathroom door just enough to peek inside and see her silhouette behind the curtain. Satisfied she was still there, he closed the door and leaning against the wall in the hall, he listened. The running water made even more noise than he'd expected. He glanced at his watch. He'd give her fifteen minutes more.

Ten minutes later, Katrina stepped out of the bathroom wrapped in a towel. Seeing him there, she was too infuriated to be embarrassed. "I can't believe you actually stood out here. Where was I going to go? You saw yourself that the window sticks."

"My father always warned me never to underestimate a determined woman."

Shaking her head at the depth of his cynicism, she entered her bedroom, pulled down the blinds, then switched on the light. Feeling a pricking on her neck she looked toward the door to see Boyd there. "I would like a little privacy."

He scowled and held up the scanner reminding her the

room could be bugged. "I won't see anything I haven't seen before," he said, continuing to play the part of the boyfriend.

Mentally Katrina kicked herself. Boyd Logan was such an irritant, he'd made her momentarily forget about Garduchi's surveillance.

Boyd schooled a husky apology into his voice as he closed the door, then wandered around the room searching for listening devices. "Look, I tried to satisfy you. I've never seen you so tense."

"I've got a lot on my mind right now. Go sleep in the guest room. I want some time alone," she returned with a curt demand.

He gave her a "forget that idea" look. "You don't really mean that." The scanner showed one bug on the back of a picture frame on the wall. Reaching her in one long stride, he leaned close and whispered in her ear. "If you want this room cleaned, stay angry with me and play along."

Staying angry with him would be easy, she mused and nodded her agreement.

He moved into a position near the picture with the bug. "Why don't you let me give you another massage. Maybe after your shower, you'll be able to relax."

"And why don't you go find that redhead from the party the other night and give her one," she retorted.

"So that's what this is all about. I told you, she's the one who came on to me."

"A likely story!" Even as she tossed back this reply with cynical disbelief, she guessed he was used to having women hit on him.

"I swear." He motioned for her to pick up something and throw it at the wall beside the picture.

Realizing what he was up to, she picked up a jar of hand cream. "Get out! You're lucky I'm letting you stay in the guest room.'' She heaved the jar as hard as she could. It hit the wall about an inch from the frame causing the frame to bounce in place.

Boyd grinned at the sound that had to have been made on the other end as he used this opportunity to remove the bug. ''Now, sweetheart...'' He motioned for her to throw something else.

She was tempted to aim for him as she picked up a book and moved closer for a better shot. Controlling herself, she again hit the wall.

Boyd dropped the bug on the floor. ''Look, you know I love you,'' he said with a husky plea. ''Forgive me,'' he mouthed to her.

She breathed an exaggerated regretful sigh. ''You're right. I'm overreacting. I suppose another massage would be nice.''

''I guarantee that this time you won't be disappointed.'' Boyd stepped on the bug smashing the device to bits.

In spite of the hold she'd maintained on her towel, it was threatening to come loose. ''Now, I'd like a little privacy,'' she snapped in hushed tones.

Boyd turned so that his back was to her. ''You've got it.''

''This is absurd,'' she grumbled, crossing to her bureau and pulling out a cotton nightgown. After slipping it on, she got a robe out of the closet.

''It goes against my grain to keep my back to a woman for too long,'' Boyd said. ''Are you decent yet?''

''Yes,'' she replied curtly. Sitting on the side of the bed, she began to dry her hair.

Boyd frowned. Nature was calling. And that shower had sounded refreshing. Unplugging the phone, he carried it across the room and set it on the bureau. Then taking out his handcuffs, he reapproached the bed. It was an antique brass affair.

"What the devil are you doing?" she demanded as he snapped one of the bracelets around her wrist and one around one of the poles making up the headboard of the bed.

"Making certain you don't use the phone or leave while I'm showering," he replied.

Her gaze narrowed on him. She'd taken about as much of his insinuations as she could stand. "I have no intention of going anywhere. I've got my own personal reasons for wanting to see Garduchi behind bars. And, in case you've forgotten, the phone is bugged."

The hatred toward Garduchi Boyd read in her eyes was real. But that didn't mean she and her aunt weren't up to something together. "I'm sure you and Leona have a code."

Katrina frowned. "No, we don't. Until she called me last night, I hadn't spoken to her for nearly ten years. Besides, I don't even know how to contract her. She's the one who's going to contact me."

Boyd was tempted to believe her, but again his cynical side won out. "I don't want you doing anything I don't know about."

"Has anyone ever mentioned that you're a real control freak?"

"I'm simply guarding my backside."

With a wry smile, Katrina watched him exit. The thought that he had a nice backside to guard crossed her mind and she frowned at herself. At the moment, she wasn't in the mood to allow herself to think there was anything nice about him.

Boyd returned to discover her standing at the bureau

brushing her hair and his handcuffs lying on the bedside table.

In the mirror she saw his reflection. He'd pulled on a pair of jeans and a T-shirt after his shower. His still damp hair had an ebony sheen. His shoulder holster was slung on one shoulder and his satchel was in his hand. At that moment, he looked so handsome it nearly took her breath away. *He's a rotten bore who thought you might even be helping Garduchi,* she reminded herself and her breathing returned to normal.

With cool haughtiness, she said, "My father had great hopes for me. By the time I was five, I could pick any lock. And you did leave me with a whole array of possible tools near at hand. It was hardly a challenge."

Outwardly Boyd scowled at her. Inwardly he found himself thinking she looked kissable when she thought she had the upper hand and he'd never seen a woman look so sexy in a simple cotton nightgown and robe. "Sexy" and "kissable" were not words he should be associating with her, he cautioned himself. "Get into bed," he ordered. "I don't know about you, but I need some sleep."

She pointed toward the door. "You can use the bed in the guest room."

He would have preferred to do just that, but he couldn't stop wondering if she had any other tricks up her sleeve. "I'm not letting you out of my sight for that long."

The determined expression on his face told her that no amount of arguing would change his mind. She considered sitting up all night but her body ached to lie down. "You stay on top of the covers," she ordered.

"Yes, ma'am."

She heard the "if I had my preference we'd be sleeping in separate countries" implication in his voice. Well, that suited her just fine.

As she climbed in under the covers, he replugged in the phone. Hanging his shoulder holster on the foot railing of the bed, he removed his gun and put it within easy reach on his bedside table. Then he lay down.

"Comfy?" she asked dryly.

"All comfy," he returned.

Switching off the light, she snuggled into her pillow. She wished she hadn't pulled the handcuff stunt. He already distrusted her enough as it was, but she hadn't been able to resist. His attitude had rankled her too much. Too tired to care anymore, she slept.

Chapter 4

Katrina awoke sometime midmorning, her back pressed against something solid. Turning over, she came face-to-face with Boyd Logan.

"Morning," he said in an easy drawl.

His mussed hair…that lazy morning look on his face…the heat of his body coming through the sheet…they all blended together causing a fire to spark to life inside her. *How could anyone so irritating be so sexy? And in the morning—when most people looked their worst?*

"Morning," she returned stiffly and quickly scooted to her side of the bed.

Damn, she was adorable in the morning, Boyd thought. Immediately pushing that word from his mind, he rose, stretched and headed to the bathroom.

Katrina was out of bed in an instant, dressing quickly before he returned.

Entering the bedroom, Boyd said, "And now it's time for you to call in sick."

Katrina reached for the phone, but Boyd caught her wrist stopping her. The urge to pull her into his arms and taste her lips was close to overwhelming. Releasing his hold, he took a step away. "Wait until we're in the kitchen. We'll do a little set up for Garduchi's men. Just follow my lead."

His touch had felt like a hot brand against her skin. But the way he released her and stepped away as if he found the contact distasteful, turned the heat to ice. With a frosty expression, she preceded him out of the bedroom.

A few minutes later while she was scrambling some eggs, Boyd said, "I've got the next couple of days off. Why don't you call in sick and spend them with me? You look like you could use a break."

"I could," she agreed, fighting to keep her tone romantic when what she really wanted to do was to order him out of her life.

Her hostility was obvious and, if she was an innocent like she claimed, Boyd couldn't blame her. If she wasn't, she was one hell of an actress. Again he was tempted to believe her and try to make friends. But he stopped himself. Maintaining his cynicism was the best way to keep them both alive.

As soon as she dished out the eggs, Katrina phoned Drake. She trusted him, but hadn't enjoyed hanging around the station all day yesterday. Her fellow officers hadn't asked why the captain had taken her off the streets, but she'd read the hint of suspicion in their eyes. Since her aunt's disappearance, she'd guessed that most of them thought she knew where Leona was and was helping her aunt get away. She hoped they weren't as cynical as Boyd and thought she might actually turn Leona over to Garduchi.

"You take good care of yourself," Drake admonished her.

He sounded sincere, but she was skeptical. The distrust she'd seen in his eyes still stung. "I will."

Sitting down, she ate her breakfast without even tasting it. With the phone call from her aunt, all the effort she'd put into proving herself to be trustworthy had been destroyed like a shack in the path of a bulldozer. The walls of the house felt as if they were closing in on her. "I feel like sight-seeing today," she announced abruptly.

Boyd raised a questioning eyebrow.

"We'll start at the art museum. My mother used to take me there often and I haven't been in years," she continued, putting her dishes in the dishwasher.

"Whatever you want," Boyd replied, wondering what she was up to.

A few minutes later as Katrina drove toward Forest Park, Boyd checked her car for bugs. There were none inside. "It's my guess they planted a tracer," he said.

"I'd say that's a good guess," she replied.

He studied her narrowly. "Is there some purpose to this sight-seeing?"

She grinned mischievously. "It'll give you a tourist's tour of our fair city and Garduchi's men and anyone else following me some exercise."

Boyd found the twinkle in her eyes enticing. He frowned at himself and at her plan. "I think we should go back to the house. What if your aunt tries to contact you while we're gone?"

"She said two days, she meant two days."

The determined set of her jaw let Boyd know that arguing would be useless.

"Besides, a little culture can't do you any harm." The tone of her voice suggested that he had more than a few raw edges that could use some smoothing out.

He gave her a dry look. "Nobody's perfect."

She heard the insinuation behind his words aimed at her. "I've never claimed to be perfect, just honest." A sudden thought occurred to her. She'd been so concerned about people not trusting her, she hadn't considered the other side of the coin. "How do I know I can trust you?"

Boyd's gaze turned to ice. "My father and his father before him were Texas Rangers. My older brother currently is a ranger. I had just finished five years in the Texas Department of Public Safety, working my way to becoming a ranger when my father was killed on the orders of a man just like Garduchi. That's why I broke with tradition and joined the FBI. I wanted the chance to hunt down the Garduchis of this world and put them behind bars. That's the only reward that interests me."

The cold hatred she heard in his voice made her believe him. She recalled that he'd mentioned knowing her father's family had, for generations, worked for the Garduchis. She guessed he also knew they had served as enforcers. That made them the same brand of men who had killed his father. "I didn't follow my father's family tradition either," she said firmly.

Boyd studied the hard set of her jaw. "I hope you're telling the truth."

They were at a stoplight. She turned to him. "I am."

Again he was tempted to believe her. *Don't let a pair of pretty brown eyes fool you!* he ordered himself, and turned his attention to the traffic.

It was clear to Katrina that he didn't want to trust her. Casting the hard set of his jaw a haughty glance, she too turned her attention to the traffic.

For the rest of the way to the art museum, they rode in silence. As they entered the huge old building, Boyd took hold of her hand.

His touch was warm and sent a current of heat up her

arm. Furious with the way her body continued to respond to contact with him, she started to work her hand free.

Boyd's hold tightened and he leaned close to whisper in her ear. "We're sweethearts, remember."

His breath on her neck again had an erotic effect and her self-directed anger increased. "That doesn't mean we have to hold hands."

"I intend to make certain you don't suddenly slip away."

"I won't. I'm the one who talked my aunt into turning herself in to the authorities," she reminded him in a curt whisper.

"That's your story. All I know is that I saw you going into Garduchi's compound and I told Drake. You had to tell us something. Now smile and look like you're enjoying yourself."

She gave him a sticky-sweet smile. Knowing his hold on her was the same as a handcuff quelled the warmth and turned his touch into an irritant.

After an hour of slowly surveying the exhibits, nature called. "I have to use the ladies' room," she informed him.

Boyd was feeling the call of nature himself, but he didn't like letting her out of his sight.

"I've counted four of Garduchi's men. The two watching me must have called in for reinforcements. My guess is that there's more outside. I doubt I could give all of them the slip."

She had a point, Boyd admitted. "I'll meet you here." Releasing her, he headed to the men's room.

Leaving the ladies' room, she found him waiting for her. She shoved her hands into the pockets of her slacks before he had a chance to get hold of one.

Boyd allowed her her freedom.

But even with him not holding on to her, the prickling

on her neck caused by Garduchi's men made her again feel closed in. "Time for the zoo," she said.

"Time to go home," Boyd corrected. "Garduchi's men have gotten a good look at me. Could be one of them recognized me from that encounter with those two hoods in front of your house yesterday and my cover has been blown."

Katrina gave him a wry look. "Only Dominic and his driver saw you up close and they think you're out-of-town talent. Of course, they would start wondering why I was letting you hang around with me, but they haven't been around and, I bet, they won't be. Dominic will want to keep his distance. I'm certain these goons have orders to snatch Leona if she shows up, or, if they can't do that, take her out. Either way, Dominic will want to be as far away from the scene as possible."

Boyd had to agree she had a point and sitting around her house for the rest of the day didn't appeal to him either. "Okay, next stop the zoo."

The zoo was just down the hill from the art museum. They parked in the lot and entered. As they strolled through the open air exhibits, Boyd set out to find out as much as he could about his companion. Deciding to play dumb about what he'd heard about her mother's family, he said, "Your personnel file lists no close relatives. What about your mother? Didn't she have a family?"

"She came from a religious, law-abiding family. My father was a handsome man and could be very charming when he wanted to be. My mother was young and naive and fell in love with him. She thought belonging to the mob was romantic. Her parents knew better. They wanted nothing to do with the Garduchis or anyone connected with them. They disapproved so strongly of the marriage, they refused to attend the wedding. Then fearing retaliation or being caught up in my father's activities against their will, they moved to California and severed all ties with my mother.''

"I'd say that if they didn't want to be tainted by Garduchi, they didn't have much choice.''

"Yeah, that's for sure. But it hurt my mom pretty bad. Still, she was in love. It wasn't until after my brother was born and she realized that my father intended for him to follow in his footsteps that her maternal instincts caused her to take a closer look at my father and the life he led. Once her eyes were opened, she wanted out of the marriage, but it was too late. She could have left, but she would have had to leave without my brother, and she refused to desert her child. So she stayed.''

"And gave your father another child," Boyd noted dryly.

Katrina shot him a hostile glance. "A man like my father would not allow his conjugal rights to be withheld. She did try not to get pregnant again but accidents happen. By the time I was born, she knew she'd lost the battle to save my brother. He already considered my father his hero. So she began to work on me, to make me see that the kind of 'work' my father did was wrong and sinful. I was young, too young to understand I should keep my mouth shut. One night I blurted out something about him killing people. I don't know what he said to my mother, but after that she stopped trying to discourage me and turned to alcohol. Then one night she took a couple of bottles of pills along with the gin, went to sleep and didn't wake up.''

Boyd was surprised. That was a stupid lie. She had to know death records were easily accessed. "I looked up the record of her death. It said she died in a single car accident.''

Katrina drew a harsh breath and her voice hardened further. "Suicides are bad for business. Those that don't leave notes get investigated by the police, and my mother didn't leave a note. The Garduchis fixed it. But I was there. I know the truth. I saw the empty liquor bottle and the bottle of pills, and I heard my father making the arrangements over the phone. They staged the accident and made certain the car caught fire and the gas tank was full so that it exploded. There was very little left to bury."

Boyd had to admit her explanation sounded plausible. It was exactly what he'd expect Garduchi to do under those circumstances. He studied the woman walking beside him. She'd been ten at the time of her mother's death. That was an impressionable age and the hatred he heard in her voice and saw on her face toward her father and Garduchi seemed genuine. But he recalled the knife wound in his back and warned himself not to be too trusting. She could be an accomplished liar and have made the whole story up. Her parents could have been deliriously happy.

Katrina read the continued skepticism on his face. "I'll be glad when this is over," she said in a low growl.

"That makes two of us," Boyd replied.

"Where to now?" Boyd asked as they left the zoo.

"I'm getting hungry. There's a restaurant on the southside of town I've been wanting to try."

Boyd wondered if she'd lied to him and there was a purpose behind her movements. He found it difficult to believe Leona would meet with her in such public places, but maybe Officer Polenari was looking for a chance to get word to Garduchi. He found himself hoping this wasn't the case and she was on the level.

A while later he was again warning himself to never let down his guard. Their food had just arrived and they'd begun to eat when he'd noticed a man in his late twenties enter. The man sort of lazily surveyed the room while waiting for a table. Suddenly his gaze leveled on their table, and grinning with recognition, he headed their way.

"Katrina," he called out with friendly greeting.

Boyd leaned back and slipped a hand under his T-shirt to the butt of the gun tucked in the waistband of his jeans.

Katrina looked up to see one of her fellow police officers approaching. He was out of uniform, dressed casually in slacks and a pullover shirt. "Evening, Russ," she said when he reached their table.

He grinned at her. "Thought you were out sick."

She shrugged. "Just decided I needed a couple of days off."

"Guess your aunt taking off is causing quite a turmoil."

Playing dumb, Boyd stared at Katrina questioningly. "Your aunt? You never mentioned an aunt. I thought you were an orphan with no family."

"As far as I'm concerned, I am. I cut my ties with my aunt a long time ago," Katrina assured him, continuing to play the role of the disinterested niece, and shot Russ a caustic look.

"Oh, yeah." Russ grimaced apologetically. "Sorry I brought her up."

"Consider her forgotten," Katrina replied.

Russ turned his attention to Boyd and held out his hand. "You look familiar."

"I've come by to see Katrina at work a couple of times," Boyd replied, refusing to release his hold on his gun to accept the handshake.

Russ shrugged at Boyd's lack of a friendly response and dropped his hand back to his side. "That must be where I saw you." He gave Katrina a wink. "Sorry I interrupted your evening. Have a good time."

Watching him walking away, Katrina frowned. "Russ

Miller never had the time of day for me before. I wonder if Captain Drake sent him to find me and keep an eye on me.''

Boyd decided that the honesty in her voice was genuine. If she'd come here to meet someone, it hadn't been Russ Miller. ''You said you'd never been here before.''

''That's right.''

The man's actions had seemed natural, but Boyd's instincts kept telling him something was wrong. ''Then I'd say either he's on the level and accidentally bumped into you or someone told him where to find you.''

Suddenly Katrina was seeing Russ in a whole new light. ''The captain wouldn't know where to find me. But Garduchi would and he's bound to have someone on the police payroll.'' Grudgingly, she admitted, ''Maybe you were right and this sight-seeing tour wasn't such a good idea. Russ could have come here just to get a closer look at you. Rebecca kept her voice low when she told me there was an FBI agent in the captain's office, but someone could have overheard and passed the word around. If Russ saw you at the station yesterday, he might put two and two together.''

''Could be,'' Boyd agreed. ''But I'll keep playing the role of the boyfriend who knows nothing about your aunt. If he is one of Garduchi's men, we don't want to tip him off that we suspect him.''

Katrina smiled wryly. ''Ironic, isn't it? I've spent five years trying to prove I'm trustworthy and failed and it turns out that one of the most-liked guys on the force could be a snitch.''

Another alternative occurred to Boyd. ''Or, maybe Drake has had a tail on us in case we needed help.''

Katrina shook her head. ''I don't think so. Until Russ

showed up, I hadn't seen anybody except Garduchi's men.''

Silence fell between them as they returned to eating. Katrina tried to act relaxed for their watchers, but by the time they'd finished their entrée, she was tense as a bowstring. She didn't mind putting herself into danger, but the full realization of how much danger her aunt was putting Boyd in had hit her full force. As irritating as the man was, she didn't want to see him get hurt. "I'm really sorry that I might have blown your cover," she said stiffly.

She seemed sincere. But then maybe that was the real reason they'd gone on this tour. Maybe she wanted Garduchi's men to get a good look at him. He shrugged. "Even if my cover is blown, that doesn't change anything. It might even work to my advantage. Garduchi's men will think they have an edge. That might make them a little cocky and men and women who are cocky make mistakes.''

Katrina caught the hint of accusation in his voice. He was obviously considering the possibility that she'd brought him out to blow his cover on purpose. She scowled at him. "I'm not cocky. I was just tense and the thought of spending a whole day cooped up with you was more than my nerves or patience could stand. You are the most irrit—''

"You're making it look as if we're having an argument. We're supposed to be in love, and you're supposed to be *enjoying* my company." Boyd smiled a smile that didn't reach his eyes as he reached across the table and took her hand in his.

Katrina forced a smile as she finished between clenched teeth. "Irritating man I have ever met and I think it's time to go home.''

"Sounds like a good idea to me," Boyd said with husky suggestiveness in his voice for the benefit of the waiter who was approaching. He looked up at the man. "We'll take the check, now."

The waiter gave him a knowing grin. "Yes, sir. Immediately, sir."

Katrina suddenly visualized herself in Boyd's arms. *I must really be exhausted to be having moments of lunacy like that.* She shoved the image out. The man honestly believed she might be capable of turning her own aunt over to Garduchi.

All the way home, his distrust nagged at her. Pulling into her driveway, she fantasized about escaping from Agent Logan's company. An unexpected rush of fear swept through her and she was stunned to realize how much safer she felt having him near. Garduchi is a dangerous man. Under present circumstances, only a fool would feel safer alone. Any help, even that of as aggravating a man as Agent Logan, is better than nothing, she reasoned.

Climbing out of the car, she kept a lookout for any freelancers who hadn't gotten the word that she was under Garduchi's protection.

Boyd too searched the shadows for any movement. When Katrina came around the car, he took a position behind her.

"I'm taking a shower and going to bed," she announced as they entered the house. "I'm exhausted."

He read the stress lines on her face. Whatever was going on, wasn't easy for her. If she was on the level, he felt sorry for her. On the other hand, his coming into the picture might have added a twist to her plans she hadn't counted on and that was what was causing the strain. "Not too exhausted, I hope," he countered, playing the part of the ardent lover, for their listeners.

She simply gave him a wry look and headed down the hall.

Boyd made a quick check of the house. No new bugs had been planted and the one he'd gotten rid of in the bedroom had not been replaced. Going into the living room, he sat down on the couch and waited until he heard the water stop running. He gave her a few minutes to towel dry and then go into her bedroom, then he went down the hall to check on her. She was in bed. Crossing the room, he lifted the covers. She was wearing her nightgown.

Katrina opened her eyes and glared up at him.

"Just wanted to make certain you weren't dressed to run the minute I left the room," he said.

"I'm not going anywhere. I may not even move all night long," she growled up at him. "Now put down the covers and let me go to sleep."

He dropped the covers back in place. Her body had looked soft and enticing. Lusty thoughts filled his mind. *Forget it!* he ordered himself.

Discarding his jacket and gun, he lay down on the bed until he was satisfied she was asleep, then showered. Returning to the bedroom, he cursed under his breath. She was gone.

Katrina entered the bedroom to find Boyd cursing and pulling his shoulder holster on. "What's happened?"

He spun around to see her in her nightgown and robe. "I thought you'd taken off."

She frowned at his distrust. "I just went in the kitchen for some water and ibuprofin. You're a walking headache." Climbing back into bed, she added, "I keep trying to tell you I'm one of the good guys."

Boyd wished he could believe her, but he'd been fooled before and it had nearly cost him his life.

Chapter 5

The ringing of the doorbell woke Katrina. Boyd was already on his feet, heading to the hall. He was holding his gun behind him so that anyone looking in the windows, wouldn't see it. Grabbing up her robe, she pulled it on as she went. "Coming," she yelled in response to another round of ringing.

Boyd stopped at the end of the hall, letting her take the lead. As she continued past him, he remained across the room but shifted his position so that when she opened the door he would have an easy shot at whoever was there.

Being careful to give him a line of vision, Katrina opened the door.

"Katrina Polenari?" the delivery boy asked, from behind an arrangement of roses of various colors.

"Yes."

"Sorry I woke you," he apologized, clearly embarrassed. "The lady who ordered these was insistent that they be delivered at nine o'clock"

Seeing his eyes looking past her to Boyd and his embarrassment turning to trepidation, she said, "It's all right. He always looks grumpy in the morning," and accepted the vase.

"Have a good day," he said over his shoulder already hurrying back to his truck.

"I'll bet you don't get many door-to-door salespeople stopping by," Katrina commented, glancing over her shoulder to see that Boyd had moved closer.

"Never twice," he replied.

She hated the way his nearness was causing her blood to race. *He thinks you're as cold-blooded as your father,* she reminded herself, and her pulse returned to normal.

Stepping back, she allowed him to close the door. Then, setting the flowers on the coffee table, she found the card and opened it. As she suspected, it was from Leona. It said her aunt was on her way out of the country. She scowled at the bouquet. She had Garduchi watching her every move, her captain now distrusted her and then there was the FBI. And all for nothing. *Or maybe not,* her little voice rebutted. If Leona had really left, why did she insist the flowers be delivered at exactly nine? Katrina's gaze returned to the roses. There were eleven.

"Do I have competition?" Boyd asked, reminding her of his presence.

"No. They're from my aunt." She saw the surprise on his face that she would have mentioned Leona openly in a room she knew was bugged and smiled to herself.

"The aunt Russ mentioned last night?" He shifted his eyes toward one of the bugs to remind her they were there.

She shrugged to let him know she remembered their presence. "That's the one. She's my father's sister. We haven't seen each other in years and it looks like it's going to stay that way. Her note says that she's on her way to some remote part of the world and doesn't plan to return,'' she repeated what Leona had written.

Boyd had to fight to keep the frustration out of his voice. ''That's too bad.''

''Not really. She's gotten herself into trouble with some people it isn't smart to cross. If she'd stayed I'd probably have gotten caught in the middle of it.'' She gave him a wry look to let him know this was all an act.

Boyd's frustration vanished. ''So that's why you're so tense.'' He added a huskiness to his voice. ''Now that you don't have to worry about your aunt, how about us going back to bed for a while?''

''I can't spend the entire day on my back.''

''We could try some other positions.''

Katrina could imagine the chuckles her listeners were having at her expense, but she didn't care. If this exchange got them off her tail, she'd be happy. ''We've got to get to the grocery store if you want something home-cooked for dinner.''

''Some of your terrific lasagna?'' Boyd asked, playing along. Clearly she wanted to get going quickly.

''Whatever you want.'' Katrina's voice took on an agitated edge. ''How did that picture get crooked?''

Boyd watched her approach a perfectly straight frame, one that had a bug behind it. What was she up to?

Katrina moved the picture around as if straightening it. ''What's this?'' she demanded angrily, pulling the bug off the back. ''Someone has bugged my house. The FBI, maybe. Or the local police. Or, maybe even Garduchi. Damn, that makes me mad.''

''Garduchi? Who's Garduchi?'' Boyd asked, playing his part of being an innocent bystander.

''Vince Garduchi, the mobster. That's the man my aunt got herself into trouble with.'' Dropping the bug on the floor, Katrina stomped on it. Knowing there was another bug in the living room that would allow Garduchi's men to continue to monitor her, she said, "I hate having my privacy invaded. We'll stay at your place. Tomorrow I'll go into work and get a bug detector and clean my house of these metal insects."

"Sure. They should be finished painting it by now," Boyd replied, giving her credit for being smart enough to come up with a reason they could both leave with suitcases.

Returning to the bedroom to dress, Katrina was aware that he was following. "You can't watch me every second," she mumbled under her breath.

Boyd knew she was right. Besides, if she'd wanted to get away she'd had enough chances already. If she had a hidden agenda, it was obvious by now that, at least for the time being, it involved him. With a nod of agreement, he stepped into the hall and closed the bedroom door.

Exiting her bedroom a few minutes later in a pair of jeans, cotton top and sneakers, Katrina was surprised to find him nowhere in sight. The thought that Garduchi's men might have come to check the card and were holding Boyd prisoner, caused her stomach to knot in fear for him and she cursed under her breath for having left her gun in the living room. Cautiously, she made her way in that direction. The scraping of a chair in the kitchen attracted her attention. Quietly taking a look, she discovered Boyd seated at the table eating a sandwich. Her stomach unknotted. *I just don't want him hurt because of my aunt or me,* she told herself, refusing to even consider the possibility that her concern for the man went any deeper than it would for anyone caught up in this situation with her.

As she entered the kitchen, Boyd nodded toward a plate holding a second sandwich. "My mother used to say never go to the grocery store on an empty stomach."

She hated taking anything from him, but she knew she should eat while she could. Once they left the house, there was no telling what would happen next. As she began gobbling down the sandwich, she glanced at her watch. "We need to get going soon," she said, between bites. "I have a hairdresser's appointment in a couple of hours." As an afterthought she added, "And I need to drop some stuff off at the dry cleaners."

Pulling out a fresh green plastic bag, she headed back to her bedroom, eating the rest of her sandwich as she went. Boyd followed, retrieving his holster and jacket while she shoved some clean clothes into the bag. "I figured we wouldn't be coming back here. I can take a few things in an overnight bag but a suitcase would be too obvious," she said in answer to his questioning look.

Boyd nodded. "I'll drive."

She knew he was hoping his car didn't have a tracer on it or any bugs in it. Still, considering how closely they were being watched, it was only smart to be cautious.

After tossing his satchel in the trunk, he helped her put her bag of clothes in the backseat, giving himself a chance to give that area a quick scan. No internal bugs there.

"So where to?" he asked, climbing in behind the wheel and giving the front a quick scan. There were no bugs there either.

"The grocery store," she replied, giving him directions.

As they pulled out into traffic, she spotted their tail a couple of cars back. "Looks like my trying to convince them Leona has taken off didn't work."

"Looks like," Boyd replied, letting her know he'd spotted their tail also.

When they pulled into the grocery store parking lot, she went inside while he feigned interest in his tires. Rounding the car slowly, kicking each tire as if checking the air, he made a quick search for any kind of tracers Garduchi's men might have attached to his vehicle. There was one in the right rear wheel case on the passenger side. Standing, leaning against the car nonchalantly, he managed to free it. Walking to the front tire, he dropped it behind the wheel so that it would be crushed when they pulled out.

Then, leaning against the hood, he pretended to be enjoying the spring day while he waited for Katrina to return. Casually, he surveyed the parking lot. The car that had been following them was one aisle over. The driver had remained behind the wheel and was keeping an eye on him, while the other man in the car had followed Katrina into the store. He guessed his cover had been blown and made a mental note to be certain to mention Russ Miller to Captain Drake.

Katrina returned a short while later with a single bag of groceries. "I decided you could take me out to dinner tonight," she said loud enough for anyone who wanted to hear. Then stowing the bag on the backseat, she climbed into the front.

"Now what?" Boyd asked.

A grin suddenly spread across her face. "It looks like we just got lucky. We get to lose our tail without being obvious."

Boyd wondered why she was smiling, then he saw. An elderly woman had climbed into the huge older model car next to the one belonging to their tail and was backing out at a snaillike speed. Pulling out at a normal speed, Boyd was out of the parking lot while the woman's car was still blocking Garduchi's men.

Katrina began giving directions. Once she was satisfied there wasn't a second tail, she began guiding him to their destination. Half an hour later they were pulling into the parking lot of the Missouri Botanical Garden. As they left the car and headed toward the entrance, she said, "When I was growing up, my aunt and I used to come here regularly. I'm counting on her message meaning that she wanted to meet us here in their rose garden. And, I'm assuming that the eleven roses meant eleven o'clock. Or the message on the flowers could have been legit and she's on an airplane winging her way somewhere into oblivion."

Boyd scowled at that possibility. "Garduchi will find her if she tries to get away on her own."

"I'm hoping she realizes that."

Inside, they bought tickets.

"Shall we have a cup of coffee in the cafeteria. We're early," Katrina suggested.

"I want to get an idea of the lay of the land," Boyd replied, catching her hand to keep her with him as he continued to the exit leading into the gardens.

Stepping outside into the scented air, Katrina experienced a giddiness like the one she'd felt the very first time a boy had held her hand. Refusing to believe it had anything to do with the man beside her, she told herself it was the spring weather and the romantic effect of being in a garden. She tried not to think of her companion, but instead found herself recalling his bared chest. Attempting to divert her mind from the sturdy look of him, she recalled the bullet hole. Before she could stop herself, she heard herself asking, "How did you get shot?"

"Bank robber. Had two hidden guns. I hadn't counted on that."

Surprised he'd answered, her curiosity took control. "And the knife wound in the back?"

Boyd realized he'd been enjoying strolling hand in hand with her. Abruptly, he released his hold. "I trusted the wrong person."

The giddiness vanished. His body language and the tone

of his voice was like a slap in the face, letting her know once again she was currently top on his list of people he didn't trust.

"Which way to the rose garden?" he asked.

"This way." Walking alongside of him, Katrina faced the truth. She'd never gain the full trust of the law officers she worked with.

"I don't like this." Boyd broke the silence between them. "There's too much large foliage."

Katrina nodded her agreement. Glancing at the denim shoulder bag she was carrying, she made sure the zipper was open giving her easy access to the weapon inside.

"You look like a strong young man," an elderly woman seated on a bench a couple of feet ahead of them called out in a voice that crackled with age. "Give an old lady a hand. I can sit myself down, but getting up is near impossible."

The woman's shoulders were stooped and both of her hands were resting on the top of her cane as if it was the only thing keeping her the least bit erect. Her makeup was heavy in the style of years past with bright red circles of rouge on the cheeks and vivid red lipstick put on beyond the true shape of the lips. She wore thick glasses with round gold frames and her hair was a mass of gray curls. Her dress was matronly, made of material with a flowery design and the collar was lace. The sleeves were long and what was visible of her legs was covered with heavy support stockings. Her breasts and hips were ample. Her shoes were sturdy.

Katrina studied her narrowly. There was nothing about the woman that resembled Leona Serrenito. Her aunt, as Katrina remembered her, was slender and stylish, dressing in the latest fashions. Her hair might be gray at the roots, but she'd become a blonde in her twenties and Katrina knew she'd die a blonde. And, Leona had always taken good care of herself. She'd been forty-nine when Katrina last saw her but she'd looked closer to thirty-five.

Just an old lady asking for help, she decided. But as Boyd complied, she saw the ring. It was a four-carat diamond with a large sapphire on either side and it was her aunt's pride and joy.

"Why don't we help you back to your car," she said, quickly approaching and placing a hand under the woman's elbow.

"Now that would be kind of you." The woman accepted the offer with a grateful smile. She looked up at Boyd. "And you, young man, can carry my knitting bag."

Boyd scowled. They didn't have time to play nursemaid. He wanted to case the rose garden and the rest of the place. Over the top of the woman's head, he gave Katrina an impatient look.

She gave him an equally impatient glance. "Sometimes you find what you're looking for in the least likely places."

Boyd looked harder at the old woman. Was this really Leona Serrenito? If it was, she was an expert at disguise. He'd spent an hour going through photos of her but he'd have never spotted her on his own. Picking up the large straw carryall that had been on the bench beside her, all doubt as to her identity vanished. The thing was so heavy he was surprised the bottom didn't fall out.

"Are you sure you weren't followed?" Leona asked as they exited the garden and started across the parking lot.

"As sure as we can be," Katrina replied, her gaze continually scanning for any trouble.

As they pulled out onto the street she continued to watch for any car following them. She didn't spot any tails, but it wasn't until they were on their way out of town, that she finally allowed herself to breathe a sigh of relief. "Looks like we made a clean getaway."

Leona had been sitting hunched down in the back. Now she straightened and smiled. "How in the world did you spot me so quickly. I was sure this disguise was perfect."

"The ring," Katrina replied.

Leona held up her hand and smiled at the huge diamond. "A gift from your uncle on our tenth wedding anniversary so I would quit complaining about how small the stone in my engagement ring was. And I deserved it and more."

Katrina glanced back at her aunt and saw the glint of greed in her eyes. That was not something she expected to see in a woman who'd had a religious conversion. It was, however, the Leona she remembered. "Did you really give all of the money you took to charity?"

Leona shrugged and dropped her hand into her lap. "Some."

"And the rest?"

"Tucked away for my old age. I didn't want to be a burden on anyone in my later years."

"You had to know that having any 'later years' would be questionable if Garduchi found out what you were up to," Katrina admonished curtly.

Leona smiled. "I was counting on you to save me."

Katrina's frown darkened. "That was taking a gamble, wasn't it?"

"So you haven't spoken to me in nearly ten years. So what? We're still blood. Besides, I know you'd like to get Vince."

Katrina groaned. "With a family like mine, who needs enemies?"

"Speaking of family, have you been in contact with your mother's parents?" Leona asked.

"I tried but they didn't want any part of me."

Leona smiled a motherly smile. "That's just as well. They were the most boring people."

"I would have preferred boring to what I got," Katrina returned.

Leona sighed and sat back. "You've never gotten over your mother's suicide, have you?"

The image of her mother lying dead in bed filled Katrina's mind. It was as vivid as the night she had witnessed it. "It's not something a person forgets."

Boyd noted the intense bitterness in her voice and, glancing toward her, he saw her hands balled into fists.

"I did my best to help you get through those rough times," Leona reminded her.

Katrina drew a harsh breath and shoved the image from her mind. "I know and I appreciate it." Not wanting to travel down memory lane any further, she turned her attention to Boyd. "Where are we going?"

"You'll know when we get there."

"Sounds like he doesn't trust either of us," Leona noted.

"He doesn't," Katrina confirmed.

Boyd said nothing, letting her comment stand. But after listening to the exchange between the two women, he was now convinced of one thing...she'd been telling the truth about her mother's death and her hatred of Garduchi. He was also willing to believe that she was telling the truth about not having had contact with her aunt for years. *But then a clever liar always tells some truths,* he reminded himself. She, or she and her aunt, could still have their own agenda.

Silence filled the car as he exited onto Interstate 70 heading west. An hour or so later, he took the Fulton exit. He continued for several miles, then pulled into a gas station. Instead of stopping at the pump, he pulled in beside a heavy-duty four-wheel drive vehicle parked next to the garage.

"I thought you'd never make a rest stop," Leona complained, quickly slipping out of the backseat and heading to the ladies' room, the pads that had provided the look of ample hips left behind.

"Stay with her," Boyd ordered.

Katrina gave him a dry look. "She's not going to run away." Suddenly recalling how unpredictable Leona could be, Katrina did as she was told.

A few minutes later when the women returned, they discovered Boyd waiting for them behind the wheel of the four-wheel drive vehicle. As they pulled back onto the road in their new transportation, he handed Katrina a hand-drawn map. "You're my navigator."

Forty minutes, one gravel road and two dirt roads later, they turned into a heavily rutted drive with a wooden gate barring their way. Katrina took the key Boyd gave her, unlocked the padlock on the gate and swung it open. Once he'd driven through, she relocked the gate and climbed back into the vehicle. She guessed they had gone another quarter of a mile before they came to a small cabin.

"It's rustic but no one should find us here," Boyd said.

"I hope it has indoor plumbing," Leona grumbled.

Katrina entered and looked around. The room she was standing in was divided into a living room area and a kitchen area. To her right was a small bedroom and left of the kitchen area was a bathroom. "Cozy" was the word that came to mind.

Brushing past her, Leona came to a halt a few feet inside. Her gaze too traveled around the interior and she crinkled her nose in disgust. "It's certainly not the Plaza. Surely the government could have come up with better accommodations than this."

Boyd followed behind the women with his satchel, Katrina's green lawn bag and overnight case and Leona's straw bag. He scowled impatiently at Leona's attitude. "It may not be plush but it's safe. You two can have the bed. I'll take the couch." Leaving his satchel in the main living area, he continued past them and put their things in the bedroom.

Well, considering her companions, "cozy" had definitely been the wrong word, Katrina mused. Aloud, she said, "I'll see what's in the refrigerator for dinner."

"And I'm getting out of this getup." Leona went into the bedroom and closed the door.

Katrina felt a pricking on the back of her neck. Turning she found Boyd standing nearby looking at her with sarcastic disbelief.

"You actually went to Garduchi and pleaded for *her*? You really told him that she'd had a religious conversion?" he asked.

"All right, so maybe she's a little difficult to take," she said. "But she can be nice when she wants too. And she was very good to me after my mother died. I don't know how I would have survived if it hadn't been for her. I didn't have anybody else I could've turned to."

Boyd's expression let her know he wasn't convinced Leona had a good bone in her body. "Your loyalty is admirable."

Katrina regarded him dryly. "And I suppose there isn't anyone in your family who's difficult to get along with, but you still have a soft spot for."

She had a point, Boyd admitted, a slow smile spreading over his face as his maternal great-grandmother came to mind. "Actually I do."

He was incredibly handsome when he smiled, Katrina thought. Her gaze traveled to his eyes and in those brown depths she saw an unexpected camaraderie. She grinned crookedly.

"Well, I certainly feel a lot better," Leona announced, coming out of the bedroom wearing an expensive silk pantsuit and carrying her makeup kit. Whisking past them, she continued on to the bathroom.

Boyd silently cursed himself for letting down his guard. What he was seeing of Katrina Polenari could be a facade. Beneath the surface, it was entirely possible that she was as cold and calculating as her aunt. Better safe than sorry.

Seeing the ice return to his eyes, Katrina knew the barrier of distrust he was keeping between them was again in place. A wave of regret washed through her. *Forget him,* she told herself and returned her attention to the food in the refrigerator. There were eggs, milk and some fresh vegetables.

"There's meat in the freezer, canned goods, powdered milk and cereal in the cabinet," Boyd informed her. Taking a small cell phone out of his pocket, he punched in a long distance number. "The bird is in the cage," he said, then hung up.

It was getting late and she was hungry. Katrina pulled out a box of frozen fried chicken. "Okay with you?" she asked, holding it up.

"Anything," he replied with disinterest.

As Katrina searched for a pan to put the chicken in while the oven was heating, Boyd pulled out a can of green beans and opened it. "See if you can find a pan for these, too," he said, turning his attention to setting the table.

Surprised that he hadn't left the kitchen chores to her, she obeyed.

"Definitely not Luigi's cuisine," Leona noted, coming out of the bathroom and frowning at the empty box that had held the frozen chicken. The heavy makeup was gone, replaced by an expertly applied light layer that restored Leona to her usual elegant self. She placed an arm around Katrina's shoulders. "Surely you haven't forgotten the absolutely marvelous meals we used to have there. The man was an artist with food."

"Oh sure, it was great fun," Katrina returned dryly. "All during the meal I used to wonder if anyone was going to come in and gun us all down."

"I should never have let you watch *The Untouchables.*" Leona turned to Boyd. "I'm beginning to think the critics are right. Television is detrimental to young minds." Issuing an exaggerated sigh, she crossed the room and seated herself in the rocking chair by the fireplace. "I hope you know that I'm not going to tell anyone anything until I've got a pardon in my hands and a written assurance that I'll become part of your relocation program."

"A federal attorney will be here tomorrow or the next day," Boyd informed her. "He'll decide how valuable you are."

"He'll discover I'm a very valuable commodity," she assured him.

"I'm glad to hear that. I'd hate to think we've all been risking our lives for nothing," Katrina said curtly. Suddenly she was recalling the fear that had swept through her when she'd thought Boyd was being held captive by Garduchi's men. *Guilt. The intensity of the fear was due to guilt,* she told herself. If he'd been hurt because of her aunt, she would have felt responsible.

"Crossing the street is a risk," Leona tossed back, then smiled warmly. "I'm glad we're going to get to spend a little time together. Remember when you were twelve and had the chicken pox?" She turned to Boyd. "She refused to let anyone but me see her for three weeks."

Katrina grimaced as she recalled her face covered with pox. "I was scary looking."

Leona studied her critically. "You could use a few beauty aids right now. Your skin is good but a little blusher, a little more eye makeup, and a fresh application of lipstick would enhance your features greatly." She turned to Boyd. "Don't you think so, Officer..." Leona frowned. "I don't believe you ever introduced yourself."

"Agent Boyd Logan, FBI," he said. "And I think she looks fine just the way she is." *In fact, she looks downright enticing.* Abruptly, he pushed that last thought from his mind.

The honesty in his voice caused a warm rush of pleasure in Katrina.

"You obviously haven't noticed that my niece has the potential for being a very pretty woman," Leona chided.

"I've noticed that she is one." Boyd mentally kicked himself, but the impulse to come to Katrina's defense had been too strong to resist. "However, her looks are of no concern. I would think that you would want me to be concentrating on keeping you alive," he added in curt tones.

Leona shrugged. "I was simply making conversation."

Katrina's body temperature returned to normal. Boyd was obviously angry with himself for even admitting he thought she was pretty. And, he was right. What he thought of her looks wasn't important. He still didn't trust her.

A few minutes later when they began to eat, Leona grimaced apologetically toward Katrina. "You're not part of his organization so Vince shouldn't hold your helping me against you. But if I were you I'd consider moving to a new town, anyway. He has a temper and your presence could weigh on his nerves. After all, you were his godchild. Your defection was a blow to his pride. The only reason he forgave you was because I was able to convince him that your grief over losing both your parents and your brother was too much for you to bear.''

Boyd's gaze narrowed on Katrina. ''Vince Garduchi is your godfather?''

''Babies don't have a say in who their godparents are,'' she replied.

''Vince disavowed her,'' Leona said, then returned her attention to her niece. ''Anyway, I think it would be best if you don't stick around St. Louis.''

Katrina nodded. ''I've been thinking the same thing myself. Even after five years on the force, my captain doesn't trust me.''

Leona smiled knowingly. ''I warned you the outside world would be rough.''

''Looks like you didn't take your own advice,'' Katrina noted.

Leona sighed. ''Handling all that money was just too tempting. Or maybe it was my midlife crisis. I considered trying to convince Vince that it was menopause that had caused me to act irrationally. But he'd have wanted the money back and I just couldn't do that.'' Abruptly, she turned to Boyd. ''And I'm not turning it over to the government either. What's mine is mine and it stays that way.''

''That's between you and the attorney,'' Boyd replied, marvelling at her greed. This was a woman who would die for money.

Leona smiled confidently. ''My little pittance will be nothing compared to what they can get out of Vince on back taxes alone.''

Katrina would have liked to have blamed her aunt's behavior on the change of life but she knew Leona was simply living up to her true colors. She saw the disdain in Boyd's eyes and that she was related to Leona caused a flush of embarrassment.

Boyd noticed her cheeks redden and again he was tempted to trust her. *Caution, man,* he reminded himself. He'd like to believe it was embarrassment but that flush could be anger that her aunt was being so openly mercenary while Ms. Polenari wanted to win his confidence or at least his sympathy for them.

The rest of the meal was accomplished in silence. When it was over, Leona watched television while Katrina cleaned the dishes and Boyd, taking the precaution of taking the distributor cap from the vehicle with him, made a sweep of the woods around the cabin to make certain they were alone.

"I'd suggest we all get some sleep," he said when he returned. It was an order.

For a moment, Leona looked as if she were going to protest, then with a shrug, she obeyed.

An hour later Katrina gave up trying to get any sleep in the same bed with her aunt. Leona was not only a restless sleeper, she snored. Getting a spare blanket out of the closet, she retrieved her gun from the bedside table and a pillow from the bed, then went into the main living area.

Boyd had conditioned himself to wake at any sound. When he'd heard one of the women moving around in the bedroom, he'd been considering checking on what they were up to when the door had been pushed open further and someone had entered the main area. Without even looking, he'd known it was Katrina. She'd showered before going to bed and he caught the vague scent of her herbal shampoo. *Nice,* he thought, then shoved the thought from his mind. Pretending to be asleep, he watched, his eyes open only a slit as she rounded the couch. The gun in her hand caused him to brace for action. Had he completely misjudged her? *It wouldn't be the first time,* his little voice mocked.

Moonlight coming in the windows gave Katrina enough light to make her way to the rug in front of the fireplace. Moving quietly she laid her gun down, then spread the blanket and rolled up in it. Boyd's steady breathing convinced her that she hadn't disturbed him. Snuggling her head into the pillow, she closed her eyes.

Mentally, Boyd groaned. When she'd laid down her gun, he'd relaxed. But when he'd closed his eyes and tried to go back to sleep he could not block her from his mind. He saw her face with those incredibly kissable lips and the remembered feel of her, when he'd held her hand or put his arm around her, taunted him. "I would think the bed would be a lot more comfortable than the floor," he said, unable to keep his irritation out of his voice.

Startled to discover that he was awake, she turned in the direction of the couch. "My aunt not only snores like a sailor, she kicks like a mule. Now I know why she and my uncle had separate beds." The "you're treading on my space" tone in his voice grated on her nerves. "If you don't want me in here, I'll go sleep in the car."

He'd heard the snoring and knew she wasn't exaggerating. He also didn't want her where he couldn't keep track of her. "No." He shifted into a sitting position. "You can have the couch, I'll take the floor."

Katrina balked. She wanted no favors from him. "I didn't come in here to take your bed. I'm perfectly comfortable here."

"Well, I'm not. The couch is too short. Besides, I've spent half of my life sleeping on the ground around a campfire. I rest better on a hard surface." Already on his feet, he tossed his blanket and pillow onto the floor. Then rounding the coffee table, he scooped her up, blanket and all.

Fear of being dropped caused her to circle her arms

around his neck. She didn't think she'd ever felt such strength in a man before.

The moment he had her in his arms, Boyd knew he'd made a mistake. He'd been wondering too long how her lips would taste. Before he realized what he was doing, he was kissing her. Her lips were soft and inviting and she tasted even better than he'd imagined.

Momentarily stunned, Katrina put up no resistance. By the time she got over her surprise, she didn't want him to stop. His mouth was warm and enticing. The flames of desire began to spark to life within her and her hold around his neck tightened to harden the kiss.

Boyd had never been so instantly aroused by a woman. He wanted her then and there. *This isn't smart!* his inner voice warned. He started to ignore it, but a sudden combination of loud snorts and snores from the bedroom reminded him of the company he was keeping and the reason he was there.

"Damn!" he growled, breaking the contact. Furious with himself for his near loss of complete control and frustrated by unsatisfied urges, he rounded the coffee table and dropped her unceremoniously on the couch. Then returning to the rug in front of the fireplace, he tossed her pillow to her and put her gun on the coffee table.

As he rolled up in his blanket, Katrina frowned at him. His behavior made it clear he was angry with himself for having kissed her. Pride caused the hairs on the back of her neck to bristle and demanded that she say something. "Don't worry, I won't go shouting about that from the treetops." *It deserved to be shouted about from the top of a mountain,* her inner voice admitted, grudgingly. Not certain who she was angrier at...him for rejecting her or herself for the way her heart was still pounding wildly...she turned her back to him and ordered herself to sleep.

Boyd made no response. He could still taste her and he still wanted more. *Keeping the women and yourself alive depends on you keeping a clear head,* he growled mentally at himself. It also depended on him not forgetting that Katrina and her aunt could be playing a game with him as a pawn.

Chapter 6

Midmorning the next day, Katrina stood at the front window. Her job was to stand guard inside the house while her aunt cut a deal with the federal attorney. From her vantage point she could see anyone approaching the porch. She could also see through the bedroom door to the window in there.

Boyd and the two agents who had come with the attorney were patrolling the outside. She found herself searching for glimpses of him to reassure herself that he was all right. *Don't you have any pride? You know he's ecstatic to be free of your company,* she chided herself and forced her attention back to the porch and the interior of the cabin.

Outside, Boyd finished a wide sweep of the woods surrounding the cabin.

"Quiet?" Fred Carrelli, the senior agent who'd come with the attorney asked.

"Quiet," Boyd confirmed.

Fred's job was to watch for any movement on the road

leading up to the house. With a pair of binoculars, he could see through the tree cover to the main road. "Nothing here, either." Giving his eyes a rest, he pressed the talk button on his walkie-talkie. "Anything?" he asked into it.

"Nothing," came the reply from his partner. Charlie Klause, the other agent who'd arrived with the attorney, was posted at the rear of the cabin.

"Guess you'll be glad to get those two off your hands," Fred said, setting the walkie-talkie aside and again peering through the binoculars.

The implication in the man's voice placed Katrina in the same category as her aunt. Boyd experienced a nudge of irritation. In the next instant he was mocking himself. She and her aunt having an agenda of their own was one of the suspicions he'd been harboring since this began. Keeping his voice conversational, he said, "You think Officer Polenari is in on this with her aunt?"

"Maybe. You know what they say about a leopard not being able to change its spots. Or, could be she's in it with Garduchi. Her whole 'leaving the family' thing could have been staged. If that's the case, then even the aunt wouldn't know. Garduchi would keep a deep mole a secret, known only to himself."

"She hates Garduchi. She blames him and her father for her mother's death," Boyd said in Katrina's defense.

Fred gave him a patronizing look. "Maybe she does and maybe she doesn't. Could be she's just a good actress. Her father was one of the best enforcers in the business. If she's as good as he was, she could take out anyone without a blink of an eye and the death of a relative would mean nothing."

"If she wanted to take her aunt out, she would have already tried."

Fred shrugged. "Could be she's got a good reason for playing along for a while."

Boyd tried to picture Katrina as a cold-blooded killer. He couldn't. But was that his gut instinct or was it coming from a lower region of his body? He didn't like to think that he could be influenced by lust, but he was human. "I'm going to make another sweep." Heading off into the woods, he recalled how easily they'd escaped their tail. Had it been luck or had it been arranged? He'd been so certain she hated Garduchi. Cursing under his breath, he again cautioned himself not to let his guard down.

Inside, Katrina marvelled at her aunt's coolness in cutting the deal with the attorney. Leona had gotten him to agree in writing to everything she wanted.

"Of course this is all contingent upon you providing us with proof of Garduchi's guilt," the attorney said, when Leona finished making her demands. "Account numbers. Their locations. Amounts, etc."

"Of course." Leona gave him a dry look. "And I have everything you need…copies of the past five years of the private ledgers I kept for Vince that record all the monies received, where they came from and how they were laundered."

"And you have these ledgers with you?"

"Don't be ridiculous."

"Then just tell me where they are and I'll have someone pick them up."

Leona gave him a caustic look. "You get your grand jury together. I, my niece and Agent Logan will pick them up."

The attorney frowned. "You'll be much safer if you let us keep you hidden. We'll need your testimony to verify the records."

"Trusting the authorities is difficult for me. I'll feel more comfortable if I keep my aces in my own hand."

"You really should listen to him," Katrina encouraged. Not only was she convinced that her aunt would be safer if she complied with the attorney's wishes, Katrina had no desire to continue her association with Agent Logan.

Ignoring her niece, Leona sat back, crossed her arms and faced the attorney with resolve. "It's my way or you get nothing."

"That means the three of you'll be on your own," he countered.

"I have as much confidence in myself as I have in your people," she returned.

For a long moment a tense silence filled the cabin as each tried to stare the other down.

Katrina's money was on her aunt. She won.

"All right," the attorney snorted. "Have it your way. I'll convene a grand jury. It'll take a few days. I'll be in touch."

Leona smiled brightly at Katrina as the door closed behind the lawyer. "This will give us some time to get reacquainted."

Grudgingly, Katrina admitted that deep inside, she liked her aunt. She wasn't certain why. Most likely because Leona had been the only family member who'd shown her any real sympathy after her mother's death. And Leona had always been able to make her laugh. When her aunt wanted to, she could be quite witty. But Katrina wasn't blind to Leona's other sides. She was greedy and self-serving and those traits ran deep. "You're up to something, aren't you?"

"I'm just trying to stay alive."

"You have a plan. There's something you're not telling me."

"My plan is to let you and Agent Logan protect me." Leona rose, approached Katrina and placed an arm around her shoulders. "But you're right. There is something more. I wanted some time with you. Other than a few distant cousins I prefer to avoid, you're the only family member I have left." She gave Katrina's shoulders a squeeze. "You were such an adorable baby and such a sweet child."

Katrina considered the possibility that her aunt was telling the truth. Maybe going through the change of life had made Leona pine for family ties. But she couldn't stop thinking that the honey in her aunt's voice was just a little too thick. *I'm letting Agent Logan's suspicious mind affect me too strongly,* she chided herself. Her aunt was a survivor and she had to know that the only way to get out of this mess was to cooperate with the authorities.

Boyd entered with a dark scowl on his face. "Apparently we're going to be spending a little more time together."

"Your enthusiasm is overwhelming," Leona noted with a smile.

"I tried to talk her into placing herself entirely under the care of you and your fellow agents and allowing the attorney to arrange to have the evidence picked up," Katrina said, wanting him to know that she wasn't any happier about this situation than he was.

Boyd studied her narrowly. The lawyer had mentioned that Katrina had tried to dissuade her aunt. But she probably knew it was futile. If she was working for Garduchi, the evidence could be the prize in the game. Once she had it in hand, she was to take care of her aunt and destroy it.

His gaze was unnerving Katrina. "Don't look at me as if I'm the one being difficult," she snapped.

She looked and sounded innocent, but Boyd had learned that the most deadly of enemies could appear innocent on the surface. "I've got a headache," he growled, stalking to the cabinets and searching for some aspirin.

Leona grinned at Katrina. "You see, you did inherit some of the family traits. I don't know how many times I've been accused of giving a man a headache."

Her aunt was enjoying this. Giving her a rueful glance, Katrina turned to watch the cloud of dust in the distance as the car carrying the lawyer and two other agents left. "Do you think it's safe to stay here after all the traffic in and out today?" she asked.

"Probably. But there's no guarantee." Boyd had found the aspirin. He took two, then an extra one.

"I want to be on our way today, anyway," Leona said. "We've got a lot of ground to cover. And tonight I would like to stay someplace with room service and a decent wine selection."

"And where are we going?" Boyd asked.

Leona smiled with exaggerated sweetness. "You'll know when we get there."

Boyd shoved the bottle of aspirin in the pocket of his jeans. He was sure he would be needing it again.

Leona directed him to a small town a couple of hours southeast of the cabin. There she had him stop at an old Victorian house with a sign out front advertising it as a bed and breakfast.

"I left the rest of my luggage here," she said.

Katrina had been surprised when her aunt had insisted on changing before they left the cabin and had emerged from the bedroom in a polyester pantsuit. Now glancing over her shoulder, she discovered Leona had again put on the gray wig, the bright red lipstick, and the glasses. It was amazing, she thought, how just the clothes, the wig, the lipstick and the glasses could change her aunt's appearance so drastically.

Boyd wasn't surprised to discover his passenger's transformation. He was now certain that whatever Leona did, she did well and that she had planned her every move in advance. He just wished he knew what the outcome of her plan was.

"You," Leona addressed him, "may come inside and carry my suitcases out for me."

Katrina went as far as the front door, then stood guard on the porch.

A few minutes later, Leona emerged carrying a small overnight case. Behind her was Boyd with two large suitcases.

"You must have packed everything you owned," Boyd muttered as he hefted the cases into the back of the car.

"Not everything. But you certainly couldn't have thought I'd leave town with only that little bit of stuff I had in that bag, did you?" Leona signed. "I had to leave my mink behind but then I can always buy a new one."

Climbing back into the driver's seat, Boyd breathed a sigh of relief. His part of the job was nearly done. "Now that we have the ledgers, I can take you to a safe house near Washington so you'll be in easy distance to testify once the grand jury is convened."

Leona gave him a wry look. "You don't actually think I would be carrying the ledgers around with me in my suitcases?"

"You mean that there really is only clothes in those bags?" Boyd demanded, his frustration showing.

"So where are they?" Katrina asked, as disappointed as Boyd that they didn't now have them in their possession.

"You'll know when we pick them up," Leona replied. "Now let's get going. Head south."

It was after dark when Boyd decided it was time to stop. Periodically, he'd turned off of the main road and taken a side road that ran parallel to make certain they weren't being followed. Again leaving the main road, he drove until he found a small, out-of-the-way motel.

"I hope the accommodations improve somewhere along the line," Leona complained.

Boyd ignored her and went inside to register them. Coming out a few minutes later, he climbed into the driver's seat, then said, "If anyone asks, Katrina and I are the Claypools and you..." He turned to Leona. "You are Mrs. Snodgrass, my mother-in-law. It seemed like a perfect role for you."

Leona cast him a haughty glance. "I'm hungry."

"The manager said there's a fast-food place down the road that's open all night. We'll get something there and bring it back to our room to eat. The less we're in the public view, the better."

"You are obviously not a gourmet eater," she complained.

"Sometimes you have to settle for what you can get."

"Well, you go get it and Katrina and I will wait in the room."

Boyd clicked the master lock switch on his door console preventing her from opening her door. "We stick together."

"Your chosen traveling companion is as stubborn as a Missouri mule," Leona said to Katrina as Boyd pulled out of the parking lot.

That she hadn't "chosen" him was on the tip of her tongue. Instead, Katrina heard herself saying, "He's just doing his job." She couldn't believe she'd come to Boyd's defense. The man didn't trust her enough to leave her alone for even a few minutes with her aunt.

"I suppose," Leona muttered.

Surprised by Katrina's response, Boyd glanced at her.

"I'm assuming that your acute stubbornness is part of what makes you good at your job," she said.

Boyd grinned. "That sounds more like what I would have expected you to say."

Katrina studied him covertly. He liked having the animosity between them. Why? Was he afraid he might learn to like her? A sudden thought struck her. "I'll bet that knife wound in your back was put there by someone you liked and trusted...probably a woman."

Ignoring her remark, he pulled into the fast-food place and stopped in front of the large menu in the drive-through lane. "What do you want to eat?"

"A determined change of subject," Leona noted, mischief in her voice. "Obviously you're right, Katrina. It was a woman."

"It wasn't a woman. And that's the end of this discussion," he replied. "Now what do you two want to eat?"

Fair's fair, Katrina reasoned. He'd felt perfectly free asking her about herself and expecting answers. "I'll bet you're lying. You probably irritated her to the point of uncontrollable rage."

Boyd realized they were not going to stop until he told them what had happened. "It was a man...my first partner. I found out he was on the payroll of the mob boss we were trying to get some evidence on. He tried to kill me to keep me quiet." His jaw hardened to let them know that he now considered the subject absolutely closed. "What do you want to eat?"

This time they placed their orders.

"I don't suppose we could find a decent bottle of wine to go with this...this meal," Leona pleaded on the way back to the motel.

"We have to stay clearheaded," Katrina replied.

"You and Agent Logan have to stay clearheaded," Leona corrected.

"We're not making any more stops than necessary." Boyd's curt tone stopped any further pleading from Leona.

She did, however, continue to glower at him until they were seated at the table in the motel room. Then with a final aggrieved grimace in his direction, she turned her attention to Katrina and smiled motherly. "So, do you have a boyfriend?"

"No." Katrina said it with a finality she hoped would stop any more questions. It didn't work.

"Why not?" Leona demanded. "You're pretty enough. And sweet. Men like 'sweet' women. Don't they, Agent Logan?"

"Men like women they can trust," Boyd returned grimly.

Tired of telling him that she could be trusted, Katrina merely cast him a caustic glance, then returned her attention to her aunt. "Most men exit quickly when they discover I'm a cop. For those that stick around for a second date, eventually the questions about family arise. So, what does your father do? My father's dead. Oh, I'm sorry. Don't be, he was an enforcer for Vince Garduchi. Suddenly, my date's looking at his watch and remembering something important he forgot to do."

Leona frowned sympathetically. "Wimps. You just haven't met the right man yet. You need someone macho, confident, fearless." She turned to Boyd. "Do you have any brothers at home with a more friendly disposition?"

An unexpected twinge of jealousy at the thought of Katrina with another man shook Boyd. Casting Leona a cool glance, he continued eating.

"I'm sure that Agent Logan wouldn't want me as a member of his family," Katrina said.

Boyd met her icy gaze. "I have two brothers. But neither of them would suit you any better than I would."

Katrina was stunned by the glint of possessiveness in the dark depths of his eyes.

Realizing how close he'd come to admitting how attracted he was to her, Boyd scowled angrily at himself and returned his attention to his food.

"That's definitely not promising," Leona muttered.

Katrina made no response. She was recalling Boyd's kiss. If she could ever break down his barrier of distrust, maybe...

"You're part Native American, aren't you?" Leona asked, continuing to study Boyd with interest.

Pride showed in his eyes. "My mother is Apache."

"No doubt she's one of those submissive women who caters to your father's every whim and spoilt her sons by waiting on you hand and foot," Leona said. "That's why you're so overbearingly authoritarian."

Boyd abruptly grinned. "Anyone who ever called my mother submissive to her face would live to regret it." The grin vanished. "As for my being authoritarian, I'm just trying to keep you alive." His gaze narrowed on her. "But I am beginning to wonder how you survived in Garduchi's service for so long. I'm surprised he didn't have you knocked off for being such an irritant."

"Don't be ridiculous. I'm not stupid. I was always polite and respectful to his face."

"The not-being-stupid part is questionable. You stole from a man who thinks that death is the only viable retribution," Katrina reminded her.

"So I showed a little bad judgment. Nobody's perfect."

Katrina shook her head and finished eating her meal in silence.

While her aunt was in the bathroom preparing for bed, Katrina's gaze traveled over their accommodations. There were two double beds. That meant sharing a bed with her aunt again. "I'll take the first watch," she said. "I'm not going to get much sleep anyway."

"There's no need to keep watch. No one followed us here." Boyd frowned at the two beds. He knew he should keep his distance from Officer Polenari but he couldn't make her spend the night in a chair and he needed to stretch out on a bed. "If you promise to keep on your side, you can share my bed."

Katrina considered rejecting his offer. His cold, businesslike manner made her feel like a pest. But she was exhausted and stiff and the desire to lie down was too hard to resist. "You've got a deal," she replied in equally cool tones.

When Leona discovered their agreed-upon arrangements, she wasn't happy. "I feel as your aunt, I should protest," she said.

"I'm keeping my clothes on," Katrina assured her.

"And I give you my word, I'll keep my hands off of her," Boyd added, then realized he was saying this more as an order to himself than as a reassurance to the aunt.

Leona shook her head. "I hope the two of you don't get in a fight over the covers and maim each other. Good night, children."

Katrina pulled the bedspread over to her side. "I'll just roll up in this," she informed Boyd. "You can sleep under the sheet and blanket."

Boyd nodded. For a long moment he studied her with indecision. Finally, he said, "I'm going to take a shower.

I want your word that you won't make any phone calls or leave this room.''

Disbelief showed on her face. "You're actually going to take my word?"

"It's going to be a long trip. I can't watch you every second."

"You have my word."

Boyd heard no hesitation in her voice. Either she was on the level or she still needed him. Or, he was playing the fool and she and her aunt would try to sneak out. *Might as well find out now,* he decided. But he wouldn't make it easy if they did decide to run. Saying he wanted to check the fluid levels in the car, he went out and loosened a couple of wires. Returning to the room, he left the keys to the car in plain view and went into the bathroom to bathe.

When he came out a short while later, Leona and Katrina were both there. Leona was snoring and Katrina was curled up in the bedspread watching television. The tiny wad of crumpled paper he'd surreptitiously dropped on the floor and pushed up against the door was where he'd left it, telling him they hadn't opened the door.

Unable to keep her gaze from drifting in his direction, Katrina felt her temperature rising. He was shirtless and shoeless, dressed only in a pair of jeans. His skin still glistened with lingering dampness and his dark hair was wet and mused. She didn't think she'd ever seen a man look more virile. Jerking her gaze back to the television, she kept it there while he combed his hair and pulled on a T-shirt.

Then going over to the phone, he pressed the redial. He got a local pizza place.

She frowned at him. "I gave you my word we wouldn't use the phone."

"Just checking," he returned.

The man was impossible, Katrina fumed. She'd allowed

herself to actually begin to think he was learning to trust her. When he stretched out on the bed beside her, she told herself to ignore him. Instead she heard herself saying dryly, "So you actually took a shower."

"I told you I was going to."

Deciding to let him know that she was aware that he'd left his keys out in plain view for the express purpose of seeing if the women would run, she said, "I considered getting up and clanging your keys. Good thing I didn't. We would have both been embarrassed if you'd come rushing out of the bathroom with only your gun."

The thought that the lusty effect she had on him could have been exposed caused his neck to redden. "This isn't a game," he growled.

"You're right," she agreed, wishing she'd kept her mouth shut. Her jabbering had caused her to consider what he might have looked like and the image that her mind had conjured up was causing her blood to race. Switching off the television, she ordered herself to sleep.

Boyd placed a call to his superior to let him know they were all right. Then lying on his back, he stared into the dark. Bedroom games he'd like to play with Officer Polenari occupied his thoughts. *Keep your mind on the business at hand!* he commanded himself for the umpteenth time and closing his eyes, he slept.

Chapter 7

Katrina awoke comfortable and rested. Feeling the pressure of something laying on her, she realized Boyd had thrown his arm over her. A sense of being safe and protected wove through her. She scowled at herself. He wasn't protecting her, he was making certain she didn't try to sneak out during the night. Even in his sleep, his distrust was so strong, he'd felt the need to hold onto her. Squirming free, she left the bed and went into the bathroom.

Boyd turned on his back and stared up at the ceiling. He'd been awake for a short while. When he'd woken and discovered he had his arm around Katrina, he'd liked the closeness. He'd told himself he could be holding on to a rattlesnake, but still he'd lain there quietly unwilling to break the contact. The remembered taste of her lips taunted him and he wanted a second serving. Angry with himself, he rose and woke Leona.

"Go away," she grumbled and covered her head with her pillow.

"Time to be on the move," he insisted.

She raised the pillow just enough to glare at him. "There's no rush. The attorney said it would take him a few days to convene a grand jury."

"I want those ledgers in hand so that when that time comes we can be in Washington within hours."

Leona continued to glower at him as she tossed off her pillow and rose.

Hearing the locks on the door being undone, Boyd's attention was jerked away from her to Katrina. "Where do you think you're going?"

The suspicion in his voice rankled her. "Nowhere. I was just seeing if they'd left a newspaper outside the door." Her gaze shifted to Leona. "My aunt likes to take her time in the morning."

"And I don't intend to rush for anyone," Leona added.

Boyd waited until Katrina had picked up the newspaper left outside their door and relocked the locks, then he again stretched out on the bed and lay staring up at the ceiling. He should have let Lewis take this assignment, he grumbled silently. Then the thought that Katrina could be exactly as she presented herself brought the realization that he wanted to be the one to protect her in case there was trouble, and that realization brought a mental groan. Sitting up, he switched on the television and found the news channel.

It was nearly three hours later before they were finally ready to begin their day's journey. Leona had insisted on breakfast at a local diner instead of a fast-food place and she'd also insisted that they keep the motel room and return there to freshen up after they ate.

"So what direction do I head in?" Boyd asked as they sat in the car and he prepared to pull out of the parking lot.

"Head for Natchez," Leona replied, handing Katrina the map.

Well, at least she wasn't keeping their destination a secret any longer, Boyd thought.

They'd been riding for nearly an hour in silence when Katrina could no longer keep the thoughts bouncing around in her head to herself any longer. Turning to look at her aunt, she said, "You were always cautioning me not to cross Vince. You used to tell me that he could hunt anyone down anywhere. And you used to say it with admiration. The one thing I never would have questioned was your loyalty to him. I still can't believe you actually stole from him."

Hatred glistened in Leona's eyes. For a long moment she was silent, then said, "Maybe I wouldn't have if I could have gotten my hands around your uncle's throat and choked the life out of him. But he was already dead by the time I found out what he'd done."

Katrina had never heard such venom in her aunt's voice. "What did he do?"

"A simple affair I could have dealt with." Leona gave a sharp wave of her hand. "Men begin to worry about losing their macho image so they play around a little. But not Carlos Serrenito. He did it in style. And Vince helped him. Carlos set his mistress up in a house, bought in her name, and fathered two sons by her. Just because I was barren didn't justify that. The wedding vows say 'for better or worse until death us do part.' And I lived up to my end of that bargain. Believe me Carlos wasn't that easy to live with either."

Katrina recalled her uncle being a very stern, cold man who demanded that everything be done his way. She even remembered seeing him slap her aunt once and guessed that wasn't the only time.

"And," Leona continued, "his mistress, the house, the boys were all paid for out of Carlos's salary and by bonuses

Vince gave him in cash, under the table. Carlos told me that he'd gotten into debt gambling and Vince was deducting his losses, some each month from his salary. Instead the money was going to his mistress. I even wrote the checks to her. The woman was Vince's niece, Stella Berrette, the one with brains but homely as sin. I never saw her around, but Vince liked to put family on the payroll if they needed a little help so I didn't think anything about her getting monthly checks. I guess Vince figured being a kept woman was as close as Stella was going to come to having a man of her own.''

"That would be a shock," Katrina said sympathetically.

"A shock? A shock? It was humiliating. Everyone knew but me. After Carlos died, behind my back, Vince arranged for Stella and the boys to come to a private viewing of him in his casket. Then she had the nerve to come openly to the funeral and bring her sons along as well. It wasn't until we were leaving the cemetery that I overheard Roseanne Garduchi and Wilma Valpreo talking and found out the truth. You know how loud Wilma can whisper. It's a wonder the Pope in Rome didn't hear her. I went directly to Vince and demanded to know how he could have allowed me to be humiliated that way.''

Apparently Vince Garduchi had never taken seriously the old saying about how dangerous a woman scorned could be, Boyd mused.

The sarcasm in Leona's voice increased. "He said that he'd suggested to Stella that perhaps she shouldn't attend the funeral but his niece had wept because of her deep love of Carlos and argued that the boys should have a chance to say a final, graveside goodbye to their father. 'She's family,' he said to me. 'And she was right. The boys should have the right to pay respect to their father.' Then he pointed out that I had a well-paid position in his organization and it would be foolish to do anything to threaten it. He also mentioned that it was tragic how so many widows followed their husbands to the grave...his little way of letting me know that if I caused any trouble, I'd find myself being taken for a ride by Louey and Victor and there'd be no return trip.''

"Now I understand why you did what you did," Katrina said. "It had nothing to do with a midlife crisis. It was revenge."

"You haven't heard the worst yet."

Katrina stared at her aunt in disbelief. "It gets worse?"

Leona nodded. "The reading of the will. Carlos legally recognized the boys as his sons and left half of everything we owned to them and their mother. The house, our savings, what was in our checking account...everything. I was in a rage. Vince showed up that evening and told me he'd made arrangements with his niece to turn down her portion of the house so that I could keep my home. In return he paid her its value out of his own pocket and kept her on the payroll. For that, I was supposed to be grateful! I knew that behind my back, the other wives were laughing at me." Leona drew a calming breath. "But I ignored them, pretended that I was pleased."

Boyd glanced at Leona in the rearview mirror. He recognized the murderous look in her eyes. This was not a woman who dealt well with wounded pride. "I'm surprised you didn't try to kill Garduchi."

"I considered it. But that would only have gotten me killed in return. So I decided to hurt him in a way that would bring me a great deal of pleasure. I took his money and, if I get away, there will be a blemish on his reputation he can never get rid of. He'll have been outdone by a woman." She laughed. "And then as icing on the cake, there's the jail time he'll be serving." She grinned at Katrina. "Don't ever let anyone tell you that revenge isn't sweet."

"You're not going to feel that way if you end up in a grave," Katrina cautioned.

Leona smiled confidently. "I'm counting on you and Agent Logan to see that doesn't happen."

Katrina had to admit that she felt a little better knowing her aunt hadn't gotten herself into this predicament simply out of greed.

Several miles outside of Natchez, Leona insisted that Boyd stop at an abandoned gas station. "You two need disguises," she said. "I'm sure Vince has sent out descriptions of both of you."

Katrina had to admit her aunt was right. Opening up one of her suitcases, Leona pulled out a red wig. "I've always thought you'd look good as a redhead," she said tossing the wig to Katrina.

"As for you." Leona turned her attention to Boyd. "I figured they'd send a man but I had no idea what you'd look like. But I came prepared with several choices. The black beard and mustache will do." She tossed them to him with a tube of glue.

Katrina was glad her hair was short. That made it easy to get the wig on.

"And now a little eye makeup and some lipstick." Leona handed Katrina a makeup kit and directed her on how she wanted it applied.

"I look like a hooker," Katrina grumbled.

"You look terrific," Leona insisted and turned her attention back to Boyd.

Grudgingly, he'd glued the beard and mustache into place.

"You're perfect," Leona said. "You look like a mountain man come into the big city for a look around. And that accent of yours will fit your disguise perfectly.''

She turned back to Katrina. ''You need to speak with a southern flair as well.'' Adding with her own southern accent, ''I watched *Gone with the Wind* twice to get mine right. How do you like it?''

''Very good,'' Katrina replied mimicking her aunt's drawl.

Boyd had to admit that Leona had thought of everything. Pulling back on the road, he wondered what other tricks she had up her sleeve.

Reaching Natchez, Boyd found them a motel. It was late afternoon.

''I've got to stretch my legs,'' Leona said. ''We'll find the main shopping district and do some looking around.''

Boyd wasn't happy with the thought of them exposing themselves so openly. But he also was feeling the need for some exercise. And their disguises were good.

Katrina, too, wasn't interested in spending the rest of the day closeted in a motel room with the two of them. She also hoped her aunt was finished playing games and was going to pick up the ledgers.

But Leona seemed only interested in shopping. Then spying a quaint restaurant, she insisted on eating there. ''I must have some decent food,'' she said and strode in before either Boyd or Katrina could stop her.

By the time they returned to the motel, Katrina and Boyd were both tense from constantly keeping an eye out for trouble. Leona, on the other hand was relaxed and very pleased with her purchases.

''I hope you plan to pick up those ledgers tomorrow so I can get you to a safe house near Washington,'' Boyd said in a tone that warned her of dire consequences if she didn't.

"We'll get them soon," she promised. "Now turn around. I'm tired and I want to get changed for bed."

With his back to Leona, Boyd looked at Katrina, impatience written on his face.

Knowing it was futile but wanting to prove to Boyd that she was trying to cooperate, she said, "Aunt Leona, it really isn't safe to keep running around the country so openly."

Leona turned and smiled at her. "I'm sure you'll do an excellent job protecting me." Then climbing into bed, she went to sleep.

Katrina gave Boyd a look that said she'd done all she could, then headed into the bathroom to take a shower.

While they ate breakfast the next morning, Leona pulled some brochures out of her purse. "I want to tour these old plantation houses," she said.

Boyd frowned at her. "I really don't think that sightseeing is a wise pastime."

"This could be my only chance. It's something I've always wanted to do and I insist upon doing it."

Boyd groaned.

"Really, Aunt Leona, I don't think this is such a good idea," Katrina protested.

Leona smiled at her. "Don't you remember how we always planned to take a trip down here but we never got to. Now don't fret. Everything is going to turn out just fine."

"Overconfidence has been the downfall of many a man," Boyd warned.

Leona simply smiled at him, then finished her breakfast.

As they climbed the stairs of the porch at the first plantation house, Leona said with disappointment, "This isn't anything like Tara in *Gone With the Wind.* It's just a big, old, white frame house.''

Katrina barely heard her aunt's complaint. She was experiencing an uneasy feeling in the pit of her stomach. She glanced around. The only people she saw other than them was a group of elderly ladies. Entering the house, they began the tour on the lower level. Katrina's uneasiness grew. Flashes of memory began to dart through her mind. When the guide paused at the door of the downstairs parlor, vivid images began to emerge. Terror threatened to overwhelm Katrina. "I have to get out of here," she mumbled and fled from the house.

Boyd and Leona caught up with her outside.

"You're shaking like a leaf in a high wind," Leona said, looking at her worriedly.

Seeing how pale she'd become, Boyd became worried that she might faint. He scooped her up in his arms. "We're going back to the motel," he informed Leona in a voice that told her she'd better not balk.

"Yes, of course," she replied, continuing to study Katrina with concern.

In Boyd's arms, Katrina felt safe and her shaking lessened. The images grew stronger and she wrapped her arms around his neck and buried her face in his neck in an attempt to stop them. It didn't work.

When her hold on him tightened, Boyd tightened his hold on her. The desire to protect and comfort her overwhelmed him. "I'll see that no harm comes to you," he vowed gruffly.

Tears welled in her eyes. Her father had controlled her with threats of reprimand. Her mother and Leona had constantly warned her to behave and keep her thoughts to herself. No one had ever promised to protect her.

When they reached the car and Boyd sat her in her seat, she felt deserted.

Sitting on the edge of the backseat, Leona placed a hand on Katrina's shoulder. "What happened in there?"

"I remembered something," Katrina replied shakily.

Boyd had climbed in behind the wheel just in time to hear her response. "Must have been one hell of a memory."

Katrina nodded.

Leona studied her anxiously. "What in the world could you remember that would cause such a reaction?"

"It was the Christmas Eve after mother died. We'd been to a party at Vince's...me, my father and brother. On the way home, my father told my brother he had some personal business that needed to be taken care of. My brother asked if he could help and my father said, 'Sure, it's as good a time as any for your initiation.' My brother was fifteen at the time."

Katrina felt dizzy and paused to draw a deep breath, then continued. "They thought I was asleep in the backseat. When they stopped the car and got out, I peeked through the window. They were walking up to a house a lot like the one we were just in. The porch light was on. I saw my father hand my brother a gun with an extra long barrel. I know now that what made it look so long was that there was a silencer on the end of the barrel. Then my father unscrewed the porch light so that the porch was dark."

"I can't believe they took you along on a hit," Leona fumed.

Katrina trembled, then continued. "My father knocked on the door. Lights came on upstairs and then downstairs. A man opened the door. My brother shot him. Through the open door, I saw a woman coming down the stairs. My brother shot her, too. My father shifted the man's feet so that they could close the door, then they returned to the car.''

Katrina paused to take another deep breath. ''I had lain back down on the backseat. I was trembling so badly, I was sure they would notice but they didn't. They wanted to get away fast so my brother didn't look in the backseat until they'd pulled away. Without the interior light on, I was just a shadow. He called out my name and I rubbed my eyes and pretended to be just waking up. I asked if we were home yet and he said no so I asked why he'd woken me. He said if I hadn't been sleeping he'd have had to shoot me, then he laughed and told me to go back to sleep.''

''You really think your brother would have killed you?'' Boyd asked.

''He might have,'' Leona replied for Katrina. ''Jimmy had a real cold streak...colder even than his father's and he liked killing.''

Katrina nodded her agreement. ''I was overcome by fear. I couldn't stop shaking. Then suddenly everything went black. I must have fainted. When I came to, I convinced myself that I'd just had a very bad dream. But it wasn't a dream. It was real.''

Boyd realized that she must have lived her entire childhood in fear. He cupped her face in his hands. ''It's over. Your father and brother are dead. They can't hurt you.''

Tears trickled from her eyes. ''I'm so ashamed to have been from the same gene pool.''

All lingering suspicion that she might be a cold-blooded killer had vanished. ''You have your mother's genes as well,'' Boyd reminded her, trying to ease the pain he saw in her eyes.

''He's right,'' Leona said.

Boyd scowled at Leona. ''There will be no more sight-seeing today. We've played this game long enough. It's time to go get those ledgers.''

Leona sat back in her seat. ''I agree that touring these old plantation houses is not a good idea. We might as well head for Memphis. I've always wanted to see Graceland.''

Still shaken by the remembered terror of that Christmas night, Katrina looked back at her aunt. ''Can I assume there is a purpose behind that?''

''Of course there's a purpose. I want to see the place. And since it doesn't look anything like this place, it shouldn't send you into shock. This could be the last trip I ever take. I intend to make the most of it,'' Leona returned.

Boyd frowned. ''Graceland is a very popular sight. By some quirk of fate, one of Garduchi's men might be there on vacation. And it might be someone who will see through your disguise. It's not a good idea.''

''I want to tour Graceland.'' Leona insisted.

So maybe Memphis was where she'd stashed the ledgers, Boyd reasoned hopefully. ''All right. Graceland it is,'' he drawled grudgingly.

As they drove back to the motel, Katrina recalled the strong feel of Boyd's arms around her and his promise to protect her. The chilling fear caused by the sudden memory of that Christmas night faded. She looked to Boyd, studying the hard line of his jaw. ''You sounded sincere back there. Does that mean you're learning to trust me?''

''Not entirely,'' he admitted honestly. ''I don't think you're a killer but you and your aunt might still have an agenda of your own.'' He glanced at Leona in the rearview mirror as he said this, wanting to see her reaction. Amusement spread over her face.

''Killer?'' she asked, at the back of his head for an explanation.

''He thought I might be working as an enforcer for Garduchi, like my father and my brother and I might be wanting to find you to kill you,'' Katrina elaborated before Boyd could respond.

"You, a killer?'' Leona laughed. "You hated killing even a fly. I always figured you'd get yourself killed in the line of duty because you wouldn't be able to fire your gun at a thug who was aiming at you.'' Her gaze shifted to the back of Boyd's neck. "As for Katrina and I having an agenda of our own, I can assure you that her only objective is to get me in front of that grand jury.''

"I really hope that's true.'' As he spoke, Boyd knew he'd never wanted anything more strongly.

"Don't you remember how we used to talk about touring Graceland?'' Leona asked Katrina a while later as they headed north.

"Yes.'' Katrina searched her aunt's face for any sign that this was not merely a whim on Leona's part. She couldn't tell. It was not normally Leona's nature to be guided by whimsy. But clearly the touring of Natchez had served no purpose as far as collecting the ledgers was concerned. "I just never would have expected you to want to go there with Garduchi on your tail.''

"He's not. Agent Logan has assured us of that.'' Leona studied the back of Boyd's head. "He might be stubborn, but it's my guess he's very good at his job.''

"If I was very good at my job, I wouldn't be letting you expose yourself so openly,'' Boyd grumbled.

"You have no choice. Consider it a possibly dying woman's last wish.''

"I wish you would reconsider,'' Katrina pleaded. "If the ledgers are there, tell me where they are and I'll pick them up.''

Leona gave her a patronizing look. "Don't be ridiculous.

I would never stash the ledgers where some nosy, preco-
cious child might stumble on them. Besides, why would I
want to tour Graceland if I'd already been there? Now don't
worry, our disguises are excellent. We'll be fine.''

Katrina shook her head. ''Agent Logan isn't the only one
in this car who is stubborn as a Missouri mule.''

''I prefer to think of myself as having taken control of
my life.'' Leona sighed heavily. ''For as long as I can remember, there has been a man telling me what I could do
and what I couldn't do.''

''You obviously needed some guidance to keep out of
trouble,'' Boyd noted.

''I really think we should skip touring Graceland,'' Katrina protested again.

''No. Whatever time I have left, I intend to do what I
want.''

It occurred to Katrina that she'd ruled out a midlife crisis
too soon. ''Have you considered talking to a doctor about
taking hormones?''

Leona tossed her a dry look. ''I know exactly what I'm
doing.''

In spite of his determination to remain skeptical of Katrina, Boyd found himself wanting to keep his vow to protect her. ''Do you realize you're putting your niece's life
in danger as well as your own? If you get spotted, she could
easily get killed in the cross fire.''

''Katrina became a policewoman. She puts her life on
the line daily. She's safer with me than she is on those
streets she patrols.'' Leona sat back and closed her eyes.
''If you want that information on Vince, you'll take me to
Graceland. Wake me when we get to Memphis.''

Boyd cursed under his breath.

Katrina covertly studied him. The beard and mustache
made him look even grimmer than usual. But she had a

question she had to ask. Waiting until she heard light snoring from the backseat, she said, "Are you really concerned about my safety or was that just a ploy to try to get my aunt to cooperate?"

"Both," he admitted tersely.

She heard the self-directed anger in his voice. "You want to protect me but you're not sure I'm worth protecting."

Again he glanced at her. "You don't know how badly I want to believe you're on the level."

She saw the flash of heat in his eyes. A responding heat swept through her. "Boyd?" she said his name softly, a question in her voice.

This time when he glanced toward her, she saw ice in his eyes and knew he was again angry with himself for having shown warm feelings toward her. The man was twice as stubborn as a Missouri mule, she fumed in frustration. Maybe even three or fours times as stubborn.

Chapter 8

It was after dark when they reached Memphis. As Katrina snuggled into the bedspread, staying as far from Boyd as possible, it occurred to her that her aunt had stopped complaining about their lodgings and the food from the fast-food places. Hopefully, Leona was finally taking her situation seriously.

But the next morning proved her wrong. As they put on their disguises in preparation for going outside of their room, Leona continued to insist on touring Graceland.

"This beard and mustache are extremely uncomfortable," Boyd grumbled at her. "I hope this is the last day I'll have to wear them."

Leona smiled sweetly. "They give you character."

Katrina gave Boyd a sympathetic look.

Again he found himself hoping they were on the same side.

"Isn't it lovely," Leona declared with a wide sweep of her arm toward the mansion and gardens, when after a wait in line they finally entered the grounds of Graceland.

"Lovely," Katrina agreed, only momentarily glancing in the direction her aunt indicated before continuing her surveillance of the other tourists.

"Relax," Leona admonished.

"I'll relax when you're tucked away in a safe house," Katrina returned.

Boyd took a position behind them. "If you see anyone you recognize or even think you recognize, let me know."

Katrina nodded.

Ignoring them, Leona continued to point out every detail she found interesting. "Your uncle—that snake—and I saw Elvis perform in Vegas," she said as they finished their tour of the mansion. "It was a wonderful show. He was a true performer. It's so sad that he died so young."

"He wasn't that much younger than you," Katrina noted pointedly.

Leona started to give her a wry glance when she suddenly paled. "What's Sammy Ramous doing here?"

Immediately, Katrina and Boyd sandwiched Leona between them.

"Where?" Katrina demanded.

"There." Leona nodded toward a group of people in the distance.

"What's he look like?" Boyd demanded.

"Short, slender, blond hair, fortyish," Katrina replied.

"Beady eyes and he's fifty," Leona corrected. The group parted and she suddenly breathed a sigh of relief and her color returned. "I was wrong. It's not him."

"Sight-seeing with you is certainly different," Katrina muttered.

Leona sighed. "You both were right. This was not a good idea. If Agent Logan will agree to splurge, or I'll even pay the bill, we'll go check into a hotel with room service, and I won't leave the room until tomorrow morning. At which time, I will take you to where I've stashed my evidence.''

"Why do we have to wait until tomorrow?" Boyd asked.

"Because I can't collect it until tomorrow," she replied. "Now how about the hotel?"

"It's a deal," Boyd agreed and Katrina breathed a sigh of relief.

"Other than my little scare and Katrina's sudden memory purge, this has been a wonderful trip," Leona said as they sat in their room waiting for their dinner to arrive. "I can't tell you how good it felt to tell someone what I really thought of Vince, Carlos and Stella."

The anger that had been building in Boyd demanded to be vented. "You knew when you sent Katrina to talk to Garduchi that he knew you'd taken the money for revenge. You put her life in danger for no reason."

Surprised by his outburst, Katrina looked at him and saw the protectiveness in his eyes. Even though he was determined not to trust her, he still cared about her. A warm feeling wove through her.

Leona shrugged. "There was always the chance he would buy the religious conversion story. Carlos's death had produced one shock after another. If he had, I could have gone back and kept the money where I'd hidden it. Of course he would never have let me do his accounting again, but I was ready to retire anyway. As for Katrina being in danger, Vince isn't stupid. He knew the FBI would be watching his house. He had to let her leave. Besides, it was me he was after. Since I'd contacted her once, he had to assume I'd contact her again."

A knock on the door interrupted further conversation.

Boyd motioned for Katrina to stand to one side, her gun at the ready while he answered. Her body tensed. If it was one of Garduchi's men on the other side of that door, he could shoot Boyd through it. "I'll open the door," she said, brushing past him.

Boyd grabbed her arm. "Stay back. This is my job."

The heat of his hand traveled up her arm and the desire to keep him from harm grew even stronger. "She's my aunt."

"If anyone is going to be shot by a bellhop, it will be me." Leona strode past them and opened the door before either had a chance to stop her.

Katrina barely had time to hide her gun behind her back before a ruddy-faced teenager and an older man pushed the food-laden carts inside. Boyd had released her arm but the imprint of his touch lingered along with the heat.

Leona gave the boy and man a big tip and saw them to the door. Once they were gone, she smiled happily at Boyd and Katrina. "Aha. The aroma of real food."

"Don't ever do that again," Boyd growled.

To Katrina, he said, "And in the future you follow my orders."

The fear for him still lingered. "I will not let you get shot because of my aunt."

He read the determination on her face. Pleasure that she didn't want to see him harmed wove through him and again the urge to trust her was strong. *Or it could all be an act to win your confidence?* his little voice warned.

"Let's not ruin our dinner with depressing thoughts," Leona said. Her smile waned a little as she picked up the bottle of sparkling white grape juice. "However, I do think your insistence on not having any alcohol is going a bit far," she addressed Boyd, then shrugged and returned her attention back to the bottle. "At least this will give the same bubbly effect as champagne. You two take the warming covers off our plates while I open it.''

Katrina's shoulder brushed Boyd's chest as she moved to obey. Images of him shirtless flashed in her mind and a fire blazed to life within her. Looking up she saw a heat in the brown depths of his eyes that matched the heat flowing through her. Then his gaze became shuttered, reminding her that he was determined to fight any attraction he felt for her.

Boyd ordered himself to move away from her. Instead, he cupped her chin in his hand and looked into her face. When she'd headed for the door, the fear that she could be shot had shaken him to the core. ''From now on, you follow my orders without question,'' he repeated curtly.

His touch made her knees threaten to buckle. ''I will not allow you to get hurt because of my aunt,'' she repeated.

He wanted to kiss her. His mouth moved toward hers. He was only inches away when he reminded himself about the knife wound in his back. Straightening, he released her and stepped away.

Katrina had watched as the fire that had again flamed in his eyes was replaced by cool distrust. Feeling deserted and frustrated, she frowned at him.

Leona approached with the wine glasses half-filled with sparkling grape juice. ''I want to make a toast,'' she said.

Katrina and Boyd, both fighting emotions that had them shaken, accepted their glasses without protest.

''To the end of our journey,'' Leona said, clinking her glass to theirs.

Boyd nodded his agreement and swallowed.

Irritated by his obvious desire to be rid of her company, Katrina gave him a dry look then downed her drink.

''Damn!'' she heard him growl just before she felt the room begin to spin. From somewhere in the fog that seemed to be closing over her mind, she heard her aunt's voice and saw Leona holding onto Boyd's arm.

"Now, just lie down," Leona was saying, easing him onto the bed. He was struggling ineffectually as if he'd lost his coordination. "If you don't cooperate, Katrina is going to fall before I can get to her," Leona reprimanded. "You wouldn't want her to get hurt, now would you?"

"Go help her," Boyd ordered, his words slurring as he tried to rise, then fell back across the bed.

Katrina tried to move forward toward him. Her legs didn't want to function properly and she began to sway.

"Now, dear, you come along," Leona said, taking her arm and guiding her to the second bed in the room.

"You put something in our drinks," Katrina accused, the words coming out with difficulty.

"It's time for us to part company," Leona said. "Now lie down."

Katrina didn't want to obey but her legs were refusing to hold her any longer. "You promised to help put Garduchi away."

"Now that really would be fatal. You rest." Leona lifted Katrina's feet up onto the bed.

The last thing Katrina was aware of was her aunt placing a light kiss on her cheek.

Katrina opened one eye just enough to see sunlight streaming in through the small space between the drapes. She tried to lift her head, then dropped it back on the pillow. "What a headache!" she moaned.

A deep-throated groan followed by a curse, sounded from somewhere nearby. She turned her head in the direction from which it had come, opened both eyes and tried to focus. Boyd's long form came into view.

She saw him slowly easing himself to his feet. Bumping

into a chair, he cursed under his breath, then continued on into the bathroom. Running water drowned out a string of expletives.

Her mind was clearing by the time he came out drying his face. "What the hell did she slip us?" he demanded.

"I have no clue," she replied, following his example and heading to the bathroom to splash cold water on her face.

When she came out, she found him sitting on the edge of the bed rubbing the back of his neck. Straightening, he said, "She left a note. She says she wanted to spend a little time with you before she took off on her own and she knew that pretending to want to give evidence against Garduchi was the only way. She says that she's going to fix it so Garduchi won't come after you but she suggests that you really should relocate."

"I should have known she'd never give evidence against him. She let her need for revenge cause her to behave somewhat irrationally, but she's not crazy." Her head still throbbing, Katrina sat down on the edge of the other bed and rested her head in her hands.

"Do you have any idea where she might have gone?"

"None."

Boyd looked at his watch. "She has a fourteen-hour start." He'd put a homing device on the car in case the two of them decided to run and managed to get away from him, but Leona had had plenty of time to get out of range. His jaw hardened. "I'll find her."

"*We'll* find her."

"You're coming along all right," he growled. "I want you where I can keep an eye on you."

She frowned at the continued suspicion in his voice. "You can't believe I had anything to do with this. My aunt was my chance to prove to people I was on the level. If I'd helped deliver evidence against Garduchi, they would have to stop distrusting my motives for becoming a police officer.''

"So far you've played straight with me," Boyd admitted. "And my instincts are to trust you, but I'm not sure I can trust them where you're concerned."

Again she saw the fire in his eyes. "You can."

"I wish it was that easy," he growled in frustration.

Her own frustration showed. "You had one bad experience and I'm paying for it."

"I trusted the man with my life and he nearly took it."

The ringing of the phone caused the pounding in Katrina's head to increase. She reached for it, but Boyd got to it first.

"Where are you?" he demanded.

Katrina knew from the fury on his face that the caller could only be Leona.

After less than a minute, Boyd dropped the receiver back in the cradle. "She gave me directions to where I can pick up the car. It's at the airport."

While Katrina took a couple of minutes to make herself presentable, he placed a call to his superiors.

"I guess they weren't too happy," she said.

"They didn't expect me to be blindsided by a fifty-nine-year-old female accountant."

"She's my aunt. I'm the one who should have known not to trust her."

She looked so unhappy, he wanted to take her in his arms and reassure her. His inner voice intervened. *This could be an act, all part of some scheme she and her aunt cooked up to help Leona disappear.* "Let's just find her," he said through clenched teeth.

Boyd pulled a picture of Leona out of the folder in his suitcase. For the next two hours they questioned every ticket seller, airport security person, janitor and car rental agent they could find, first showing them the photo and when that didn't produce results, describing Leona in her disguise. Their inquiry was futile.

Back at the hotel, they found a message from Lewis Hamond to call him.

"Leona called Garduchi a little over an hour ago. She told him that she'd tricked Katrina into helping her because she wanted to see her niece one last time before disappearing for good. She assured him that she hadn't turned over any evidence to any law enforcement agency, but said she would if anything happened to her niece," Lewis informed Boyd.

Hanging up a few minutes later, Boyd told Katrina what her aunt had done.

Katrina groaned. "Garduchi doesn't like to be threatened."

The phone rang. Again Boyd answered. As he listened, the grim expression on his face sent a chill through Katrina. Hanging up, he said, "The word on the street is that the reward on your aunt has been upped to a quarter of a million."

"I have to find her."

The grim expression on Boyd's face deepened. "No. You're going home."

Her eyes rounded in surprise. "I thought you didn't trust me out of your sight."

"Every small-time hoodlum up through the top ranks of professional hitters is going to be looking for your aunt. Being anywhere within ten miles of her is going to be like being a target in a shooting gallery." His gaze narrowed on her. "I don't care what part you're really playing in this. Whatever it is, it's too dangerous."

Again she saw the protectiveness in his eyes. "Admit it, you like me just a little." Inwardly, she gasped. She couldn't believe she'd said that. But what really shook her was how much his answer meant to her. *Maybe blurting that out wasn't such a bad thing,* she reasoned, seeing the coldness return to his eyes. *He'll say no and that will put an end to this attraction I keep experiencing.*

"If I liked you just a little, this would be easy," he said curtly.

A smile spread over her face at the implication in his words. "You like me a lot."

"It's only lust and I don't plan to give in to it."

She liked the idea that he was lusting after her. Her gaze traveled over him. "I've heard that animal attraction is what draws couples together from across crowded rooms." She suddenly flushed. That sounded like a come-on line from a bar. "Not that I believe in instant intimacy. I'd have to get to know someone first. I'd want to know we had a relationship that would last."

For a moment he'd thought she was going to try to seduce him and he'd been considering letting her. Sometimes a taste of honey was the cure. But she'd clearly decided to move more slowly. Well, that was the end of that. She was a distraction he didn't need. "You're going home."

She knew that Garduchi exerted a lot of power but so did the reward he was offering. "A quarter of a million dollars is a lot of money. Even if Garduchi has put out the word that I'm to be left alone, there's always the chance someone will get greedy enough to pay me a visit to ask if I know where my aunt is."

"You'll be watched over. I'll have some of our people keeping an eye on you and I'm sure Garduchi will have some his men protecting you as well. He won't want to take a chance on you getting hurt and Leona keeping her word about turning over the evidence."

"And what if Garduchi decides I know more than I'm

telling and decides to try to persuade me to cooperate with him. When I can't help him, his temper could easily take control. Or, what if my watchers get greedy?'' She saw the protectiveness beginning to show on his face. ''Either I hunt my aunt with you or without you, but I'm not going home and I'll shake any tail you try to put on me.''

The thought of her being out on her own chilled Boyd to the bone and she had a point about Garduchi and her watchers. He envisioned her being tortured for information and wanted to pull her into the secure circle of his arms and hold her there forever. *This could all be an act,* he reminded himself for the umpteenth time. Maybe she just wanted to hang around to see if the FBI could find her aunt. It could be a way of testing Leona's ability to remain hidden. Once she and her aunt were certain they knew how to hide from anyone, she'd disappear as well.

''So what now?'' she asked.

Even if she were using him as a pawn in a game, he couldn't bear the thought of her getting herself hurt or killed. ''We go back to Washington and wait.''

Katrina frowned thoughtfully. ''We could fake my death and make it look like Garduchi was involved.''

Boyd studied her for a long moment, then said curtly. ''You'd have to stay dead. If your aunt turns over the evidence and then you reappear, Garduchi is sure to put a contract out on you.'' Sudden enlightenment showed on his face. ''Is this a way you and your aunt cooked up so that you could become part of our relocation program…have the government protecting you while you and she enjoy the money she embezzled?''

''You're impossible! Here I am offering myself as a sacrificial lamb to get Garduchi and you're twisting it into some sort of scheme. I can't believe I'm attracted to you.'' Her fit of anger had caused the pounding in her head to increase. "I need some of those aspirin you brought along."

Boyd produced the bottle, took three for himself and gave her two.

"You're definitely a three-aspirin pain," she retorted and held her hand out for one more.

He dropped it into her palm, then went into the bathroom to run a couple of glasses of water. After swallowing down his aspirin, he said tersely, "Even if you are on the level, I wouldn't let you do it. You'll have to spend the rest of your life in hiding, always looking over your shoulder, knowing that if Garduchi discovers you're still alive, he'll come after you. Then there's always the possibility that your aunt is playing liar's poker and doesn't even have any evidence, in which case you would have placed yourself at risk for nothing."

"I still think we should consider it."

"No. If your aunt really wanted to turn over the evidence on Garduchi, she'd have done it." He cupped her face in his hands and looked into her eyes. "And, I'll admit, I have a selfish motive as well. If you are on the level, I'd like the chance to get to know you better. If you disappear into the witness protection program, that can never happen."

"That would definitely be a downside to my plan," she admitted, the heat of his touch causing her blood to feel like molten lava.

Boyd forced himself to release her. "We'd better get going or we'll miss our plane," he said gruffly.

Katrina frowned as he turned away from her. What if he never allowed himself to fully trust her? She could do no more than she had already done to prove herself. She wanted to cry. Life wasn't fair! *But then nobody ever told me it would be.* Her head still pounding, she rose and packed quickly.

Chapter 9

On the way to the airport, they stopped at a mall and bought Katrina a satchel to replace the plastic bag she'd been using for her clothes. The car had been a rental. They returned it at the airport and flew back to Washington, D.C., arriving in the early hours of the morning. During the flight Boyd had questioned her about places her aunt had mentioned as being locations she'd like to live in or visit.

"Almost anyplace where she can get good room service," Katrina had replied. "Miami, Las Vegas, San Francisco, New York, Denver, Paris, Rome, London, Morocco, the Virgin Islands, the Bahamas, etc."

"That takes in about half the world and her tastes may have broadened in the past few years," Boyd had grumbled and allowed a silence to fall between them for the rest of the flight.

"You'll be staying at my place," he told her as they left the terminal and he hailed a taxi.

She didn't object. She liked being with him. Even if he

didn't trust her, he cared about her and for the first time in a very long time, she didn't feel alone in the world.

His apartment was small but neatly kept.

"You can have the bedroom," he said.

He looked tired and she wanted him to be comfortable. "I'll take the couch."

Boyd read the determined line of her jaw. "Fine."

A short while later, snuggled comfortably on the couch, she smiled softly to herself. He'd closed the bedroom door, leaving her alone with a phone and an easy exit. Maybe he was allowing himself to begin to trust her. Abruptly the smile changed to a frown. Or, maybe he thought she might contact her aunt and he had a trace on the line. Or maybe, he was hoping she'd leave and lead him to her aunt. With his acute sense of hearing, she was certain that even with the door closed, he'd be aware of her movements. *Don't start liking his company too much,* she cautioned herself and, trying not to think about him, she closed her eyes and slept.

Boyd woke at seven. He couldn't believe he'd slept so soundly. Wondering if he still had a guest, he pulled on a pair of slacks before leaving his bedroom. As he opened the door, his gaze went immediately to the couch. He saw her curled up, still asleep and a smile played at one corner of his mouth. Her presence added a warmth to his apartment that had been lacking. In the next instant, he was frowning at the paths his mind was taking. Reminding himself of how short a time he'd known her, he headed into the bathroom to shave.

When he came out she was up, dressed and her bedding neatly folded.

"We'll get some breakfast on the way to headquarters," he said continuing into the bedroom.

"Fine," she replied to his retreating back. The smell of his aftershave filled her senses. Silently, she cursed his hardheadedness.

A while later when they entered the operations room where all the information about Garduchi and Leona was being routed, a man who looked to be in his late fifties rose to greet them. He was medium in build and height. His hair was still thick but had turned completely white.

"Lewis Hamond, Boyd's partner," he said, extending his hand toward Katrina. "And I can certainly understand why he wanted to be the one to keep an eye on you."

Katrina had been prepared to face the same distrust she'd grown to expect from law officials. Instead, the man's broad smile was genuine and there was a mischievous gleam in his eyes as he winked at Boyd. "I'm pleased to meet you," she said accepting the handshake.

"Boyd been giving you a hard time?" Lewis asked solicitously. "Getting stabbed turned him real cynical. Sometimes I wonder if he trusts any of us, anymore."

She cast Boyd a rueful look. "He does have a problem on that point."

Boyd didn't hide his surprise at seeing his partner. "I thought you were watching Garduchi."

"I left the locals to keep an eye on him. Figured finding Leona was more important. Slippery, uh?"

Boyd's neck reddened with embarrassment. "I'll admit she blindsided me."

"I'm really sorry," Katrina said quickly. "I thought she honestly meant to cooperate."

Boyd's manner became sternly businesslike. "Have you had any possible sightings?"

"Nothing that's proven worthwhile." Lewis gave Katrina another sympathetic look. "The truth is Garduchi has a lot more men out there looking for her than we do. No matter how clever she thinks she is, she's in deep trouble." A plea entered his voice. "Are you absolutely certain you have no idea where she might have gone?"

Katrina shook her head. "Until she called me a few days ago, I hadn't seen or spoken to her for years."

"Too bad." Quickly, Lewis added, "I didn't mean it was too bad you had broken all ties with her and the rest of Garduchi's 'business' associates. I just meant it's too bad you don't know where she might be."

"I can tell you that it'll be somewhere luxurious. She does like her creature comforts," Katrina offered.

"That'll help some," Lewis said encouragingly. "At least we'll know not to waste our time checking bag ladies."

"I wouldn't put anything past her," Boyd interjected. "She'll need a good disguise to fool the men Garduchi has looking for her. Being a bag lady for a while to give herself time to get out of the country might be just the thing she'd try."

Mentally, Katrina groaned. Boyd probably thought she was trying to throw them off her aunt's trail. "You're right, she might," she agreed. "I wouldn't put anything past her."

"Bag ladies are back on our list," Lewis said and returned to the computer he'd been sitting at before they entered.

"I wasn't trying to throw anyone off my aunt's trail," Katrina whispered defensively to Boyd.

"I didn't think you were." Surprised that he hadn't suspected her made him uneasy. Again he cautioned himself not to let his lust do his thinking for him.

Katrina smiled. So maybe she was breaking through that shell of his.

As the morning progressed, it became evident to Katrina

that others in the office weren't as willing to accept her on her word as Lewis. By noon, she'd taken all the suspicious glances she could stand. All she wanted to do was escape. Tapping Boyd on the shoulder, she said, "I need to do some laundry."

He too was growing tired of the tension her presence was causing. "Me, too," he replied, not wanting to let her out of his sight.

Katrina wiped the sweat from her brow on the sleeve of her shirt as they left the laundry room in the basement of Boyd's apartment house and entered the elevator. He'd called Lewis while the clothes were drying to discover they were following up on several leads but none looked promising.

Leaning back against the wall of the elevator, Katrina frowned glumly. "I feel like we're looking for a needle in a haystack."

"A needle who has set herself up with at least one other identity, is my bet," Boyd said, thinking aloud.

Katrina looked at him questioningly.

"She has to be getting money somehow and none of her credit cards have shown up and she hasn't withdrawn anything from her checking account. Considering how well she's planned everything so far, a second identity seems like a reasonable explanation."

Katrina nodded. "You're right. She might even have a couple more."

"So who would have helped her with the documentation?"

Katrina thought for a long moment then said, "No one. She had to know Garduchi would come after her. She didn't dare trust anyone. She would have done it on her own. And it's obvious she's been planning her escape a long time.

She probably searched out gravestones, got birth certificates for women who would be her age now but who passed away a long time ago and used those to set up new identities.''

Boyd nodded in agreement.

Seeing the tired lines in his face, Katrina wanted to mother him. "Why don't we go by the grocery and pick up a few things and I'll cook dinner."

Boyd looked at her. He saw the softness in her eyes. He also saw his own exhaustion reflected there. "Thanks, but I think we should save that for another night. You look as tired as I feel. There's a little Chinese place I frequent. How about going there?"

"Sure," she replied, unable to stop a yawn. "And you're right. I'd probably fall asleep standing at the stove." Her shoulder muscles felt tight and she moved them around, trying to stretch out the kinks.

Seeing her movement, Boyd reached over with his right hand and began to massage the back of her neck. Immediately he regretted the friendly gesture. Her skin was soft and his ministrations threatened to become a caress.

"That feels delicious," she purred.

The thought that she tasted delicious played through his mind. A heat began to build inside. The elevator came to a halt on his floor. Breathing a mental sigh of relief, he released her and stepped out. *Don't do that again,* he ordered himself, the texture of her skin still strong in his mind.

Katrina held in a groan of displeasure at the loss of his touch. It had been so very soothing. It had also been igniting embers, warming her in a mellow sexy way.

Changing for dinner, she found herself wishing this was a real date. A sly smile played at the corners of her mouth. She could pretend it was. In which case, she would center the conversation on him. Her curious side liked that idea a lot. She wanted to know all there was to know about him.

She'd packed hastily, but she had thrown in a lightweight summer dress. The feminine effect, however, was ruined by her tennis shoes. And since they were the only footwear she'd thought to bring along, she had to settle for wearing slacks and a blouse.

At the restaurant, she waited until they'd placed their order then said, "I'm tired of talking about my aunt. Tell me about your family."

"There's not much to tell."

Katrina wasn't going to let him get off that easily. "I know you have two brothers. I suppose they have names and ages."

"Slade is four years older than me. Jess is five years younger."

"And you're how old?"

He grinned at her perseverance. "Thirty-two."

"And I know your mother is Apache and your father was a Texas Ranger. How did they meet?"

Normally he would have said he didn't like talking about himself and changed the subject. He preferred to keep his private life private. But this time, he heard himself saying, "She was out in the desert hunting plants when she found my father. He'd been tracking a couple of killers who had backtracked and shot him. They'd left him for dead. She's always believed it was the Great Spirit that led her to him. My father said he opened his eyes and saw this lovely face in front of him and thought it was an angel."

In her mind's eye, Katrina pictured the Apache maiden kneeling beside the nearly dead body of a Texas Ranger. "That's a lovely story," she said wistfully. "It must be nice to have a family you can talk about without feeling ashamed."

Boyd read the pain on her face. "No one can choose their parents. As long as you're on the level, you've got nothing to be ashamed about. I've seen your record. You've worked hard to save kids from getting caught up in drugs and prostitution."

"So how do I prove to you that I'm on the level?" she asked.

"By not playing any games."

She looked hard into his eyes, willing him to believe her. "I'm not."

"I believe you." The words were out before he'd even realized they'd formed. They'd come from deep inside, but was it instinct or had he said it because he knew that was what she wanted to hear and he couldn't resist pleasing her? He recalled her reaction to the memory of her brother's killings and the protectiveness he'd seen in her eyes when the bellhops had knocked on the hotel room door and chose to believe it was instinct.

Tears welled in her eyes. "You really mean that?"

"I just hope you don't prove me wrong," he said gruffly. "That'd make me lose all my faith in humanity."

"I won't," she promised.

Their dinner arrived at that moment and a silence fell between them as they ate. Katrina tried to think of some subject to make small talk with, but failed. She felt like a teenager on her first date…nervous and uncertain but wanting desperately to make a good impression.

Studying her covertly, Boyd considered his feelings for the woman seated across from him. They were strong and he was tempted to explore their strength, but they were dealing with some very dangerous men and it wasn't safe for them to be distracted by emotions.

As they finished their meal and returned to the apartment, Boyd couldn't help but notice how happy Katrina was. That he had caused the smile on her face, pleased him. But, he found himself admitting, it was another look, a look of passion he really wanted there. Stepping out of the elevator, their arms brushed. This simple contact was like a bolt of lightning striking him and he wondered how long he would be able to maintain the boundary he'd set for himself. *For as long as it is necessary to keep us alive,* he affirmed.

But later that night, lying alone in his bed, he wished he wasn't such a cautious man.

Snuggled on the couch, tears of joy brimmed in Katrina's eyes. Boyd Logan believed in her.

Chapter 10

The following afternoon, Katrina hummed as she entered Boyd's apartment with a bag of groceries in each arm. She'd left him and Lewis directing the following up of leads and had come back early to prepare a home-cooked meal.

A knock on the door interrupted her before she could begin unpacking her groceries. Looking through the peephole she saw Lewis, his expression grim. Panic that something horrible had happened to Boyd caused her knees to weaken. Opening the door, she tried to speak but her vocal cords refused to work. All she could do was stare at Lewis with a question on her face and fear in her eyes.

"May I come in?" he asked.

She stepped aside.

Once inside, he closed the door, insuring their privacy.

"Boyd?" she managed to choke out at last.

"He's fine." Lewis's features had relaxed into a more comfortable expression but his gaze remained cold.

Katrina tensed. Something was wrong. "What's going on?"

Lewis drew his gun and motioned her further back into the living room area. "You might have managed to convince Boyd that you're legit, but I'm not buying it. You and I are going to find your aunt."

"I don't know where she is," Katrina insisted in clipped tones.

"You'd better. Your life depends on it. Otherwise, I'll have to shoot you, make it look like one of the hoodlums after the award did it, and hope your aunt meant it when she said she'd turn over the evidence if anything happened to you. However, I'd prefer not to go that far."

There was a fanatical glint in his eyes that told Katrina he meant what he said. Thinking quickly, she said, "All right. I'll help. But we need to contact the rest of the team for backup."

He sneered at her. "I'm not stupid. You've got Boyd hoodwinked. The minute he and the others showed up, you'd tell them that you didn't know anything and he'd believe you." He motioned toward the desk against the far wall. "Sit down. You're going to write a farewell note. You're going to tell Boyd that you're going to meet your aunt and that it's no use for him or any of us to continue looking for you because you and she have devised a plan that will make it impossible for you to be found."

Fear for herself was outweighed by the thought that Boyd would think she'd betrayed his trust. "This is kidnapping. You're supposed to be upholding the law, not breaking it."

"Write the note." He gave her a shove toward the desk.

"I suppose a quarter of a million dollars can corrupt anyone," she muttered, seating herself.

Lewis snorted. "The money means nothing to me. I want the evidence to put that scumbag Garduchi behind bars."

Katrina heard the hatred in his voice. She took a calming breath. She had to think clearly. Taking a blank sheet of paper out of the desk drawer, she began to write:

Dear Boyd,
   I realize that because of our intimacy you thought we'd formed a partnership.

"Keep it simple. Just say what I told you to say," Lewis ordered curtly.

"You want him to believe the note, don't you?" she replied.

"I said keep it simple," he repeated threateningly and began to reach for the paper to destroy it.

"I care about Boyd. I don't want him coming after us." Her gaze met his. "I get the feeling that you don't intend to let anyone stand in your way."

He stopped in midmotion. "You're right. I don't want Boyd getting suspicious. I'd hate to have to hurt him. Go on, but keep it as short as possible."

Mentally Katrina patted herself on the back and continued writing:

   I enjoyed our time together, but you were right about trust. Sometimes it gets misplaced. I do feel badly about this. Perhaps in your line of work, not trusting anyone is for the best. I'm on my way to meet my aunt. It will be a waste of your time to try to find us. We have devised a plan of escape by which we will disappear forever.

                                      I will miss you,
                                      Katrina

"Good," Lewis said reading over her shoulder. "Now

put it on the kitchen counter by the bags of groceries and get your things together.''

Pretending to scratch her ear, she loosened an earring and carefully dropped it out of Lewis's view between the two bags of groceries as she placed the note in plain view. She hoped the wording of the note and finding a single earring would cause Boyd to realize she hadn't left voluntarily. More importantly, she hoped he would get the message about not trusting anyone.

After making certain there were no weapons in her satchel, Lewis followed her as she moved around the apartment picking up her things. When that was done, she casually reached for her purse hoping her behavior would make him think there was nothing of importance inside.

"Just leave that where it is," he said. "And step back."

Mentally cursing the fact that he was so thorough, she watched him open the purse and take out her gun. Tossing the purse to her, he slipped her gun into the pocket of his jacket, holding it ready to be fired and aimed at her through the fabric. Then he reholstered his gun.

Clever, she admitted. If he shot her, it would be with her gun and Boyd would think some hoodlum had found her.

"We're going out the back door. Anyone who sees us had better think we're just a couple leaving on a trip, or you're dead and them, too. I can't leave any witness to identify me."

She didn't doubt he meant it. His car was parked by the Dumpster. He opened the trunk, had her toss her things inside, then opened the back door for her and waited for her to climb in. Taking a prescription bottle out of his pocket, he handed it to her. "Take two."

She recognized the name of the drug. It was a sedative. She read the directions. "It says to only take one."

He scowled threateningly. "Don't argue. There's bottled water on the seat."

She took two pills out of the container, then opened the bottle of water. Plopping the pills in her mouth, she held them under her tongue and took a drink of the water.

He put his face near hers. "I'm being nice keeping you alive. It'd be a lot easier to just leave you dead in the Dumpster. Now swallow the pills."

She scowled at him. "You're keeping me alive because you're not certain my aunt will keep her word about turning over the evidence."

"I'm keeping you alive because I don't like killing people unnecessarily and I'm hoping you'll cooperate. But if you make this difficult, I'll take my chances Leona meant what she said."

She believed him. And as long as she was alive, there was hope she would escape or be rescued. With another gulp of water, she let the pills go down.

Lewis closed the door and climbed in behind the wheel. "We'll just sit here for a minute and give them a chance to work. You should be feeling drowsy already. I remember the first time I took one. It was after my daughter's death. I hadn't slept for a week."

Katrina felt a fog closing in over her mind. Giving up a useless fight to stay awake, she curled up on the back seat as a blank darkness enveloped her.

Boyd had given Katrina his car to run her errands. Taking a taxi home, he had the cabby stop on the way so that he could pick up a bottle of wine and some flowers.

"Heavy date?" the man asked with a knowing grin.

"Maybe," Boyd replied. He knew getting more deeply involved with Katrina at the moment wasn't smart but he hadn't been able to keep his eyes or his mind off of her all day. After she left, she'd continued to haunt him. It was time to throw caution to the wind.

Opening the apartment door, he was surprised that there was no aroma of cooking food. He called out to her, but got no answer. Striding through the living room to the kitchen area, he saw the bags of groceries still on the counter and the sheet of paper nearby. Glancing through the note, he felt as if he'd been kicked in the stomach. He'd played the fool.

"It's what you *really* expected," he growled at himself. Her face filled his mind. No, it wasn't what he'd *really* expected! He had truly believed she was being honest with him.

Grabbing up the phone, he called the task force and had them put an all-points bulletin out on her. It was Jane Forester who answered and he could almost hear the snicker in her voice. They'd all thought he was an idiot to trust her...everyone but Lewis.

He paced the floor to cool down. As he got his temper under control, something about the note began to nag at him. He read it more closely a second time.

She talked about intimacy, but there hadn't been any between them. He frowned at the unpacked bags of groceries and a glint of gold caught his eye. It was one of her earrings.

She hadn't left of her own free will! He fought a bout of panic as he read the note a third time looking for any clues as to who had taken her.

The part about not trusting anyone was most likely a warning. Could someone on the task force be involved? He studied the note again. The word "partnership" taunted him. Surely she couldn't be implying that Lewis was involved in her disappearance. Lewis was the best, most by-the-book lawman he'd ever worked with. And, after partnering with him for three years, Boyd would have sworn Lewis was one of the most honest. He was reading more into the note than was there.

He started for the door then stopped and went to his computer. Connecting with the department files, he called up Lewis's file. What was available to him was short and concise...name, family members, marriage status, address and brief summary of Lewis's career.

The man had a distinguished record. "This is ridiculous," Boyd muttered to himself. Still, he read through the personal data in the file. He'd known Lewis had a daughter who'd died about five years ago from a drug overdose. He'd been to Lewis's home and seen the photos of the girl in the living room. She'd been pretty. And he knew that the death of the girl was a driving force in Lewis's life, but it was no reason for Lewis to cross the line in this case. They'd worked together nailing another crime boss and Lewis had insisted they go by the book. And he'd been the same way in the Garduchi case. He hadn't wanted to do anything that would get evidence thrown out of court.

Boyd looked back at marital status. From the dates in the file, about a year after the daughter's death, Lewis's wife had divorced him. But there wasn't anything unusual about that. There was a high divorce rate among lawmen. If there had been any problems in the marriage, the death of a child could easily have been the final rift. Boyd noted that Lewis's address hadn't changed following the divorce and recalled someone mentioning that Lewis's wife had moved back to California to look after her parents.

He leaned back in his chair and rubbed the back of his neck. But if it wasn't Lewis why would Katrina use the word "partnership." There were a dozen other phrases she could have chosen..."because of our intimacy you thought

I was someone you could trust" or "we'd formed a bond."
But she'd used "partnership."

"They say everyone has a price," he muttered. Maybe
Lewis's was a quarter of a million. The expression on his
face turned grimmer. He didn't want to believe that.

Forty minutes later he was parking in the driveway of
Lewis's home. The meticulously maintained ranch-style
house was located in one of the older middle-class com-
munities beyond the beltway.

Lewis opened the door as Boyd reached it. "You look
like hell. Come on in," he said sympathetically, stepping
aside to give Boyd room to pass him.

Boyd accepted the invitation.

"I thought Katrina was going to fix you a nice home-
cooked meal. What happened? You find out she can't
cook?" Lewis said teasingly.

"She's gone."

Lewis's expression became serious. "Gone? As in left
your apartment to go to a hotel or 'gone' as in disappeared?" Worry etched itself into his features. "Do you
think one of Garduchi's men got her?"

Boyd had to admit the man seemed genuinely surprised
and concerned. Still, he decided to pretend he believed the
note. "Gone as in left town on her own."

"Did she say where she was going?" Lewis motioned
for Boyd to go into the living room.

"She's on her way to join her aunt. The two have devised a scheme to disappear for good."

Lewis shook his head. "I've always been able to trust
your instincts before. That cynicism of yours makes it difficult for anyone to earn your approval. You said she was
on the level and that was good enough for me."

"I thought she was." Boyd lowered himself into a chair.

Lewis eased down on the couch. "How about we order

a pizza, have some beer and watch a football game? I've got the sports station on my cable."

Boyd had been studying Lewis closely. The man showed no hesitation in asking him to stay. In fact, there was nothing, absolutely nothing, in Lewis's manner that suggested he could be involved in Katrina's disappearance. This had been a futile trip. Boyd pushed himself to his feet. "No, thanks. I think I'll go and get some sleep."

"That'd probably be best." Lewis rose and placed an arm around Boyd's shoulders as he walked him to the door. "Don't feel so bad. We men are always being fooled by women."

"I suppose," Boyd conceded.

Lewis laughed. "You're only human. A pretty face and nice figure can cause a man to do his thinking with something a lot lower than his brain."

Boyd nodded and left. During the drive back to his apartment, a new possibility occurred to him. Had Katrina left the note and earring in order to cause him to doubt Lewis and send Boyd on a wild-goose chase? She knew he'd been double-crossed by a partner in the past and if he was busy investigating Lewis, he wouldn't be looking for her and her aunt. Anger that he could be so gullible washed through him.

Back at his apartment, he threw out the two bags of groceries. He didn't want anything to remind him of what an idiot he'd been. After making a sandwich, he ate it glaring at the couch where she'd slept.

Then cursing himself, he went into his bedroom, kicked off his shoes and stretched out on the bed. Images of her face played through his mind. The desire to trust her was still strong. Maybe he'd misinterpreted her message. He knew it by heart. Closing his eyes, he went through it word by word. Nothing new came to mind. Exhaustion overcame him and he slept.

He woke in the small hours of the morning, shaken by the dream he'd been having. In it a frightened Katrina had been holding her arms out and calling to him for help. Splashing water on his face to bring himself fully awake, he couldn't rid himself of the feeling that she needed him to rescue her. "All right. All right. So maybe I'm the biggest fool of all time, but I believe in her," he declared to his image in the mirror.

So where was she and who had taken her?

Whoever it was hadn't forced his or her way in, which meant she must have let her abductor in. Since she was too smart to admit a stranger, it had to have been someone she knew. Maybe "partnership" had been the only word she could think of under stress. Maybe she'd really meant "comradeship" to indicate that it was another agent. That would explain the warning not to trust anyone.

Getting out a pad of paper, he made a list of the agents she'd met. It was a fairly short list, just the task force and his superior, Gerald Eldridge. Then, taking the time she'd left him, adding in some time for her to go to the grocery, he determined what time she'd probably arrived home. Since the groceries hadn't been unpacked, whoever had taken her must have been waiting or following her and showed up at the door almost immediately. He checked off the names of the agents who had left when he had. Everyone of them had offered him a ride home. He'd declined because he'd wanted to stop for flowers and wine. And on his way out, he'd seen Eldridge in his office. When he finished, he could account for everyone except Gwyne Simmons and Lewis.

Just after Katrina had left, Gwyne had received a call. She'd said it was her mother calling from the hospital. Her father had taken a turn for the worse. Checking her records, he found her father's name and began calling hospitals until he found one that said they had a patient by that name. Needing to be active, he drove there, got the room number and found it. Peeking inside, he saw Gwyne along with a couple of other women.

"Are you a family member?" a nurse paused to ask sympathetically.

"No, just a friend of Gwyne Simmons."

The nurse gazed compassionately at the three women. "She and her mother and sister haven't left his bedside for hours."

"I think I should leave her and her family alone," he said, backing away before Gwyne could look up and see him.

"I'll tell her…"

"I'll give her a call later," Boyd interrupted and left before the nurse could ask his name. He and Gwyne had never been close and he didn't want her wondering why he'd stopped by the hospital.

Back in his car he frowned. Lewis too had left the task force room soon after Katrina's exit. He'd said he was going back to his office to take care of some paperwork. But he wasn't there when Boyd had gone by to tell him he was leaving.

The path kept coming back to Lewis.

Or maybe it was an agent he hadn't considered. Word must have gotten around the building about who Katrina was. And a quarter of a million was a temptation. But would she have opened the door to someone just because they had a legitimate badge. Sure, why not?

Returning to his apartment, he paced the floor. If it was any agent in the building, it would be like looking for a needle in a haystack. Katrina was clever. She knew he'd

need some clue as to whom to pursue. "Don't trust anyone" implied that it was someone he would trust. And, he
was certain, "partnership" had to be important.

Katrina was being roughly shaken to consciousness.

Vaguely she recalled that this had happened once before
and she'd been given another pill, maybe two. She was too
groggy to remember accurately.

"Time to wake up," a familiar male voice ordered
curtly.

"O...kaay. O...kaaay." Her mouth was dry and she had
a hard time making her muscles work properly causing the
words to come out almost unintelligibly. She opened her
eyes. Multiples of the same image blurred in front of her.
She rubbed at her eyes with the palms of her hands. The
multiples decreased to three.

"Take a drink," the male voice ordered, holding her up
high enough to swallow.

"Nooo...mo-o-o...pillllss," she said, then clamped her
mouth shut.

"No more pills," the voice assured her. "We need to
talk. Now drink."

This time she obeyed. Swallowing was hard and some
of the water dribbled down her chin. After she'd drunk, she
was lowered back onto something soft and the man or
men—she still wasn't certain if there was more than one—
stepped out of her vision. As her eyes began to focus she
realized she was on a bed. It was of a four-poster design.
Overhead was a white canopy with frilly pink ruffles
around the perimeter. She turned her head to the side and
saw that the bedspread and pillow shams were also white
with pink ruffles. Her wrists hurt. Focusing her gaze on
them, she saw red lines. At some time while she slept, she'd
been tied up.

Shifting into a sitting position, a bout of dizziness forced her to sit holding her head in her hands. When the world finally stopped spinning, she began to look around. The room appeared to be decorated entirely in pink and white. The tassel from a high school graduation hung on a corner of the dresser mirror. There were photographs stuck into the sides of the frame and a collection of dolls sitting on the dresser. It reminded her of a teenage girl's room.

"This was my daughter's room," the male voice broke into her thoughts.

This time she recognized it. It belonged to Lewis. Looking over her shoulder, she saw him sitting in a rocking chair.

"She was so pretty and sweet and innocent. Then one day, she ran away. Teenagers do that. They get frustrated with the rules their parents set down." He breathed a tired sigh. "She didn't understand the dangers she could get into. She was only seventeen."

Katrina had dealt with a lot of runaways. Seventeen was a late age to start. "She'd never run away before?"

"A couple of times. The first time, she went to her grandparents' house. Her mother's parents. I made it clear I didn't want them to interfere in our family matters. The next time she went to her girlfriend's house. I let that girl's parents know, in no uncertain terms, I didn't appreciate them trying to break up our home."

Katrina marveled at the double image Lewis presented to the world. At work, he was friendly and jovial. Here at home, the self-righteous way he spoke indicated he must have been a tyrant. "Maybe you should have sought counselling."

"Psychologists are idiots. They refuse to understand that a child needs stern supervision and guidance. The world is a dangerous place. Brenda had everything she could possibly want right here,'' he waved his hand around the room.

"Except a little freedom, I'll bet."

"Freedom." He spat out the word. "You sound like her mother. I'll tell you about freedom. It can destroy a life, even kill." His features formed a snarl. "She claimed her friends were all good kids but how could she know for sure? She was so sweet and naive. How could she know they wouldn't try to get her to drink or take drugs? And then there were the boys. They were always hanging around. I knew what they wanted. If they'd had their way, she would have ended up pregnant or with some socially transmitted disease. She claimed I was smothering her when all I was doing was saving her from the pitfalls just waiting for a pretty, innocent girl." Tears welled in his eyes. "But she refused to understand. The last time she left, she went with a friend to St. Louis and got mixed up with Garduchi. He made a prostitute and a drug addict out of her. She died of an overdose."

"I'm sorry." Katrina's sympathy was for Brenda not for Lewis. In her mind, he was as much to blame for the girl's death as Garduchi. However, now, she decided, was not a good time to voice that opinion.

"Garduchi's the one who's going to be sorry when I put him behind bars." His gaze narrowed on her. "Contact your aunt, tell her to bring the evidence if she doesn't want to read about you in the obituaries."

Katrina forced herself to think. It was evident Lewis wasn't totally sane. He'd threatened to kill her if she couldn't reach Leona, and Katrina was certain that he would do just that. She had to buy some time. "I can't contact her directly. I call my home answering machine and leave a message to remind myself to pick up my dry cleaning when I get home. That's our signal that I feel the coast is clear for us to meet.'' Katrina paused, then asked, ''What day is this?''

''Tuesday.''

He'd kidnapped her on Monday. She felt like she'd been out for days but it had only been one night. ''My aunt wouldn't check my messages until Friday. When she hears the signal, then she'll be at our designated location on Sunday at two o'clock.''

''And where is this designated location?''

Think! She needed someplace in the states, but far enough away that it would require a long drive or, if he waited until closer to time for the meet, air travel would be required to get there. A country and western song popped into her mind. ''Santa Fe.''

''New Mexico?''

''Yes.''

A knowing look came over his face. ''She's in Mexico, isn't she?''

''I don't know where she is at this moment.''

He frowned. ''But it doesn't make sense that she'd come back across the border if she's already out of the country.''

''Then she's probably still here. We do have an extradition law with Mexico and she's not the type to risk spending even one night in a Mexican jail.''

His gaze turned coldly cynical. ''I suppose you and your kind would know all about jails. It's probably part of your childhood training.''

''I was never part of Garduchi's organization.''

''You were born into it. It's in your blood.''

''It was never in *my* blood,'' she snapped.

He shrugged, letting her know that anything she had to say meant nothing to him. ''Make the call.''

Katrina obeyed.

''If you'd like to use the facilities, go ahead. But don't

try anything funny. I won't peek, but I insist on keeping the door open a crack."

The residual effect of the pills was still strong. Katrina had to concentrate hard to make her legs carry her into the adjoining bathroom. It too was all pink and white. Her gaze searched for a weapon. Lewis was thorough. There was nothing she could use. Splashing cold water on her face, neck and arms, she tried to wake her body up. It worked a little. Taking her time, she used the facilities. Then she splashed more cold water on herself. Her body continued to respond sluggishly…too sluggish for her to attempt any long-distance lunge.

Leaving the bathroom, she considered getting close enough that she could fall into him. Her coordination wasn't good enough for a struggle but if she knocked the gun free and luck was with her, she might reach it before he did. As if he'd read her mind, he kept enough distance between them to make that plan unworkable.

He motioned for her to precede him out of the room.

A clue. She needed to leave a clue for Boyd so that he'd know she'd been in Lewis's house. Momentarily, pretending to be having an extremely bad dizzy spell, she leaned against the doorjamb and held her head in her hands. Surreptitiously loosening the remaining earring, she lowered her hand and let it drop on the floor, then scooted it into a corner of the door frame.

"Come on, move along," Lewis ordered.

Slowly she continued down the hall. To her relief he didn't notice the earring left behind.

"Through there," he said, indicating a door to her left.

She opened it to discover wooden steps leading into a blackness below. He switched on the lights. It was a basement converted into a recreational room.

"I didn't have any trouble carrying you into the house,

but I figured I could get us both killed if I tried to carry you down those,'' Lewis said.

He was smiling triumphantly and her stomach knotted. ''If you're planning to kill me, you'll never make contact with my aunt.''

He gave her a patronizing look. ''I'm not going to kill you. I'm simply going to make sure I don't have to worry about you while I'm at work.''

She started to teeter as she took the first step. The pills were making her very unsteady, forcing her to hold onto the rail.

''Quit dawdling,'' he grumbled.

''You've got me doped up on pills,'' she hissed back.

''I'm sure you've tried your share of drugs. Those sleeping pills should be nothing.''

''I've never used drugs!''

He gave a snort of disbelief.

When she reached the foot of the stairs, he had her cross the rec room and go through the door into the unfinished part of the basement where the laundry area was. At the far wall a metal cabinet had been pulled out and turned sideways exposing a door the cabinet had obviously been concealing. ''That's our destination,'' he said.

She frowned in confusion. How could there be a door there? The basement should have ended at that wall.

''Open it,'' he ordered.

The door was heavy and looked as if it was made of metal. It took all her strength to obey.

''There's a light switch to your left,'' he said.

She flipped it and a cold shiver ran through her.

''Bet you can't guess what this is?'' he challenged jovially.

''It looks like a solitary confinement cell only larger and

with more stuff inside,'' she replied, his pleasure giving her the creeps.

"It's a bomb shelter." He patted the walls. "Fifteen inches of solid concrete. I had it built underground, adjoining the house so we could enter without having to go outside. In case the bomb was dropped, I didn't want to fight off those who were less prepared."

She looked around at the interior. Shelves stocked with dehydrated food and bottled water lined the wall. In one corner was a small chemical toilet.

"Don't waste your time searching for any kind of weapon. I moved anything useful out to the garage." Lewis motioned toward a counter where a couple of bottles of water and a six-pack of high nutritional drinks were sitting in a row. "Drink down one of those cans," he instructed.

Knowing she needed sustenance if she was to survive, she did as she was told.

"Now sit." He motioned toward a cot in the center of the concrete tomb.

Her legs still too shaky to make an attempt at escape, she seated herself.

He held out a pill of the same kind she'd taken before and one of the bottles of water. "Now be a good girl and swallow it down."

"You promised no more pills."

"So I lied. Now take it."

Again she tried to hold the medication under her tongue.

"Now why don't I trust you? Must be your heritage." He held her nose forcing her to open her mouth. Scowling threateningly, he released his hold. "Swallow it!"

Katrina knew from the hatred in his eyes that he was only keeping her alive to get the evidence. He'd planned to kill her all along. Again she considered trying to make a play for the gun but her body felt leaden. All she had on her side was time. With any luck, Lewis would keep her here until close to the time to meet with her aunt. Saying a silent prayer that Boyd had understood her message, she took another drink of water, this time letting it carry the pill down.

"Now open wide."

She opened her mouth.

With a nod of satisfaction, Lewis motioned for her to lie back down.

"Oh, by the way, if you're thinking Boyd might rescue you, forget it. He's furious that you left. As far as he's concerned, he never wants to see you again."

Hopelessness threatened to overwhelm her. She reminded herself that if Boyd had understood her message he would know not to trust Lewis. But what if he hadn't understood? What if his faith in her did not run deeply? What if he did believe she'd been tricking him all along?

The bit about the intimacy and the earring had to have tipped him off, she assured herself. *Or,* he could decide she had a weird definition of intimacy and maybe he'd missed the earring. No! She refused to believe that. Boyd would find her, she assured herself.

Standing, leaning against the door frame, Lewis studied her like she was some kind of insect. "I called my Brenda 'Princess' because that's what she was to me. A princess. And Garduchi and his ilk killed her."

In spite of the fact that she knew Lewis deserved some of the blame, Katrina admitted he was right about Garduchi and people who worked for him. They ruined young lives to line their own pockets. That she'd even cared about her aunt showed a weakness in her. *You can care about someone and not like what they do,* she argued. But that didn't make her feel any better. She was almost glad when the pill took effect.

Chapter 11

Tuesday morning, knowing Lewis would recognize his car, Boyd sat in a rented vehicle down the street from Lewis's house. When Lewis came out, dressed for work, he followed him, always careful to stay well behind. Lewis drove straight to the office.

Entering the building a couple of minutes behind him, Boyd again told himself he must be on the wrong trail. Lewis appeared perfectly at ease. And the friendly way he'd invited Boyd into his home the evening before was a strong indication that Katrina wasn't there. *So, maybe he has an accomplice who has her stashed somewhere.* A quarter of a million bucks, even split two ways, was a lot of money.

He drew a terse breath. If Lewis had taken her, it was because he thought she knew where Leona was. What would he and his accomplice, if he had one, do when they found out she didn't? Or had they discovered that already? They couldn't let her go free. The thought that he might already be too late to save her caused his stomach to tighten. Purpose showed in his eyes. He refused to believe she was dead.

Schooling himself to show no suspicion, he went into the operations room to check on any phone calls that had come in during the night.

"You still look like hell," Lewis said, solicitously. He motioned toward the others in the room with his eyes. "Why don't we go get a cup of coffee," he encouraged, clearly wanting to get Boyd alone.

"Sure."

In the hall, Lewis nodded toward his office. "In there. You and I need to have a talk."

Was Lewis feeling guilty and wanted to confess his part in Katrina's abduction? Boyd wondered hopefully.

Closing the door to ensure their privacy, Lewis looked at him with a fatherly expression. "I didn't have a chance to get to know Katrina, but she seemed real nice. I believed her when she said she didn't know where her aunt was. I can understand how she fooled you. She was one terrific actress. But you can't let her departure get to you."

Lewis seemed so sincere, Boyd's doubt that he was on the right trail increased. "I know you're right."

"There's something else you have to brace yourself for."

Boyd didn't like the sound of that.

"When she does join up with her aunt, that will make her a target as well. It's likely that if we find Leona dead, we'll find Katrina alongside her."

Boyd felt as if he'd been kicked in the stomach. If Lewis did have her, he was obviously planning to kill her along with her aunt. "She doesn't deserve to die."

"Garduchi has caused the death of many innocents. However, you have to realize that Katrina is not as innocent as you want to believe. After all, she did lie to us. She said she didn't know where her aunt was and she does.''

Boyd experienced a ray of hope. Clearly, Lewis believed Katrina knew where Leona was. That meant that if he was her abductor, she'd convinced him of that and, being the clever woman she was, she would also have convinced him that they had to keep her alive in order to contact Leona.

Lewis placed an arm around Boyd's shoulders. ''I don't like being the bearer of bad news, but I wanted you to be prepared.''

Boyd forced himself to sound grateful. ''I appreciate that.''

Lewis released him. ''Now, let's get back to work.''

''I'm going to stop by my office for a while,'' Boyd said as they started down the hall.

Lewis gave him a fatherly, knowing look. ''When this is all over, I'm going to find you a nice girl. Barbara down in accounting might suit you.''

''I think I'll stay away from women for a while,'' Boyd returned.

A headache had built by the time he reached his office. Lewis had seemed so sincere. If he was in on the abduction, there had to be a side of the man Boyd had never glimpsed. Again doubt assailed him. He could be wasting his time and the one thing he was certain of was that he didn't have time to waste. He scowled at the chair behind his desk. He couldn't sit around and wait, he had to do something.

Stopping by the operations room, he told them he thought he was coming down with the flu and was going home.

''Sounds like a good idea,'' Lewis said approvingly.

Driving directly to Lewis's neighborhood, Boyd parked near a small park, then carefully made his way to the back of Lewis's house. Even though he'd reasoned that Katrina wouldn't be there, during the drive he'd let his hopes that he was wrong grow. The place was big enough an accomplice could have been hiding with her in one of the rooms the night before. And, maybe he and Katrina were still there.

Picking the lock on the back door, Boyd entered stealthily and made a cautious but quick sweep of the entire place including the attic and basement. There was no one there.

Going out the back door, he entered the garage by the side door. There was no one there either.

He fought a rush of disappointment. "So now I go back through the house and make a thorough search," he ordered himself. He wasn't certain what he was looking for. But if Lewis wasn't involved, then he was back to square one with no idea where to look next.

Going from room to room, he found nothing unusual. Granted, the pink and white room was a little out of the ordinary. It had obviously been Lewis's daughter's room and it looked as if everything had been left the way it was when she died. But maybe neither Lewis or his wife had been able to bring themselves to go through the girl's things and, after his wife left, Lewis had simply found it easier to leave the room as he'd found it.

Again standing in the hall, Boyd looked upward at the string from a ceiling ladder giving access to the attic. The undisturbed dust he'd seen up there on his first sweep of the place convinced him making a search there would be a waste of his time.

Descending into the basement, he made another walk through, this time looking more closely. The recreational room offered nothing to support his suspicions. Continuing into the utility and laundry area, he could find nothing out of order there as well. It was, in fact, neat as a pin. His gaze paused on the three-shelf, metal utility unit against the

far wall. He'd checked it on his first sweep. It was fully
stockpiled with boxes and packages of spare laundry and
paper products. Lewis was clearly a well-organized house-
keeper.

Returning to the upper level, Boyd again worried that
he'd misinterpreted Katrina's note. Or maybe he was playing the fool and the note was a red herring. Maybe she was
having drinks with her aunt right now and laughing at the
gullibility of men. He realized that he was actually wishing
that was the case. All he wanted was for her to be alive
and safe. "Boy, do I have it bad," he admitted, glumly.
He also wasn't ready to believe she'd deceived him.

Returning to the garage, he looked around. There were
some boxes of camping equipment. He'd never thought of
Lewis as a camper, but then he'd never expected to suspect
Lewis of being one of the bad guys either.

Convinced that if Lewis was involved, he had an accomplice who was watching over Katrina, Boyd returned to the
house and went through Lewis's desk. There was nothing
to indicate who the accomplice might be or where he was.
Picking up the phone, he hit the redial number. He got a
pizza parlor. Apparently Lewis had ordered a pizza.

Recalling that there was a phone by Lewis's bed, he went
in there and hit the redial button. He got headquarters. Feeling more and more as if he was following the wrong trail,
he started back down the hall.

At the door of the bedroom decorated in pink and white,
he paused. There was a phone by the bed in there as well.
Still, he hesitated. The room gave him the creeps. It had
the air of a shrine. "I suppose everyone has to deal with
their grief in their own way," he muttered.

He doubted the phone in that room had been used in
years. But on the verge of desperation, he went inside. Lift-
ing the receiver and looking at the buttons, he saw that it

was too old a model to have a redial. He dropped it back in the cradle and strode toward the door. Frustration raged within him. Nothing! He'd found nothing.

Abruptly he stopped. He'd been glowering at the floor and a glint of blue in a corner of the door frame had caught his eye. Almost afraid he'd imagined it, he bent down for a closer view. It was an earring...the mate to Katrina's earring. She'd been here. But when?

Turning back, he began to search the room for clues. There was nothing to give him a time frame. Going into the bathroom, he noticed that the pink hand towel had been used. He felt it. It was still damp and there was a small puddle of water on the floor as if someone had been using the sink and splashed water around. He'd been watching the house since before dawn. No one other than Lewis had left.

"By the front way," he growled at himself. But they could have left by the back. If they'd crossed the back lawn, keeping to the right, and come out on the street running parallel to this one, he wouldn't have seen them.

Striding through the house, he went out the back door and, with the skill of a man who had learned to track almost before he'd learned to walk, he studied the wet grass. His footprints were the only ones he could find. Most likely Lewis's accomplice had taken Katrina out of the house while he was following Lewis to work.

His hand formed a fist crushing the earring into his palm until it cut into his flesh. He'd been so close and he'd let her slip out of his grasp.

Dropping the earring into his pocket, he called headquarters from his cellular phone and asked to speak to his partner. When Lewis came on the phone Boyd said that he was running a temperature and would be staying home for a few days. Lewis was solicitous as usual. He offered to bring by some chicken soup from the deli on his way home, but Boyd said he just wanted to sleep. After ringing off, he drove back to headquarters and parked where he could keep an eye on Lewis's car.

When Lewis left, he tailed him…first to the grocery, then to the movie rental place and then home. When he was certain of Lewis's destination, he continued past Lewis's street, circling the block coming in from the opposite direction. Before reaching Lewis's house, he pulled into a driveway on the opposite side of the street. During his early morning vigil, he'd noticed that this house was for sale and unoccupied. High hedges to one side of the driveway and overgrown forsythia bushes at the front edge of the lawn and along the side gave him some cover from nosy neighbors and Lewis. Settling in, binoculars in one hand and the hero sandwich he'd bought at the sub shop while Lewis was picking out movies in the other, he began his vigil. He had a clear view of Lewis's front door and the walkway from the house to the garage.

Katrina again felt herself being shaken awake.

"Time for another pill." Lewis's insistent voice broke through the fog.

"No," she groaned.

"Yes. Now be a good girl and swallow."

He shoved the pill into her mouth and held a glass of water to her lips. Her mouth was too dry to resist the temptation to take a drink. The pill went down and she felt herself again being lowered onto the cot.

Boyd yawned and looked at his watch. It was midnight. All the lights in Lewis's house had been turned off about an hour ago. The last had been in Lewis's bedroom, indicating his partner had settled in for the night.

Abruptly, Boyd cursed under his breath. A police patrol car had pulled into the driveway behind him. They hadn't used a siren but they did have their lights flashing. Hoping Lewis was sound asleep, Boyd quickly climbed out of his car.

Jacketless with his gun in its shoulder holster in clear view, he held his hands above his head with his FBI badge in his right hand. "I'm here on an FBI surveillance. Could you fellows turn off those lights?" he asked keeping his voice as low as possible.

The patrolman, who had gotten out of the car and was walking toward Boyd, waved to his partner and the lights were turned off. "What's going on?" he asked, reaching Boyd and playing his flashlight on Boyd's ID. Meanwhile his partner exited the patrol car, drew his gun and took a position where he had an easy shot at Boyd, in case Boyd wasn't on the level.

"It's my partner. He's been working on a dangerous case and his life's been threatened. He refused to let the department put a guard on him. He can be real bullheaded when he wants to be. Doesn't like to feel like he's being nursemaided. So I'm doing it on my own without his knowledge. You guys know how it is, partners should watch each other's backs."

"Yeah, you're right on that one," the patrolman nearest him said, giving his partner a nod to let him know everything was okay. "We'll let Mrs. Riker know you're on the level." He grinned. "I'd call her a nosy busybody but, the truth is, she's a real help. She keeps an eye on the neighborhood and lets us know if anything isn't kosher."

"Thanks." Boyd said, keeping an eye out for any lights coming on in Lewis's house. None did.

Hours later, Boyd watched the sun come up. Once he was certain Lewis was in for the night, he'd let himself doze at fifteen-minute intervals. He'd dreamt of Katrina. Always she was calling out to him for help.

Patience was something he'd been taught from a young age, but his was wearing thin. The urge to go inside and wring the truth out of Lewis was strong. Reason made him fight it. Lewis would never admit to knowing anything about Katrina's disappearance. And the earring wasn't proof enough to scare him. He could claim that Katrina had probably come by his place while he was gone and left it just to make Boyd suspicious. Even more importantly, if Boyd faced him now, Lewis would be put on his guard. He might even decide that keeping her alive was too dangerous and dispose of her.

"Come on, lead me to her," he growled, when Lewis came out of the house.

Instead, Lewis went to work.

His patience now almost gone, Boyd was considering the possibility of getting hold of some sodium Pentothal drug and using it on Lewis when the man came out of the building at noon, climbed into his car and drove away.

Boyd followed him to a bank. From there, Lewis went to a travel office. His next stop was at a medical supply house. He came out with a wheelchair.

A rush of adrenaline surged through Boyd. Lewis had to be getting ready to move Katrina. "And she'd better be unharmed," he growled, the promise of retribution if she had been etched into his face.

From the medical supply house, Lewis went home, unloaded his purchases and went back to work. The rest of the day was routine.

"Just keep cool," Boyd told himself that evening as he again pulled into the drive of the empty house. But that wasn't easy as the night dragged on. By the time dawn broke he was ready to beat the truth out of Lewis.

The time for Lewis to leave for work came and went. The lights in the house had come on at the usual time, indicating that the man was up and moving about. Boyd took a couple of long calming breaths. Today had to be the day. Lewis had his supplies and he was obviously not going into work.

In her concrete prison, Katrina was again shaken awake. "Time to go," Lewis said, helping her to her feet.

"I need to use the toilet and I want to use a real one," she pleaded. Through the fog that clouded her mind, her instinct for survival ordered her to fight for time to let her body shake off the effect of the sleeping pills.

"Sure, why not? We have to go upstairs anyway." Lewis helped her to the pink bathroom.

As they went through the door, she looked for her earring. Her vision was slightly blurred but she thought it was gone. Had Lewis found it or had he unknowingly kicked it under the door? Or had Boyd understood her message, come looking for her and found it? She prayed it had been Boyd. But if it had been Boyd, why hadn't he rescued her? Her hopes sank. If she was going to survive, it would be up to her.

In the bathroom, she splashed cold water on her face before taking care of her bodily needs. Nothing helped. She got dizzy just sitting and rising. Splashing more cold water on her face, she fought a bout of threatened nausea.

"Come out of there," Lewis ordered.

When she did, he nodded toward the bed. "Change into those."

A fresh pair of her slacks along with a lightweight pullover top and underwear were lying on the bed. "I figured you wouldn't mind if I chose your wardrobe," he said, backing out of the room. "I'll be outside the door and I'm leaving it partially open so I can hear you if you try anything stupid.''

Katrina was glad to have a change of clothes. The ones she had on were in pretty bad shape. Even more importantly, this would give her more time to work off the effects of the pills.

Sitting on the side of the bed, she took off her shoes and socks. Again bending over made her dizzy. Standing, she stripped out of the rest of her clothes. She felt sweaty and rank. If she was going to die, she'd die clean. Going back into the bathroom, she climbed into the shower and turned on the water. It felt incredibly good cascading over her.

''What the hell are you doing?'' Lewis demanded, barging into the bathroom and throwing back the shower curtain. His face was a contortion of rage.

''I was dirty.'' That he was seeing her naked didn't even embarrass Katrina. Survival was her only concern and overcoming the effects of the drugs was the only way she could save herself. ''You wouldn't want me drawing attention to us because I smelled so badly.''

Lewis's rage faded into impatience. ''You have five minutes.''

She turned the water on cold and stood under it. All it did was give her a chill and make her nauseous. Turning the temperature back to warm, she rubbed herself with soap, then rinsed. She was feeling better as she toweled herself dry, but her body continued to respond sluggishly. It was as if she was moving in slow motion.

''I've waited long enough.'' Lewis threw the bathroom door open again. ''You've got two more minutes to get dressed.''

She looked around for a weapon as she returned to the bedroom. There was nothing. Even if there had been something, she wouldn't have had a chance to pick it up. Lewis was standing glaring at her. "Could I have some privacy?" she requested.

"No. Now get dressed."

She was more alert than she had been in the shower. This time the thought of discarding the towel and exposing herself in front of him caused an embarrassed flush to begin to creep over her body. Then she saw his expression and the embarrassment vanished. He was glaring at her with icy hatred as if she were some horrible creature whose company he was forced to endure.

She managed to get the panties on reasonably quickly but fastening the bra was difficult.

"I'll do it," Lewis snapped after she'd fumbled with it several times. Completing the task quickly, he stepped back. "Now get finished."

Clumsily, she slipped the slacks and shirt on. Again sitting on the bed, she pulled her sneakers on. She'd barely completed that task when Lewis grabbed her arm, jerked her to her feet and shoved her toward the hall.

"Time to go," he said. There was a wheelchair just outside the bedroom door. He shoved her into it. "Sit." Taking a bottle out of his pocket, he produced three pills. "Take these."

They were different than the ones she'd been taking. "What are they?"

"Muscle relaxants. You're going to be my very ill sister whom I'm taking to a specialist in New Mexico. I want to get there ahead of your aunt so I'll have time to take a look around."

Ordering her body to fight the effect of the pills, she downed them.

"They'll work fairly quickly." Lewis smiled. "I used them when I had a back problem. One makes you comfortably relaxed. Three should make you limp."

He pushed the chair to the living room and seated himself on the couch. "We'll give them a few minutes to work."

The grogginess Katrina had been fighting began to creep over her mind once again, but worse was the sensation that her muscles were all turning to jelly.

"Lift your arm," Lewis ordered.

She tried. It trembled from the effort and after only a couple of inches, sank back down. When she attempted to speak, the words came out in nonsense mumblings.

Lewis smiled and rose. All she could do was sit helplessly as he slipped a pair of sunglasses on her, tied a large scarf on her head so that it covered her hair and obscured her face, wrapped a light blanket around her, then pushed her out of the house.

Boyd stiffened with surprise when he saw Lewis coming out of his house pushing an occupied wheelchair. The occupant's identity was hidden by a blanket, scarf and sunglasses, but he was certain it was Katrina. Lewis's accomplice must have brought her in through the backyard. He looked for the accomplice but saw no one.

Calling for backup, he pulled out of the driveway and blocked the exit to Lewis's. "Get away from her," he ordered, his gun leveled at Lewis through the window. "You're under arrest for kidnapping."

"I'm doing our job," Lewis growled back.

Boyd glanced back at the house, then to each side of it, never letting Lewis out of his sight for more than a second. "Where's your accomplice?"

"I have no accomplice."

Lewis maintained his grip on the handles of the wheelchair. "You let a pretty face fool you. She knows where her aunt is."

Keeping his gun leveled on Lewis, Boyd got out of his car and moved toward him. "I never thought you'd sell out."

"I don't give a damn about the money. It's Garduchi I want. He's responsible for my daughter's death. He turned her into a prostitute and drug addict. I'm going to get the evidence we need to put him behind bars."

Tears of frustration welled in Katrina's eyes. It was important to her that Boyd know she hadn't lied to him. She shook her head in a lolling manner. "Doon't knoow wheere Leeeoona isss." The words came out slurred as if she were drunk. "Doon't knoow wheere Leeeoona isss," she repeated, trying to make herself understood.

"What did you give her?" Boyd demanded, her limpness scaring him.

"Just some muscle relaxant. She'll be fine."

She didn't look fine. Knowing he needed to keep his mind clear, Boyd fought panic. "Get away from her," he ordered again.

"Don't you get it?" Hatred glistened in Lewis's eyes. "She's not worth your concern. She's the spawn of one of Garduchi's top killers. Her blood is tainted."

Her muscles trembling from the effort, Katrina lifted her arm and let it drop to the side of the wheelchair. Using every ounce of willpower she had, she moved her hand between the spokes and curled her fingers around them.

Boyd was studying Lewis. The man had clearly gone over the edge. "You were planning to kill her and her aunt once you had the evidence."

"They deserve to die."

"Katrina never worked for Garduchi. She's tried to do good with her life."

"She lived among them. If she wanted to do good, she

would have gotten evidence on Garduchi that would have put him out of business.''

"She was only seventeen. All she wanted was to get away from Garduchi with her life.''

"How do you know she wasn't lying about that? She told you she didn't know how to contact her aunt and she does.''

"Dooon't knoow. Wasss playing for time,'' Katrina insisted.

"Step away,'' Boyd ordered again.

Police sirens sounded in the distance.

"You're a fool!'' Lewis screamed in frustration and gave the wheelchair a hard shove in Boyd's direction.

Katrina let out a cry of pain as the spokes cut into her hand. The chair spun, crashing into Lewis sending him to the ground. Before he had time to recover, Boyd had turned him over and handcuffed him. Then rolling Lewis onto his back, Boyd retrieved Lewis's gun from its holster.

A police car arrived at that moment.

"Agent Logan.'' Boyd identified himself, holding up his badge as the officers left their car, guns drawn and approached. "I'm the one who called for backup. The man on the ground is Agent Lewis Hamond. I'm charging him with kidnapping.'' He handed Lewis's gun to the nearest officer. "This is his weapon.''

"He's nuts. I was just keeping a witness undercover for her own protection,'' Lewis said, struggling into a sitting position.

"Doesn't look like you were doing too good a job of protecting her,'' one of the officers observed, as Katrina began to fall forward out of the wheelchair.

Boyd rushed to catch her. "She's unconscious. I've got to get her to the hospital.''

"We'll take care of Agent Hamond.'' The officer who

had taken Lewis's gun into his custody nodded toward a second patrol car that had just arrived. "Davis and O'Riley can take you to the hospital."

Boyd scooped Katrina up in his arms. "Check Hamond's pockets. He's been drugging her. The doctors will need to know with what."

"There's two bottles here," the second of the first two officers said, hurriedly following Boyd's instructions, then rushing to hand the bottles to the driver of the car that was going to take Boyd and Katrina to the hospital.

Boyd had been acutely aware of the shallowness of her breathing as he got her into the patrol car and then climbed in with her. Holding on to her as the car whisked them through the streets, he looked down and saw her bloodied hand. Taking out his handkerchief, he wrapped it around the wounds. "You're going to be all right," he said softly in her ear.

She remained limp, giving no indication she'd heard.

His hold on her tightened, and he prayed.

Chapter 12

Boyd's gaze traveled from Katrina to the saline solution being administered by IV, then back to her pale features. The doctors had assured him that she was merely sleeping off the drugs. She was also dehydrated, but they didn't expect any residual complications from that either. Still, he refused to leave her.

"How's she doing?"

Boyd looked to the door to see Gerald Eldridge. "The doctors say she'll be fine."

"Good." Eldridge sat down. "I've just come from interviewing Lewis."

"I searched that house. Where'd he have her?" Boyd asked.

"In a bomb shelter built onto the basement. He'd hidden the door behind a metal cabinet filled with paper products and laundry detergent, stuff like that."

Boyd remembered that wall with the metal cabinet. Mentally he kicked himself for not having ripped everything away from all the walls in his search.

"How'd you know Lewis had her?" Eldridge asked.

"The note he made her write saying she was leaving. She managed to incorporate a message."

Eldridge scowled. "Why didn't you come to me?"

Deciding it would be prudent not to admit he hadn't known who he could trust, Boyd said, "I wasn't certain I had interpreted it right. I don't like making accusations I can't prove."

Eldridge nodded his acceptance of that explanation. "Lewis is insisting he was merely doing his job."

"He planned to kill her."

"We can't prove that. But he will be tried for kidnapping." Gerald Eldridge's gaze turned to Katrina. "He says she contacted her aunt and arranged a meeting in Santa Fe on Sunday. I've alerted our men there and sent extra."

"Leona won't be there. Katrina was merely playing for time. She doesn't know where her aunt is." There was no doubt in Boyd's mind that he was speaking the truth. A tiny smile tilted one corner of his mouth as he realized how fully he trusted her.

"Better safe than sorry," Eldridge said with calm nonchalance. "I'm going to fly out there tonight to oversee the investigation. If you're wrong, I don't want Leona slipping through our fingers again."

Boyd knew Eldridge. The man was being polite. He believed Lewis's claim that Boyd had allowed his feelings for Katrina to make him less efficient, thus providing an easy opportunity for Leona to get away from him. But then, Gerald Eldridge had never dealt with Leona Serrenito. It was equally obvious Eldridge thought Boyd was allowing his feelings to blind him to the truth...that Katrina was in cahoots with her aunt. But Gerald Eldridge didn't know

Katrina. And, right at this moment, Boyd didn't give a damn what his superior thought. "Enjoy the scenery because that's all you're going to find there."

Eldridge rose and gave him a fatherly pat on the shoulder. "I'm sorry this happened."

Boyd watched him leave, then eased back in the chair and closed his eyes.

Katrina awoke groggily. It took a couple of minutes for her mind to clear enough for her to realize she was in a hospital room. Easing herself into a sitting position, she was forced to drop her head into her hands for a moment to let the dizziness subside. One hand hurt. Realizing it was bandaged, she remembered putting it between the spokes of the wheelchair.

The dizziness subsided and she straightened. Boyd was asleep in the lounge chair by the side of the bed. His clothes were rumpled and his hair mussed. Her gaze traveled over him. Comforting was the word that came to mind, quickly followed by breathtakingly handsome. Abruptly, memories of Lewis telling him that she knew where her aunt was flashed through her mind and she wondered if Boyd was there as a trusting friend or a distrustful guard.

As if he felt her watching him, he opened his eyes. "Morning." Rising, he stood by the bed. "Thirsty?"

The concern she saw on his face eased her mind. Her mouth too dry to speak, she nodded.

He poured a glass of water, put a straw in it, then helped her get the straw in her lips.

"How do you feel?" he asked when she'd finished drinking.

"Better." She smiled crookedly. "Thanks for finding me."

"Got your message."

She recalled her fear that he would assume the worst of her and pay no heed to what she'd written. "I guess I really should say thanks for believing in me."

"With my life," he vowed, easing a strand of her hair back behind her ear.

His touch spread fire through her while his words filled her with joy. "I owe you mine."

"I'm sorry about Lewis."

Feeling the need to make it clear that she had never lied to him, she said, "I invented that story about knowing where my aunt is for Lewis. I honestly don't know where she is or how to contact her."

"I know." Figuring she'd find out that Eldridge did think she knew, he said, "I told Eldridge he was going on a wild-goose chase."

She breathed a frustrated sigh. "He sent men to Santa Fe?"

Boyd nodded.

"That's going to be a real waste of taxpayers' money." Wanting to change the subject, she asked, "What day is this?"

"Friday."

She saw the tired lines in his face. "You look like you could use a shower and a good night's sleep."

"I hope you're not trying to get rid of me," he teased.

She gently touched his cheek. "No. I'm just tired. I think I'll sleep some more and I'll rest better knowing you're someplace more comfortable than that chair."

He kissed her gently. "That chair and I have become bonded together."

Concern for him spread over her features. "Please, go home for a while. I'll be fine."

Admitting that he could use a shower and a change of

clothes, he placed another light kiss on her lips. "I'll be back soon."

Lying back, she closed her eyes. When he lingered for a moment to brush wayward strands of hair from her face, every fiber of her being was aware of his touch. Feigning sleep, she waited until she heard him leave the room, then opened her eyes.

Like a hazy dream, she recalled seeing him drive up and order Lewis to get away from her. Boyd would always be her hero. Her mind returned to the present. Closing her eyes, she saw his face when he'd approached her bed. There had been a tenderness there that had warmed her to the core. The feel of his lips and the touch of his hand lingered on her skin.

She lifted her hand as if she could once again touch his cheek. A tear escaped, trickling down the side of her face, and she dropped her hand down to her side. She loved him and because of that, she had to walk away from him and never look back. And the sooner the better.

Sitting up, she noticed that there was no dizziness this time. Relieved, she buzzed for the nurse.

"Mr. Logan said you'd woken," the nurse said cheerfully, entering the room and striding to the bed. "But he also said you'd gone back to sleep."

"I woke up again." Resolve glistened in Katrina's eyes. "And I want to get up and move around."

"The doctor did say we could get you up when you were ready. But you can't try to move around without help." The nurse put down the side of the bed as she spoke. "Now try to swing your legs over."

Katrina's muscles were slow to respond but they did. The more she moved, the more in control she felt.

After they had walked the corridor a few times, she talked the nurse into letting her take a shower and by the time Boyd returned, she was seated in the lounge chair in a clean hospital gown combing her damp hair.

He entered carrying a huge arrangement of red roses. "Looks like you're feeling a lot better," he observed with relief.

"You're looking better, too." The sight of him caused her blood to race. *Stay cool!* she ordered herself. But when he grinned at her compliment, her heart skipped a beat.

"Thought this room could use some cheering up." He set the vase on the bedside table, then pulled up a chair and sat down facing her.

"Thanks for the flowers. They're lovely." She knew what she had to do but he wasn't making it easy.

"I stopped by the nurses' station. They told me that your doctor came by and he's signed a release saying you can go home tomorrow." His voice took on a husky edge. "I'm not going to rush you into anything but I plan do some serious courting."

Unable to face him, Katrina shifted her gaze to the window. "I'm not staying in Washington. As soon as I'm out of here, I'm catching the first plane to St. Louis."

Boyd caught her chin in his hand and forced her to face him. "I know I haven't always been the most charming companion. But you didn't make my job easy. You were a constant distraction. All I want is a chance to redeem myself."

Again the heat of his touch traveled through her igniting the fires of desire. She pulled back from his hold. "I don't think that's such a good idea."

Boyd scowled. "I don't understand. I could have sworn you're as attracted to me as I am to you." Cynicism spread over his features. "Is this where I learn that I have been a fool?"

"No." She met his cold gaze. "I do care for you. That's why I'm leaving."

"That doesn't make any sense."

Impatience flashed in her eyes. "It makes a great deal of sense. I've lived with the taint of my family history all my life. Lewis isn't alone. There are others like him, others who have been harmed by Garduchi and his thugs…my brother, my father, my grandfather, etc. being among those thugs."

"You can't hold yourself responsible for what they did."

"But others can and will. And then there's the matter of trust. If your informants knew you had a connection to me, they'd suddenly become worried that I'd squeal on them. And your fellow agents would feel uncomfortable around me because they'd always be worried I'd pass on any information I got to the criminal element. Your career will be ruined."

"They'll learn to trust you like I do." He cupped her face in his hands. "We'll work through this together."

"No."

He nibbled on her lips then leisurely kissed her.

Reasoning that she should have some memories, she did not fight him.

He smiled triumphantly. "Can I assume you've changed your mind?"

Tears welled in her eyes. "No. Someday you'd find out I was right and you'd wish you'd never met me. I don't want to be there for that."

"I don't let what others think bother me," he growled.

She forced herself to push him away. "My mind is made up."

For a long time he studied her in silence. Reading the resolve on her face, he said finally, "I'll drive you to the airport."

It was taking every ounce of determination she had to remain firm in her decision. "If you'll just bring my things here, I'll take a taxi."

He rose. "This isn't the end," he declared, and strode out.

"For his sake it has to be," she promised herself.

Boyd cursed her hardheadedness. He couldn't blame her for how she felt, but he was determined to find a way to change her mind. For now he'd give her some space. But not a lot.

Chapter 13

Well, you're on your own again, Katrina mused dryly, boarding the plane for St. Louis. She fought back the urge to cry. Boyd apparently hadn't felt as strongly as he'd declared. He'd brought her things by the hospital last night, wished her well, then left and she hadn't seen him since.

You were the one who insisted on making it a clean break. You can't have it both ways, she chided herself. She'd told him to get lost for his own good and he'd obviously realized she was right. Still, it hurt to know he could walk away so easily while she felt as if a part of her had been ripped out. *It'll mend. Better to discover now how shallow his feelings were than to find out later.* Clamping her seat belt closed, she turned her mind to plans for the future.

Seated in the back of the plane, his black hair streaked with gray, wearing a false gray beard and mustache and dark glasses, Boyd watched the passengers boarding until he saw Katrina, then he settled back in his seat and slept.

* * *

Entering her home, Katrina set her suitcase on the floor in the living room, then proceeded from room to room removing the bugs from the phones and the various other hiding places Boyd had indicated. During the plane ride her anger had built. She was tired of being spied on and she was tired of people using her as a pawn in whatever games they'd devised. Carrying the devices into her garage, she found a hammer and smashed each and every one, swept up the pieces and threw them in the trash.

Returning to the living room, she picked up the now-dead arrangement of flowers sent by her aunt and dropped them, container and all, into the trash as well.

Then carrying the suitcase into her bedroom, she threw herself on the bed and had a good cry. Frustration was behind her tears. She cried because as hard as she'd tried to prove she was a good person, she was still a suspect in the eyes of many. And, she cried because she couldn't stop thinking about Boyd even though he'd been able to walk away from her without a backward glance.

Finally the sobs subsided and she slept. Waking late into the night, she bathed, changed into her nightgown and went back to bed. Lying in the dark she made a mental list of what she would do the next day beginning with resigning from the police department and putting her house up for sale. She'd paid her dues. She'd tried to make up for the life her father and his family had led. Now it was time for her to have a life of her own. She'd move out of this town, out of this state, and start fresh.

Again she slept.

A knocking on her front door woke her.

Opening her eyes, she saw sunlight streaming in from around the blinds. A look at the clock told her it was past ten. Not worrying about putting on slippers, she grabbed her robe and pulled it on as she padded barefoot to the door.

"Sorry to wake you," Dominic Ruzito said with polite apology.

She saw Victor and Louey flanking him and knew she should be scared. Dominic's polite tone was not reflected in his eyes and that generally meant trouble for whomever he was talking to. But she was in no mood to be intimidated. "I've had a really bad few days. Just state your business and leave."

"That's not very gracious," he chided. "Don't you think you should ask me in?"

It was an order, not a request. "*You* may come in," she replied, making it clear his two thugs weren't invited.

He smiled patronizingly at her, then glanced first at Victor and then at Louey. "You two stay here. Enjoy the fresh air."

"You sure?" Victor asked, eyeing Katrina suspiciously.

Dominic gave him a dry look. "I'll yell for help if I need it."

Victor didn't look happy, but he said no more.

Entering the house, Dominic closed the door, proceeded into the living room and sat down in one of the chairs by the couch. "Louey's having a little trouble hearing. We heard you were on your way back and wanted to make certain you got home safe. He was checking on you when you decided to play exterminator."

Remaining standing and keeping a distance between them, Katrina gave the impression of leaning casually against the wall while keeping every muscle braced for action. If Dominic had come here to do her harm, she would go down fighting. "I'd say I'm sorry but I'm not."

Dominic shook his head. "You have always been a problem child." Exaggerated sympathy spread over his features.

"We heard about the trouble you had in Washington. I'm sure your father warned you not to trust the authorities. You should have heeded his words."

Even after what Lewis had done to her, having a man like Dominic Ruzito talk about him with such condemnation grated on her nerves. "The man had lost his daughter."

"That's a very generous attitude considering he planned to kill you."

"He was insane. When you take out someone, you know exactly what you're doing."

"Now, now. You shouldn't make such accusations. That's slander."

The warning in his eyes caused a cold chill to run along her spine. *Remarks like that could be considered suicidal,* she cautioned herself. "I doubt you came here to sympathize with me over my escape from death's door. So why did you come?"

Dominic shook his head sadly. "You are like a thorn on the rosebush."

"I like to think I'm the rose and you're the thorn." She knew tossing an insult at him was living dangerously, but she didn't care. Because of her family's connection to this man and his kind, she'd been fighting a losing battle all her life.

Dominic sighed a patronizing, fatherly sigh. "Vince is concerned about you. After all, he once was your godfather. This city isn't as safe as it used to be, especially for a young woman living alone. And this career you've chosen, it's dangerous as well. He feels you would be safer in a new location."

Katrina got the message. She'd become too much of an embarrassment to Garduchi. He wanted her gone, but she didn't like being told to leave. *You were already planning to go,* her practical side reminded her. *Better to leave on your feet than in a casket.* Still she was unable to make herself appear to be caving in to him. "I'll give what you've said some serious thought."

"You do that." Smiling politely he rose. Reaching into his pocket, he took out a small object, placed it on the coffee table, then strode out.

Katrina couldn't see what he'd left behind. It was hidden behind a decorative bowl. She didn't care. Her whole attention was on him, her body poised for action should he suddenly decide she'd caused enough trouble and choose to terminate her. When the door closed behind him, she moved to the window and did not relax until she saw the three men drive away.

"Washington, D.C.'s a nice place to live."

Katrina whirled around to discover Boyd, his disguise gone, standing a few feet behind her. "Where'd you come from?" she managed to gasp out.

"The guest room."

She stared at him in disbelief. "How long have you been here?"

"Since pretty soon after you got home. I let myself in the back door. You were having a good cry, so I chose not to disturb you." Leaning against the wall, he added in an easy drawl, "You didn't really think I'd let you come back here to face possible retaliation from Garduchi alone, did you?"

"Actually, I did," she confessed.

He scowled. "You must think I'm as shallow as a dry creek."

"I'm just not used to having anyone who really cares what happens to me." She wanted to rush into his arms, but held herself back. Reminding them both of why she'd insisted they belonged apart, she asked, "How's the hunt in Santa Fe going?"

He grinned. "You and I both know they're going to come up empty-handed."

She didn't grin back. "You know they'll simply think I warned Leona that they were waiting for her."

"I'll tell them I was keeping an eye on you every minute and you didn't contact anyone." Approaching her, he slid his arms around her. "You look awfully cute in the morning." He drew her closer. "You feel good, too."

"Stop it!" She tried to squirm free, but his hold tightened. "They'll just think I corrupted you."

"Being corrupted by you could be fun." He nibbled on her earlobe then kissed the hollow behind it.

Her body wanted to melt into his. "It won't work. I won't ruin your..."

His mouth found hers stopping her protest. The embers his embrace had sparked blazed into a raging fire. She ordered herself to again attempt to free herself but her muscles refused to obey. She wanted to be in his arms more than she had ever wanted anything in her life.

Boyd smiled when she stopped resisting him. "I got used to waking up beside you," he said, his lips moving tantalizingly against hers as he spoke. "I've missed sharing a bed with you."

"I've missed that, too," she confessed.

His hands traveled caressingly over her back then lower, pulling her more tightly against him.

She felt his need and her own burned hotter.

"You are so soft," he murmured against her neck.

"You're definitely not soft," she returned huskily.

He ran his hands along the curve of her hips, then up along her rib cage to her breasts. Her robe and nightgown provided little barrier to the feel of her. "Nope. You have that effect on me."

She smiled and nipped his earlobe. "You have a very stimulating effect on me as well."

"We're going to have to do something about this."

"Definitely."

Scooping her up in his arms, he carried her toward her bedroom.

Katrina had always heard about uncontrolled desire, but she'd thought it was a myth. Or, if not a myth, something that she would never fall victim to. She'd always prided herself on her control. But with every fiber of her being, she wanted to be joined with Boyd. Before they had reached the bedroom, she was unbuttoning his shirt.

This would be her first time with a man and she had always expected to be afraid or at least a little nervous, but this felt right. She craved him as if her body had been waiting for this moment forever.

Standing her beside the bed, Boyd let her finish taking off his shirt, then he removed her robe and nightgown. "You are a tasty sight," he said, his gaze traveling over her.

The heat in his eyes was so intense, she could feel it touching her naked body like a fiery caress. Desire made her legs weak and she reached for the buckle of his belt.

Sensations…excitement, pleasure, joy…swept through Boyd like waves as she finished undressing him.

"I can't wait much longer," he warned as she moved away from him and lay down on the bed, her arms out to him, inviting him to join her.

"Neither can I," she replied.

A masculine smile of triumph played at the corners of his mouth as he joined her on the bed and began to take possession of her. He moved slowly, savoring the moment.

Abruptly, he stopped. Something was wrong. He was meeting resistance. The truth shook him.

"I know there's more of you than that," she breathed huskily.

"You're a virgin," he returned, an edge of guilt in his voice. "You were saving yourself for your wedding day."

"I was saving myself for you," she corrected.

Mentally he breathed a sigh of relief. "I'm really glad to hear that because I don't think I could have turned back now." That he would be the first had added strength to his need to possess her. She would be his woman and only his woman.

Katrina lifted her hips, her body begging for his fullness and Boyd complied.

Her pain lasted only a moment and was vastly overshadowed by a sense of oneness with him. As they began to move together, all thought vanished until there was only her physical being stimulated beyond pleasure to a realm of excitement that caused every nerve to tingle with delight.

Boyd's breathing became ragged. She fitted him perfectly. He began to move with final purpose. Feeling her climaxing, he joined her.

Afterwards, he continued to hold her as they lay side by side, still panting from their exertion.

Her breathing finally becoming more regular, Katrina grinned sheepishly, "That was terrific."

Boyd grinned back. "And now, since I'm an honorable man and I have deflowered you, you'll have to let me marry you."

Katrina's smile vanished. "No." Worried that if she stayed in his arms, her resolve might weaken, she slipped out of his grasp, left the bed, pulled on her robe and exited the room.

Startled, Boyd was momentarily frozen into inaction. But

as she left, he bolted from the bed, pulled on his jeans and followed. He caught up with her in the living room. "You can't mean that. We belong together."

"I will not ruin your life." She backed away from him, putting the chair Dominic had been sitting in between them.

"Katrina." He started toward her, determined to change her mind.

She held up her hand. "Don't come any clo..." Her words died in her throat. Out of the corner of her eye she'd glimpsed a sparkle of blue. Her gaze shifted from him to the coffee table.

Boyd saw the color drain from her face. "What's wrong?"

Her hands grasped the back of the chair. "Dominic left something on the coffee table. I forgot about it when you suddenly appeared." She felt sick to her stomach.

Boyd's gaze followed hers and his expression turned grim. The object on the coffee table was Leona's ring.

Tears began to trickle slowly down Katrina's cheeks. "She always said the only way anyone would get that ring off her finger was to take it off her dead body."

"She shouldn't have tried to make it on her own," Boyd growled.

"She always thought she was cleverer than others."

"Apparently she overestimated her ability." Reaching her side, Boyd placed a protective arm around her shoulders. "Everyone needs someone when the going gets rough. You're stuck with me whether you like it or not."

Her chin trembled. "You are so tempting. But I've made up my mind and one day you'll thank me for not letting you link your life to mine."

"You're one stubborn woman. But I can be just as stubborn." He kissed the tip of her nose. "We'll talk about the future later. Right now, you've had a shock. Come in the

kitchen and I'll make you some coffee, then I'll call headquarters.''

By the end of the day, word had filtered through the
streets and the local agents had learned from informants
that the hit was made in Canada the day before. But no one
knew who the shooter was. The guess was that it was outside talent. There was also word that what Leona had taken
with her had been returned to Garduchi and he was satisfied
that he was safe.

Late in the evening, sitting on the couch, her feet
propped up on the coffee table, Katrina stared into space.
The ring was where Dominic had left it. She hadn't been
able to make herself touch it.

Boyd sat beside her, his arm around her. "Penny for your
thoughts.''

She liked sitting there with him. He made her feel warm
and safe and wanted. Tomorrow she would make him go,
but for now, she would allow herself this final time in his
company. "They're dumb.''

"All right, half a penny.''

"I was wondering what my life would have been like if
I'd been born into a normal family.''

"You'd probably be married with two kids, spending
your days carpooling and going to PTA meetings and we'd
have never met. And I'd have to spend my life wandering
alone, sad and forlorn, wondering where my soul mate
was.''

Tears burned at the back of her eyes. She forced herself
to her feet. "I cannot be your soul mate. You have no clue
what it's like to have people constantly watching you as if
they expect you to suddenly metamorphose into some horrible beast.''

Boyd rose. His hands closing around her upper arms, he

looked hard into her face. "My mother is full-blooded Apache. When my father married her, half of those he considered friends turned away from him. The other half took a while to accept her. My mother's people weren't pleased with the marriage either. But my parents didn't let what anyone thought bother them. They loved each other. That's all that mattered."

She pictured a man very much like Boyd and a young Apache maiden looking lovingly at each other. Tears of frustration welled in her eyes. "It's obvious how much your family means to you. They might never accept me. My father was the same breed of man who killed your father."

"My family judges people for who they are, not who their parents were."

"You can't be certain of that."

His gaze bore into her. "There is only one question that concerns me...do you love me, Katrina?"

She dropped her gaze to the top button on his shirt. "No," she lied. "Now go away."

"Look me in the eye and say that," he ordered.

Steeling herself, she met his gaze. The soft brown depths of his eyes drew her in, threatening to drown her in their warmth. "Go away," she managed to choke out.

"You're not answering my question."

She tried to lie again. The words formed on the tip of her tongue. Instead, she heard herself blurting, "Yes. I love you. I love you. There, are you satisfied?"

Triumph spread over his features.

She twisted out of his grasp. "Now get out!"

He frowned impatiently. "You don't seriously think I'm going to give up on you now."

Her jaw firmed. "It's over between us. Absolutely over."

"I guess that means you want me to sleep in the guest room tonight. That doesn't sound like much fun."

She scowled at him. "Go tell your family all about me. See their reaction. Then remember how even Eldridge went to Santa Fe. If you're honest with yourself, you'll see I'm right and someday you'll be grateful I sent you away."

He shook his head at her obstinacy.

His stance and the set of his jaw told her that arguing would be useless. The desire to invite him to share her bed once again swept through her. But the fear that if she did, she might never be able to send him away held her back. "You're the most exasperating man! I'm trying to do right by you," she snapped, then needing to flee before she gave in to the fire burning within, she added, "I'm going to take a shower and go to bed *alone*."

Boyd frowned at her departing back. She was his woman and he was determined to convince her of that.

Lying in bed, staring into the dark, Katrina wished with all her heart there was some way she could prove her good intentions to the authorities and Boyd's family.

A plan began to form in her mind. It wasn't a great plan but it was the only one that might possibly work. She knew he'd try to stop her if he found out what she was up to. Besides, it was risky and she didn't want him involved. "So I just have to choose the right time to get away from him."

The next morning she rose early, wanting to be up and dressed before Boyd. She was in the kitchen when he came in wearing only his jeans. Her gaze traveled over his broad shoulders and muscular chest. "You're not playing fair," she said. "Go get dressed."

Reaching her in two long strides, he drew her into his embrace. "All's fair in love and war."

Knowing that meeting his gaze could be fatal to her resolve, she leaned the top of her head against his chest and stared down at his bare feet. Even they looked enticing and mentally she groaned. "I'm trying to do what's right."

He kissed her hair. "Did you miss me last night?"

"If I say yes will you please go shave and get dressed?" she pleaded.

He smiled down at her head. "If that's what you really want."

"Yes, that's what I want." *Liar!* What she wanted was to stay in his arms forever.

"So did you miss me?"

"Yes, now go."

"I'm going to take a shower. I don't suppose you'd consider coming in and washing my back for me?" he coaxed.

"No. Now go." Straightening away from him, she gave him a determined push to send him on his way.

He kissed her lightly. "Too bad."

The moment he was gone, she wrote a note saying she had an errand to run and would be back soon. Then, waiting until she was sure he was in the bathroom, she grabbed her purse, left and drove straight to Garduchi's estate.

"Didn't expect to see you here," Joey Green, the guard at the gate said, his tone unfriendly.

"Just tell Mr. Garduchi I want to see him," she snapped.

Joey placed a call to the house. "He says I have to search your car and then frisk you to make sure you don't have any wires or weapons."

Katrina smiled to herself. Vince was so worried she'd come seeking revenge, he wasn't letting her through his gate until she was checked. Well, she had come to bring him harm, but not his way. Stepping out of the car, she spread her arms to allow the search. The malicious glimmer in Joey's eyes caused her stomach to knot. "Just make sure all you do is look for wires and weapons," she warned. "Or I'll scream loud enough your wife will hear about it."

"Joey." Dominic's voice came over the speaker. "Remember she's a guest. Mr. Garduchi wouldn't want her to feel misused."

"You ain't my type, anyways," Joey muttered. He made a quick inspection of her and a more thorough one of the car, then opened the gate.

Boyd was scowling at the note Katrina had left when his cellular phone rang.

"This is Agent Harlow," the man on the other end of the line said, when Boyd answered. "I'm out here keeping an eye on the Garduchi estate."

Boyd's stomach tightened. "What's going on?"

"Maybe you can tell me. We were told you were babysitting Ms. Polenari," the agent said.

"I am."

"So what's she doing at Garduchi's?"

Boyd's hand balled into a fist, crushing the note as he fought a rush of fear for Katrina. "When did she get there?"

"Just now. Doesn't look like she got too friendly of a welcome either."

Boyd's fear for her safety multiplied. "Damn!"

"You want us to do something?"

"No. I'll take care of it." Hanging up, he punched in another number.

At the house, Katrina was subjected to a second, more thorough search by the maid who had searched her on her last visit. Apparently Garduchi wasn't taking any chances that she might be here to avenge her aunt, she mused. Finally, she was led into his study. Dominic was standing to one side of his father-in-law. Louey and Victor took positions behind Katrina. A curl of fear wove through her. She thought of her life without Boyd and it disappeared. She would stroll through Hell if it meant being able to spend the rest of her days with him.

"I'm truly sorry about Leona," Garduchi said, his voice too sticky-sweet with sympathy. "But when you trod a dangerous path you must expect adversity."

Katrina schooled her voice into one of respect. "I appreciate your words. My aunt was thoughtless in her actions. You treated her well and she betrayed you. I accept the consequences she brought on herself."

Vince nodded his head approvingly. "That's very reasonable of you. Dominic tells me that you are considering moving to a more comfortable environment. Have you made a decision?"

"Yes, I'll be moving soon." Katrina was aware that he'd given her no indication that he wanted her to sit so she remained standing. This too was another show of respect, and she wanted him to think that her aunt's death had shaken her so badly, she was completely cowed.

"Good."

"But I would like to bury my aunt before I go."

He spread his hands in a gesture of helplessness. "With that I cannot help you."

Continuing to keep the respect in her voice, she added a plea. "Surely you cannot begrudge her a Christian burial so that her soul may rest in peace."

"Professionals are careful people. They send photographs and personal belongings, and, in your aunt's case, property that was stolen, as proof the job is done. But the body, they prefer never to be found. A person cannot be brought to trial on rumors." He rose. "If there is nothing else..."

His dismissal was cut short by the sound of a helicopter.

Dominic hurried to the French doors that opened onto the patio as the machine landed on the back lawn. Katrina followed with Victor and Louey close behind, their guns drawn. Continuing outside, Dominic motioned for Victor and Louey to take positions behind him and to either side. Seeing the police markings, he cast Katrina a threatening look.

"I had nothing to do with this," she yelled above the sound of the machine.

The moment it landed, Boyd climbed out. When he was out of range of the propellers, he waved to the pilot and the helicopter took off.

"Put your guns away," Dominic ordered Louey and Victor, never taking his eyes off of Boyd. "And to what do we owe this visit, Agent Logan?" he asked as Boyd reached the patio, letting Boyd know his identity was now known to them.

"I've come for Miss Polenari," Boyd said curtly.

Dominic smiled at the anger he saw Boyd direct at Katrina. "Women can be very difficult." He glanced at Katrina. "Some more than others. You are welcome to her."

"Thanks." Reaching her in three long strides, Boyd captured her by the upper arm. "Shall we leave before they change their minds?"

She considered telling him that Dominic was happy to see her go, but decided that keeping silent would be prudent. She'd never seen Boyd so angry. His hold was like a vice as they followed the pathway around to the front of the house. Reaching her car, he opened the passenger door. "Give me your keys."

Obeying demurely, she then climbed into the passenger

seat. As he slammed the door shut and strode around to the driver's side, she looked back at the house to see Vince watching them from the front window. Bitterness swept through her. Her plan to bring him down had failed. He'd won again.

They were two miles from the estate before Boyd was able to control his emotions enough to trust himself to speak. "What the hell did you think you were doing going to Garduchi's compound? The man's made it clear that he is barely tolerating you."

The grim set of his jaw told her that his anger was still strong. "I'm sorry if I caused you concern," she said meekly.

Pulling sharply over to the side of the road, he slammed on the brakes and turned to look at her. "Concern? You scared me half to death. You and I both know Garduchi would like to see you dead."

She read the love in his eyes. She'd never expected to find anyone who would care so deeply for her. And she had been willing to die for him. But that didn't change anything. Turning away from him, she stared out the front windshield.

"Why did you go there?" he demanded.

"I went to ask for my aunt's body. I thought if I could get it, it might provide evidence as to who the shooter was. Most professionals have some kind of trademark. Then if we could trace the killer, he might be willing to admit Garduchi paid him and then we'd have Garduchi. And since I would have helped get him, maybe your fellow agents and your family would be willing to accept me."

"You don't need to get yourself killed for my family to accept you," he growled.

Deciding that arguing with him was useless, Katrina simply sat back in her seat and remained silent.

With a final scowl in her direction, Boyd pulled back onto the road and drove them to her home. As they entered, he said, "Pack a suitcase."

She looked at him questioningly.

"Pack," he ordered.

"There's no reason for me to run. I've told Garduchi I'm leaving town and he's satisfied."

"We're not running away from Garduchi. I'm taking you to meet my family."

Fear caused her to pale. "I don't think that's such a good idea."

"I think it's an excellent one. Now pack."

She considered protesting again but stopped herself. Maybe it was a good idea. He'd see how his family reacted and have to admit she was right.

Chapter 14

With an air of resignation, Katrina climbed into the driver's seat as Boyd put their bags in the trunk. This trip was not going to be fun, but to prove her point, it was necessary.

Boyd was climbing into the passenger's seat when his cellular phone rang.

"Agent Logan, this is Agent Webber from the Kansas City office. They flew some of us in as reinforcements." The woman on the other end of the line identified herself. "We've had a break in the Garduchi case and we'd like you to be in on it." Voices sounded in the background. "Hold on a minute," Agent Webber requested. A moment later, she added, "If Officer Polenari is with you, she might like to come along, too."

It was about time something went their way, Boyd thought. "She is with me and I know she'd like to be included."

Katrina saw his quirky smile. Whatever was happening was good news.

"Where are you now?" Agent Webber asked.

"Officer Polenari's house."

Boyd heard Agent Webber telling someone his location. A moment later a man's voice came on line and began giving directions to a farmhouse on the outskirts of a small town several miles north of St. Louis. "Should take you about an hour to get here," the man finished. "Better get moving. You don't want to miss the fun."

"Right," Boyd replied.

"So what's up?" Katrina asked as soon as he pressed the end button.

Boyd's grin broadened. "There's been a break in the case. Let's go. Take 270 to 70 west."

"What kind of a break?" she asked, backing out of the drive.

"Agent Webber wasn't specific but the implication was that there's a good chance it will put Garduchi behind bars."

The hope for a future with him was reborn. "I'll keep my fingers crossed."

As she guided the car down the street, Boyd touched her cheek caressingly. "And you should note that the fact that you were invited along proves you were wrong about my fellow agents not trusting you."

"Well, maybe some are a little more open-minded than others," she conceded, her hope nurtured further.

Following the directions Boyd was given, close to an hour later they arrived at a large three-story farmhouse set in the midst of several acres of wooded land. Katrina parked beside the two cars already there.

As they mounted the steps, a slender woman with long, full red hair opened the door and stepped aside to allow them to enter. "Everyone's in the front room," she said, nodding toward a door to their right.

"You look familiar," Katrina said, passing the woman, then pausing in the hall for a longer inspection. "Have we met bef—?" Her words died sharply. The hair was wrong. *A wig.* From a distance, it had obscured the woman's features but up close, Katrina recognized their greeter as the maid she'd noticed lingering in the background on her last visit to Vince's estate. She'd been surprised that he'd allowed a lesser employee to be present. Now she realized that this woman wasn't a maid. The ice that suddenly glistened in her dark eyes told Katrina this was one of Vince's enforcers.

Boyd read the abrupt panic on Katrina's face and went for his gun.

"Relax and no one will get hurt," a man's voice ordered with cold threat, stopping Boyd in midmotion.

Katrina recognized the voice and her blood ran cold. They'd walked into a trap. "I should have suspected something was wrong when I was invited along," she muttered, looking past Boyd to see Louey approaching from wherever he had been lurking on their arrival.

Boyd moved closer to her, placing a protective arm around her. "In case you've forgotten, Katrina is under Vince's protection," he reminded their two captors. "Besides, she doesn't have any knowledge that could prove profitable to either of you."

"Inside," Louey ordered.

Braced to act on any chance to escape, Katrina and Boyd grudgingly obeyed.

Dominic Ruzito was waiting for them in the front room. He motioned toward two, straight-back wooden chairs placed in the center of the room. "Please, be seated." His icy tone belied the politeness of his words letting them know this wasn't a request.

"I thought I was to be allowed to leave town," Katrina said easing herself into the chair. "Or is Vince's word worth nothing these days?"

"Maybe Vince doesn't know about this." Boyd's gaze leveled on Dominic. "From what I've heard, your father-in-law is as cold-blooded as they come but he prides himself on keeping his word." Warning entered his voice. "You go against him and you could get burned."

Dominic continued to eye them both coldly. "His word was given when he believed Katrina was telling him the truth about knowing nothing that could cause him some unpleasantness."

"I don't know anything," Katrina spit back. "If I did, he'd already be behind bars."

Dominic raised an eyebrow skeptically, "If you know nothing that would interest the FBI, then why did Agent Logan come swooping down out of the sky to rescue you?"

"So he's a little overly protective."

"That is just the point. We were under the impression that you were no longer of any interest to the FBI. That Agent Logan is still watching over you causes concern to both Vince and myself. What was stolen has been returned and we have been assured that no copies were made."

The malicious glimmer in his eyes told Katrina something she had suspected but had not wanted to think about. "Your killer tortured my aunt before she died," she accused between clenched teeth. "I hope you, he, Vince...the whole lot of you, burn in Hell."

"You should be hoping that you don't meet the same fate as your aunt. Besides, the hitter wasn't cruel. Leona never could stand pain. The mere threat of it, caused her to tell him everything. At least that is what we believed."

His gaze bore into her. "What do you know about Vinc
that makes you continue to be of importance to the FBI?"

Her chin stiffened with defiance. "Nothing. I wish I did
but I don't."

His expression of disbelief mocked her denial. "If you
know nothing, then why is Agent Logan still protecting
you?"

The realization that Boyd's love for her had placed hi
life in danger shook her to the core. She couldn't bear the
thought that harm would come to him because of her. "He
wants to marry me."

Dominic looked at Boyd, amusement replacing the ice
in his eyes. "You actually want to marry her?"

Boyd met his amusement with cold disdain. "Yes."

Dominic's amusement vanished as quickly as it had ap
peared. For a long moment, he regarded Boyd in a stony
silence, then said, "I thought the FBI frowned on people
using their equipment for personal business."

"They do. But when I'd found out where she'd gone, I
wasn't going to let a few regulations stop me."

Again Dominic considered Boyd's words in silence, then
said, "Sources I have been able to trust in the past have
assured me that the FBI has no further interest in Katrina."
After another pause, he added, "I believe you. And you
have my sympathy. Katrina is a difficult woman. Myself, I
prefer a wife who understands that the husband is the head
of the family and should be obeyed. I doubt very much that
Katrina believes that."

"I like strong women," Boyd returned.

Dominic rewarded this declaration with a patronizing
shake of his head. "You are a glutton for punishment.
However, since Katrina's love life is of no concern to
Vince, I have no reason to kill either of you." He smiled
patronizingly at Katrina. "You see Vince does have a be-

nevolent side. He doesn't like to see people die without purpose.''

With difficulty, Katrina bit back a sarcastic response. She would not risk placing Boyd's life in any more jeopardy than she already had.

Dominic's attention spread to both of them. ''I hope you will be prudent and not mention our little visit. If you do, it will only cause embarrassment to you.'' He lifted his hands to show that he was wearing gloves. ''There will be no evidence that I or any of my associates were ever here and we can all produce witnesses who will place us in St. Louis all day.''

His expression became mockingly innocent. ''Unfounded accusations from the two of you will only look as if Katrina is seeking revenge for her aunt's death, which she, mistakenly of course, blames on Vince and because she cannot get him, she has gone after me. And you, Agent Logan, will appear to be going along with her because you're in love with her. In the end, you could both find yourselves discredited.''

Katrina glowered at him. ''Someday, you'll make a mistake.''

Dominic turned to Boyd. ''I strongly suggest you reconsider your choice of women before you are led to an early grave.'' This warning hanging in the air, he strode out of the house.

''Lucky you,'' the fake female FBI agent said, holding a gun on them while the others exited. ''You'll get to see the sunrise tomorrow.'' Then emptying Boyd's gun, she put the bullets in her pocket and keeping her weapon aimed at them, backed out.

Knowing there was nothing they could do, Katrina and Boyd watched from the window as the woman dropped

Boyd's gun in the front seat of Katrina's car, then drove away with the others.

As the cars disappeared from view, Katrina broke the silence between them, "You could have been killed because of me. I am not merely a threat to your reputation and career but to your life."

Boyd heard the horror in her voice and guessed where this was leading. "The possibility of getting killed is something I face daily in my job," he countered.

"Well you're not going to face it because of me."

His hands closed around her upper arms and he looked hard into her face. "I'm not the kind of man who runs at the least little bit of trouble."

She twisted free, furious that he didn't recognize the dangerousness of the situation. "The least little bit of trouble! You call this the least little bit of trouble?"

"We survived without a scratch."

Refusing to argue with him, she strode out of the house and climbed in behind the wheel of the car.

Sliding into the passenger seat, Boyd looked at his watch. "We missed our flight."

"*Your* flight," Katrina corrected, her inner vision filling with the image of him lying dead on the floor of the farmhouse because of her. "I'm going home, calling Captain Drake and quitting my job. Then I'm going to put my house up for sale and leave town just like I promised Vince I would."

Boyd smiled with purpose. "Good. You'll like Texas."

Her jaw tensed even more. "I am not going to Texas."

"Where do you have in mind?"

"I'll throw a dart at the map."

"Then I guess I'll have to learn to like wherever the dart hits."

"You aren't invited," she said curtly.

Boyd leaned back in his seat, his manner that of a man staking a claim. "We Logans are one-woman men. You're my woman. Where you go, I go."

Frustration swept through her and, hitting the brake, she turned to look at him. "I'm trying to do what's best for you. Can't you understand that?"

"What's best for me is to have you by my side."

"My aunt drugged you. You were nearly killed by your own partner. You've been held at gunpoint and your life was threatened. Isn't that enough for you?"

"This will give us something to tell our grandchildren."

Katrina shook her head at his stubbornness and pressed on the gas. For the rest of the ride back to St. Louis she allowed a silence to hang between them. There was no reason to continue their argument. She was determined to push him out of her life before their association caused him harm and nothing he said was going to stop her. When they reached her home, she popped the trunk. "Get your satchel and be on your way."

Climbing out, he slammed down the lid of the truck. "You're not getting rid of me that easily."

"I could never live with myself if something happened to you because of me." Her voice turned harsh with plea. "Take Dominic's advice. Go." Her head beginning to pound too violently to stand there and argue with him, she reopened the trunk, pulled her bag out and strode into the house. Dropping the bag on the floor of the living room, she phoned Drake.

"I'm sorry about your aunt," he said, recognizing her voice immediately. "But she was involved with some very nasty people."

She noticed that he didn't ask when she would be returning to work. "I warned her she should cooperate with the authorities." Even though she doubted he would believe her, she wanted him to know she'd done all she could to get Leona to testify.

He surprised her by saying, "I can understand her hesitation. Vince Garduchi doesn't like to be crossed. But she made the wrong choice."

"Yes, she did. And Vince has made it clear to me that any memory of her is distressful to him. He wants me to relocate and I've decided to do just that." Even as she spoke the words, she knew she wasn't going to let Vince Garduchi get away scot-free. He'd ruined her life and she was determined to ruin his. She'd leave, but she'd come back in disguise and find a way to nail him.

"I think that's a wise choice. As a cop there are too many ways he can have you killed and never let it get traced back to him."

She could swear she heard relief in her superior's voice. "I'll be dropping off my resignation, badge and gun sometime tomorrow."

"Take care of yourself," he said and hung up.

"Ain't nobody going to weep over my leaving," she muttered.

"It's for the best." Boyd had followed her inside and listened to her side of the conversation.

She hid the pain of sending him away behind a mask of cold control. "I thought I told you to go home."

"Only if you come with me."

He reminded her of a mountain rooted firmly in the earth on which it stood. She pictured him with a bullet hole in his head and her resolve solidified into granite. "What I'm doing, I'm doing for your good," she snapped. Then seating herself at her desk, she scribbled out a resignation.

Boyd sat quietly on the couch watching until she was finished. "And now it's time for you to meet my family," he said.

She tossed him a scowl over her shoulder. "Now it's time for me to take a shower and get a night's sleep. Tomorrow, I start life anew without you. You know where the door is, use it." Without looking back, she headed down the hall.

Boyd watched her departing back. An uneasiness stirred within him. The Katrina he'd grown to know and love was no quitter. He was certain she planned to go after Garduchi on her own. He couldn't allow that.

While she was in the shower, he retrieved his bag from the car and made certain the house was securely locked. He was again seated on the couch when Katrina came into the living room. He knew she was wearing nothing under her robe and his blood heated.

"You're still here," she grumbled. "I thought I told you to get out."

"I'm not leaving you on your own. Not now, not ever. Dominic was right about one thing—you have too much of a penchant for trouble."

Too tired to deal with him, she promised herself she'd find a way to get rid of him tomorrow. Going into the kitchen she took a couple more aspirin, then went to bed.

Boyd waited until she was in bed, then took a hot shower. Afterwards, he didn't even debate about whether he should sleep in her room or the guest room. Wanting her to know that he meant what he said no matter what the danger, he went into her room and stretched out on her bed. It took all of his self-control, but he stayed on top of the cover.

Katrina had heard him taking a shower. She'd tried to ignore the sound of the water and go to sleep, but when she'd closed her eyes, she'd pictured him lathering himself and embers of desire sparked to life. *You have to forget him*, she'd ordered herself. But that proved impossible.

Tears of frustration burned at the back of her eyes. Why couldn't her aunt have been on the level? Just once, why couldn't something in her life have gone right? Her jaw hardened with determination. She would see Vince brought down even if it was the last thing she ever did.

Then Vince was forgotten as the bed moved and she realized that Boyd had lain down beside her. She'd been too tired to pull on a nightgown and with only the sheet between them, she could feel the heat of his body. The embers that she'd managed to quell blazed to life. Making sure she remained covered, she turned over to tell him to go away. Instead she heard herself saying with a husky edge, "You're a hard man to get rid of."

He smiled crookedly. "Impossible, actually."

He made her feel safe and secure and alive with excitement all at the same time. *For his sake you can't weaken,* she fumed and commanded herself to order him out. But the words refused to issue. *What harm could one more night with him do?* she argued. Didn't she deserve some pleasure before she devoted herself to bringing Vince down? The fire he fueled within her grew hotter. "You can stay the night, but tomorrow you definitely have to leave."

His smile broadened as his mouth found hers. "We'll talk about tomorrow, tomorrow," he said against her lips.

She drew back a little. "I want your word."

"You have my word," he replied, then claimed her mouth fully.

That this would be their last few hours together caused a wave of bittersweetness to wash through her. Then refusing to let anything darken this final precious time with him, she forgot about everything but the moment and let his touch fill her senses.

Boyd was startled by the intensity of his passion for Katrina. Their first night together now seemed like nothing more than an appetizer feeding his hunger. Getting rid of the sheet separating them, he drew her close. "We were meant for each other," he whispered in her ear.

Every fiber of her being agreed with him. But the urge to protect him was stronger. "Remember your promise," she returned, barely able to speak as his caress threatened to take her breath away.

"I remember," he assured her, reveling in the feel of her body beneath his hands.

Telling herself that she had to store memories for a lifetime in this one night, Katrina allowed herself to forget everything but the sweet, delicious sensations of his lovemaking.

Boyd caressed her and kissed each inch of her, marking his claim to all of her.

Each touch, each kiss, Katrina imprinted in her mind like a bouquet she could press in a book and have forever.

So desperate was their desire to enjoy each other to the fullest that together they soared to the heights of ecstacy neither had believed possible.

Afterwards, they fell asleep in each other's arms. Later they woke, ate, made love again, then again fell asleep in each other's arms.

Chapter 15

Katrina awoke early the next morning snuggled next to Boyd. For several minutes she lay quietly gathering memories for the bleak future ahead without him. Finally, she forced herself to move away from him, but before she could leave the bed, he caught her and pulled her back into his arms.

She considered allowing a final bout of lovemaking but was afraid she would not have the strength to make him go. Putting her hand up between his face and hers to stop him from kissing her, she said, "This is tomorrow. You promised to leave."

"I promised that we'd talk about it," he corrected.

She frowned. "That's not what I meant when I asked for your word and you know it."

"It's what I meant." His expression turned serious. "You can't possibly believe I would leave you on your own. I know you, my darling Katrina. You're not going to run out of town like a frightened dog with your tail tucked between your legs. You're planning to come back and bring down Garduchi. Well, you're not doing that without me.''

"It's my personal fight, not yours."

"Yours or mine, it's all the same. We belong together." Boyd's voice held no compromise.

"No, we don't. Even if Garduchi was behind bars, my name would still carry the taint of what my father, brother and those before them did." She tried to push away from him.

Boyd's hold tightened. "Leaving you behind would be like leaving a part of myself. That's not going to happen."

Tears of frustration filled her eyes. "This isn't easy for me, either. But it's for the best."

"You promised me you would come to Texas and meet my family. You'll see. You'll fit in just fine."

"Like a skunk among kittens."

"They make some of the most expensive perfumes from skunk oil."

Katrina studied the line of his jaw. It was determined. There was clearly only one way to prove to him that she was right and he was wrong. She would go. Not only would her family history turn his family against her, but there also was her vendetta against Garduchi. They were sure to realize that she was no good for Boyd and, for once in her life, she would be grateful that she was not wanted. Keeping him safe was all that mattered to her.

The trip would serve another purpose as well. It would convince Dominic that there was a romantic link between her and Boyd. When she returned alone, she would spread the word that his family hadn't approved of her and she was striking out on her own. Dominic would believe that without any trouble. Besides, it would be the truth. "All right, I'll go to Texas with you. But I don't want to be an unexpected shock. You call and tell your mother about me and my family before we leave.''

"As soon as I've made the reservations, I'll give her a call," Boyd promised.

"And on our way to the airport, I'll stop by the station and turn in my resignation, badge and gun," Katrina added.

Boyd smiled triumphantly, then released her and reached for the phone to make the reservations.

A look of purpose glistened in Katrina's eyes as she rose from the bed. Once she and Boyd's family had convinced him that she would never fit into his life, she would return here a free agent to pursue Garduchi on her own.

All the way to the airport, she'd told herself that meeting his family was nothing to worry about. It was simply a necessary gesture to prove to Boyd that they had no future together. Still, she was nervous...too nervous to remain silent. "So which members of your family will I be meeting?" she asked as the plane took off.

Boyd grinned. "First, there's my two brothers, Slade and Jess. One or both will be meeting us at the airport."

She read the affection he felt for them in his eyes. "I recall you mentioning them. Slade's the older one and a Texas Ranger. Jess is the younger but you never said what he did for a living." It was amazing, she thought, how she remembered everything Boyd had ever told her and Leona about himself.

Pride mingled with the affection. "Jess majored in animal husbandry and accounting in college. My mom wanted at least one of us to stay home and take over running the ranch."

"The ranch?" Looking at him in his jeans, shirt and western boots, she could easily visualize him riding and roping. He did, in fact, fit the romanticized image she'd had of cowboys when she was young. But then he'd looked great even in the fake beard and mustache. *Get over it!* she ordered herself. In a day or two he would be out of her life forever.

"My great-grandfather on my daddy's side always said a man needed a place to call home. He purchased a few hundred acres, built a house, bought some cattle and horses, then left my great-grandmother to tend the place and raise their children while he was out chasing bad guys. She did a real good job, same as my fraternal grandmother and my mother.'' His smile softened and he kissed the tip of her nose. "The men in my family have always married strong-willed women. You'll fit in just fine."

Strong-willed women from honorable families, she corrected mentally. "Who else will I be meeting?" she asked, determined to remain indifferent to the negative reactions she was braced for.

"My mother, White Moon, and my maternal grand-mother, Evening Flower. Blue Flame, my maternal grandfather has passed away and so have my father's parents."

Four people isn't very many disapproving faces to face, she told herself. But as they disembarked from their plane in Lubbock, the indifference she wanted to feel became more difficult to maintain. The only thing that kept her legs moving was knowing that his family's disapproval would be proof that she was right.

Noticing her tenseness, Boyd smiled reassuringly. "You're going to meet my family, not walking to the gallows."

"Facing the dislike of a family who want to protect one of their own from making a disastrous choice, isn't easy. I'm only doing this to convince you that we have no future together," she replied stiffly.

"You've got to have more faith in people."

"I have a lifetime of experience." The question that had been haunting her since the trip started, demanded to be asked. "So what did you tell them about me?"

"I told them about your father and his family and how you've spent your adult life trying to do good. I also told them I'm in love with you and I'm going to marry you."

"And how did they react?"

"Cautiously. It's their nature," he answered honestly.

"I hope you made hotel reservations for me," she returned dryly.

"No need for that," a male voice said in an easy drawl. "There's plenty of room at the ranch."

Katrina turned to see a man in jeans and a blue button-down, western-cut shirt. He looked slightly older than Boyd, but had the same muscular build and similar features. The star of a Texas Ranger was pinned to his shirt. He had to be Slade.

"Good to see you." The man held out his hand to Boyd, with warm welcome.

"You're looking fit," Boyd replied accepting the handshake.

The firmness of their grip and the way they smiled at each other told Katrina that these men cared deeply for each other.

Releasing Boyd's hand, Slade's attention turned to her. "And you are obviously Katrina." He extended his hand to her. "I'm Slade."

The smile remained on his face but she noticed that it had gone from his eyes. "I guessed as much," she said, accepting the handshake.

As they shook, he studied her narrowly. His gaze was cool and shuttered giving her no idea what he was thinking. Sure he disapproved of her, she said stiffly. "I shouldn't have come."

Boyd slipped an arm around her waist before she could head to the ticket counter and book a seat on the next plane out. "Slade has an especially irritating effect on most women. Saw one actually take a swing at him once."

"I apologize." Slade removed his Stetson hat in a gesture of respect. "Takes me a while to warm to newcomers. I didn't mean to seem inhospitable." Returning his hat to his head, he added, "We'd best be picking up your luggage and getting on our way. Mom's expecting us for dinner."

Katrina followed, but she doubted Boyd's older brother was ever going to warm up to her.

Leaving Lubbock, Slade asked Boyd to fill him in on the details of the Garduchi case. Katrina cringed when Boyd told about how her aunt had drugged them.

Slade shook his head and laughed. "Women. I keep telling you to keep a close eye on them. You never know when they're going to deliver a sucker punch."

Riding alone in the back seat, Katrina pressed into the corner, wishing she hadn't come.

Boyd gave his brother an impatient look. "Just because you have the kind of effect on women that makes them want to either slap you in the face or give you a hard right to the stomach, doesn't mean they're all untrustworthy."

Slade glanced over his shoulder to Katrina. "Sorry." Returning his attention to the road, he added, "I've had some bad luck with women. Makes me a little cynical. Didn't mean any offense."

"None taken," she replied levelly, reminding herself that she hadn't expected to be liked.

"So what happened next?" Slade directed the question to Boyd.

"Not much. Leona got herself caught and killed and Garduchi got his books back. So we're back to square one and we've turned the case over to the locals again."

Again, Slade glanced back at Katrina. "Sorry about your aunt."

She noted that there was honest sympathy in his voice. "Thanks."

It disappeared as he added grimly, "But when you ride with the Devil, you're bound to get burned."

She was certain that warning was directed at her. It was Slade's way of saying he wasn't buying her story that she'd severed all ties with Garduchi. Her shoulders straightened with pride and she narrowed her gaze on the back of his neck. "I didn't come here because I'm hoping to marry your brother. I came here to prove to him that his family would never accept me and that we can have no future together."

Slade tossed Boyd a dry grin. "Don't reckon what any of us thinks will make any difference. He'll do what he wants to do." He glanced at Katrina in the rearview mirror and his expression sobered. "But just to set the record right, I was talking about your aunt. Boyd says you're straight and I'm willing to believe him."

He sounded sincere. Still, she doubted he'd ever approve of her as a wife for his brother.

"So what case are you working on right now?" Boyd asked, turning the conversation to Slade.

"Just helped the Feds round up some bank robbers," Slade replied, then launched into the details of the chase.

It was nearly an hour after leaving the airport that Slade turned onto a dirt driveway blocked by a swinging gate. While Boyd opened the gate, Katrina's attention was held by the ranch house in the distance, her stomach knotting tighter with each passing moment.

Slade was parking in front of the well-maintained, large, rambling structure when a cowboy rode up. He looked younger than her companions but the features were similar and she guessed he was Boyd's younger brother, Jess.

"You sure can pick'um," the younger version of Boyd said, giving Boyd a wink as he dismounted in one lithe movement and opened the door for Katrina. Pulling off his gloves, he offered her his hand. "I'm Jess. Welcome."

He seemed genuinely pleased to meet her and she smiled back. "Thank you." Then she saw the hint of uncertainty in his eyes and knew that behind his friendly greeting, he too wasn't so sure she was a good match for his brother.

A pretty Native American woman, her black hair streaked with gray, came out onto the porch. Slipping an arm around Katrina's waist, Boyd guided her forward.

The woman's eyes glistened with joy at the sight of Boyd. Coming off the porch as he and Katrina approached, she gave him a hug. "It's good to have you home."

"It's good to be here," he replied, his love for the woman written on his face.

Boyd had released his hold on Katrina to return his mother's hug. Now he again slipped his arm around her waist. "This is Katrina, Mom. Katrina, this is my mother, White Moon."

"I'm pleased to meet you," Katrina said, noticing the woman's smile cool slightly and her eyes become shuttered.

"As a friend of my son's, you are welcome in my home," White Moon replied.

Again Katrina wished she hadn't come. White Moon's manner was polite but it was clear that she also was uncertain if she should be pleased to meet Katrina. "I appreciate your hospitality." Katrina wondered how much more her stomach could tighten before she threw up.

"Come along." White Moon waved them all into the house. "I need to get back to the kitchen to help your grandmother. I gave Angela and Pilar a couple of days off so that we could have a totally family time.''

Katrina glanced questioningly at Boyd.

''Angela is Mom's cook and Pilar is a live-in maid. The family struck oil on the ranch about ten years ago. Life's gotten a lot easier for her since then,'' Boyd elaborated.

''Oh, that's nice,'' Katrina managed to get out past her shock. Not only was Boyd from an honorable family but a rich one to boot.

''Apparently, Boyd told you very little about us,'' White Moon noted, clearly surprised Katrina had not known about their wealth.

Katrina noticed a shadow of relief on Boyd's brothers' faces and realized the family had been worried that, in addition to her having an ancestry no one would wish for, she was a gold digger to boot. ''He told me some. Not a lot,'' she said levelly.

An uneasy shadow crossed White Moon's features, then, her gaze encompassing the group of them, she said, ''You have ten minutes to wash up and get to the table.''

Katrina guessed White Moon had sent the cook and maid away because Boyd's mother wanted as few people to know about her as possible. She cast him an ''I told you so'' glance as they continued inside.

In the front hall, White Moon paused and turned back to Boyd. ''I gave Katrina your room. You and Slade can bunk together.''

Boyd nodded and guided Katrina to her room. Left on her own while he settled in, she leaned against the door and took several long breaths in an attempt to unloosen her taut muscles. ''This trip should cure him of any illusions he has about me being accepted by his family,'' she muttered under her breath. Then straightening away from the door, she pulled her makeup kit out of her suitcase and went in search of a bathroom. There was one next door.

Coming out of the bathroom after having washed her face, applied a light amount of fresh makeup and given her hair a brushing, she found Boyd waiting in the hall. "Am I late?"

"Right on time," he assured her, slipping an arm around her waist and guiding her down the hall.

His arm around her was the only thing keeping her going forward, Katrina admitted.

Slade and Jess were in the living room. As Boyd and Katrina were about to enter the room, an ancient-looking Native American woman, her face deeply lined, her body so frail and bent with age she looked as if she would teeter over without the cane she was using to aid her, came toward them from what Katrina guessed was the direction of the kitchen. "I have escaped my capturers and come to greet you," she said.

Boyd's back muscles tightened, ready for trouble, as he came to an abrupt halt.

Katrina saw the look of surprise on his face followed by concern in his eyes. This was someone he had not expected to be here. Was this frail, elderly woman what had caused the anxiousness on his mother's face as well?

"Morning Hawk," he said. "It's good to see you."

The old woman laughed. "Don't lie to me, Boyd Logan. You were hoping I was a hundred miles away visiting with my sister. But your mother respects her elders. She does not lie to me. When she tried to cart me off so fast, I demanded to know why and she told me." Her gaze raked over Katrina. "So this is the one you've chosen."

White Moon and another Native American woman, who looked to be somewhere in age between White Moon and Morning Hawk, came hurrying from the direction the el-

derly woman had come. "Mother," the woman with White
Moon said sternly, her tone cautioning the ancient woman
to say no more.

Amusement twinkled in Morning Hawk's eyes. "They
hover over me like a pair of watchful eagles. I am an old
woman. What harm can I do?"

"You have a sharp tongue that can sometimes be cruel."
The woman who had spoken, turned to Katrina. "I'm Evening Flower, Boyd's grandmother. This…" she motioned
toward the ancient woman, "…is Morning Hawk, his great-
grandmother."

"I merely speak my mind," Morning Hawk defended
herself.

Jess and Slade had joined the group in the hall, Jess
taking a position beside Katrina and Slade behind her. She
knew they weren't certain they approved of her, but clearly
they felt compelled to protect her from this tiny withered
old woman. "I'm Katrina Polenari and I'm pleased to meet
you," she replied to Evening Flower. Then stepping forward, out of the protective niche formed by Boyd and his
brothers, she said to Morning Hawk. "I'm pleased to meet
you, too."

The old woman continued to study her narrowly. "We
shall see."

"Dinner is ready," White Moon said sharply, motioning
them all toward the dining room.

Katrina wanted to flee. It was obvious the great-
grandmother had already made up her mind to dislike her.
The others probably had too, they were just too polite to
be as inhospitable as Morning Hawk. Pride came to Katrina's aid. No matter what happened, she would make it
through this visit with dignity. Accompanying Boyd into
the dining room, she took the chair he offered.

As soon as they were seated and everyone had served

themselves, Boyd turned to Jess. "How's the ranch doing?"

Immediately the three brothers launched into a discussion of the care and breeding of cattle and horses. Katrina knew what they were doing…they were keeping the conversation from centering on her and for that she was grateful.

The women allowed the diversion, but Katrina was aware that Boyd's mother and grandmother continued to study her covertly. Morning Hawk, however, made no attempt to hide her scrutiny. When her attention wasn't on her food, she watched Katrina like a hawk keeping a sharp eye on its prey.

Dessert was being served when Morning Hawk broke her silence. "Your aunt should have trusted Boyd to protect her."

"Yes, I know. I thought she knew that, too," Katrina replied.

Morning Hawk nodded and returned her attention to her food.

"We are sorry about her death," White Moon said.

She sounded sincere, Katrina noted. "Thank you."

"Boyd said you and your aunt had not spoken for many years?" Evening Flower remarked, her tone making the statement a question.

"That's correct." Katrina prepared herself for wherever this was leading.

"You do not believe in close family ties?" Morning Hawk demanded.

Nice Catch 22, Katrina thought. "I've greatly missed having family to be close to. But to escape Vince Garduchi, I had to break all ties to anyone who worked for him."

"Boyd also mentioned that you have no connection to your mother's family," Morning Hawk persisted.

She guessed Boyd had explained all of this to them, but

clearly they wanted to hear it from her. "My mother's family disowned her when she married my father." *A good time to remind Boyd of why I can't marry him.* "And, even after I went out on my own, they refused to have anything to do with me. They are afraid I will bring the taint of my father's family's association with Garduchi upon them."

"This is delicious blackberry cobbler," Jess said, abruptly changing the subject.

Morning Hawk gave him an angry look, but Evening Flower immediately launched into a reminiscence about how she met her future husband while hunting for berries as a young girl.

As his grandmother ended her story, Boyd decided it was time to cut this evening short. Pushing back his chair, he rose. "Katrina and I have had a long day. I'm sure she's ready to retire."

She was. Nothing would suit her more than to escape to her bedroom and into the darkness of sleep. But, she was determined to be a polite guest. And, she admitted grudgingly, even though it would not change the path she had chosen, she still found herself wanting to make a good impression on Boyd's family. She did not want them to think he had no taste in women. "I'll help with the dishes."

"No. Not tonight," White Moon said, honest concern in her voice. "You do look exhausted. Get some sleep."

Too tired to argue and guessing they preferred to be free of her company so that they could discuss her, Katrina thanked her and the other women for the meal, said her good-nights and left the room with Boyd.

Reaching her bedroom door, Boyd came to a stop, and drew her into his embrace. "Don't let Morning Hawk get to you."

"She's merely behaving the way the others would like to but are too polite to."

Boyd frowned. "Give them a chance to get to know you."

Tears welled in her eyes. "It doesn't matter what they think of me. I am not going to marry you and put your life in danger."

"I'm not letting you go."

Jerking free of him, she went into the bedroom and closed the door. Tears trickled down her cheeks as she changed for bed. This was a fool's errand. Slade was right. Boyd wasn't the kind of man who would turn away from her just because his family didn't accept her. It was up to her to walk away from him. And that was exactly what she was going to do. Tomorrow morning she would leave even if she had to walk all the way back to Lubbock.

In the hall, Boyd frowned at the closed door. This wasn't going well. He'd expected his family to be cautious about accepting Katrina. They were all very protective of each other. But Morning Hawk's outspokenness was too destructive. She was behaving the way Katrina had predicted. He'd read the desire to flee in Katrina's eyes when they went into dinner and guessed that very soon she was going to demand to leave. And, under the present circumstances, leaving would probably be for the best. His jaw firmed with determination. But this wasn't the end. It was only the beginning. He refused to give up. He would make her his wife.

Chapter 16

Katrina felt herself being shaken and none too gently. "Wake up," a voice ordered in a harsh whisper.

Turning onto her back, she opened her eyes. Illuminated in the moonlight streaming in the window was a frail, bent shape.

"Be quiet. You must get dressed and come with me," Morning Hawk ordered.

Panic spread through Katrina. "Has something happened to Boyd?"

"No. Now, hush and do as I say. Have you no respect for Boyd's elders?" Morning Hawk demanded in a disapproving whisper.

"Yes, of course I do," Katrina returned, following Morning Hawk's lead and keeping her voice low.

"Then do as I say. Do you have jeans with you and a heavy shirt? There is a chill in the air."

Katrina glanced at the clock. It was a little after 2:30 a.m. Wondering what Boyd's great-grandmother was up to, she pulled on a pair of jeans, a sweatshirt and sneakers.

"Give me your arm," Morning Hawk whispered as they started toward the door. "I came without my cane. I didn't want to wake the boys. This is women's business."

And just what was "women's business"? Katrina wondered, slipping her arm under the woman's. She considered making a clumsy slip in the hall and waking Boyd but her curiosity was too strong. Very quietly, she and the elderly woman made their way down the hall, continuing through the house to the kitchen. Katrina expected to find Boyd's mother and grandmother there, prepared to question her thoroughly about herself. But they were not.

Morning Hawk picked up a sack lying on the table and slipped the ropes holding the sack closed over her shoulder and head so that it hung at her side.

"I'll carry that for you," Katrina offered, starting to retrieve the burden.

"No. I have something else for you to do." Morning Hawk motioned Katrina toward the kitchen door.

Once on the back porch, Morning Hawk exchanged Katrina's arm for a walking stick that was taller than she was. With a crooked finger she pointed toward a clump of burlap. "Fill that sling with wood. But do not be clumsy. I doubt you will wake the others, but it is good to learn to move silently." She cocked her head to one side. "You must know how to do that. Being a policewoman, it would be necessary for you to know how to approach a suspect undetected."

"Yes, I know how to move silently," Katrina assured her, but she balked at following more orders without an explanation. "And I will follow your instructions as soon as you tell me what is going on."

"I wish to have a private talk with you." Morning Hawk began to fill the burlap sling with wood herself.

Afraid the elderly woman would strain herself, Katrina took over. "What do you want to talk about?" she asked, hoping to get this conversation over with quickly and get the woman back safely inside the house.

"We will talk of that which interests us," Morning Hawk replied, still in a whisper.

Katrina began to wonder if the elderly woman was simply unable to sleep and bored with spending the long hours of the night alone.

Seeing the sling was full, Morning Hawk showed Katrina how to slip her head and shoulder through the loop of burlap and adjust the load on her back. "And now it is time to go," she announced, again seeking Katrina's support with her free hand.

Katrina was worrying more and more that Morning Hawk was at least a little senile and leading them both into trouble. "Are you sure this is wise? Maybe we should invite your daughter and granddaughter along."

"I wish to speak to you alone," Morning Hawk insisted.

"We'd be more comfortable in the house," Katrina coaxed.

The old woman cocked her head to one side and looked up at her. Challenge entered her voice. "Does this land frighten you?"

Katrina looked out at the shadowed shapes of barns and corrals to the darkened landscape beyond. "It's strange to me. Anything strange is a little frightening," she answered honestly.

"Do you dislike it?"

Katrina was aware of a couple of horses milling around in one of the smaller corrals. She'd always had a fondness for horses. And, the air, in spite of the animal scents it carried, had a freshness to it. "No. It's invigorating."

"Then come, we have a distance to travel before dawn." Morning Hawk gave Katrina a hard nudge.

Katrina remained where she was. "I don't think it's smart to go wandering around in the dark. I should, at least, get a flashlight."

Morning Hawk gave her an impatient scowl. "The night is clear. We have the moon and stars to light our way just as my ancestors did."

Katrina thought fast. "I should get a gun. There must be snakes and wild animals out here. Do you know where the key to the gun cabinet in the study is?" Her plan was to make enough noise when she reentered the house to wake someone up.

"We have no need of a gun. The snakes prefer the heat of the day and the night predators have their own game. They will not bother us."

A coyote howled in the distance sending a chill along Katrina's spine. "I really think we should wait until morning."

Morning Hawk's impatient scowl deepened. "A woman should know the man whom she weds. To know my great-grandson, you must know the land that sired him and you must not fear it."

"I am not going to marry Boyd." The words tore at her, but she knew she was doing the right thing.

Morning Hawk stiffened and looked up at her. "You don't love him?"

"I do. That's why I'm not going to marry him."

For a long moment, Morning Hawk studied her, then again nudged her onward. "We will still make the journey."

Katrina frowned at the uncivilized land beyond the corrals and barns. "I really don't think this is such a good idea."

"If you will not go with me, then I will go alone. I feel the need to renew my bond with the land."

Katrina heard the determination in Morning Hawk's voice. "I can't allow you to go out there alone."

"Then come."

"I really think I should wake the others and invite them to come with us." Katrina looked toward the woodpile. The kitchen was on the farthest end of the large rambling ranch house away from the bedrooms. However, she was sure that if she kicked at the wood and knocked some over, there was at least a chance it would wake Boyd and possibly some of the others.

Morning Hawk followed her line of vision. "If you wake them, I will disappear into the night before they get here," she threatened, leaving the porch and heading into the shadows of the night.

Fearing for her safety, Katrina had no choice but to follow quickly. "All right, we'll go alone." Morning Hawk's staff and two pair of footprints would leave an easy trail for Boyd and his brothers to follow and find them, she reasoned. Besides, how far could they go? Morning Hawk had to be over ninety.

As they left the house and barns behind, the moon and stars illuminated the landscape with an eerie white light. A coyote's howl sounded in the distance and Katrina was certain she saw something dark and furry scurry away at their approach. Well, Boyd had protected her aunt…risked his life only to be caught up in one of Leona's games. Of course he'd had a gun and her at his side. She glanced at the withered old woman beside her. Morning Hawk would be easy prey. A rabbit could probably take her out. Mentally, she cursed. If she'd known his great-grandmother had this in mind, she would have slammed her bedroom door and woken everyone. But it never occurred to her that Morning Hawk would want to take a predawn stroll.

They had walked for over an hour when Morning Hawk broke her silence. "Do you feel the power of the land?"

"I feel like I do when I'm chasing a suspect down a dark alley I've never been in before only the scenery is better and the smell is definitely an improvement," Katrina replied.

"Aha, you are frightened but invigorated at the same time," Morning Hawk said with approval. "Yes. It is not 'a walk in the park'.... I believe that is the phrase for a comfortable stroll."

"That depends on what park you're strolling through and what time of night it is." Hearing a rustling in the brush, Katrina glanced to her right to see a dark shape hovering at a distance. "I wish you'd let me bring a gun."

"I could not have you firing at everything that moves in the night," Morning Hawk admonished.

"I am very careful at what I fire at," Katrina snapped back, her nerves wearing thin.

"Well, if carrying a gun makes you feel better." Morning Hawk reached into her sack and produced Boyd's gun still in its shoulder holster.

Well, at least she wasn't totally crazy, Katrina acknowledged, slipping the holster on, then checking the gun to see how much ammunition it contained. To her relief there was a full clip.

"Are you more comfortable now?" Morning Hawk asked.

Katrina heard the hint of amusement in her voice. The old woman was toying with her. "It's time to turn back," she said with stern authority.

Morning Hawk came to a halt and straightened to her

full height of just over five feet. "Surely you are not a quitter. Boyd would never choose a woman who would not see a task through to its end."

"He also wouldn't choose a woman who would allow his great-grandmother to pursue a dangerous path."

"We are in no danger and we have no time for discussion. We must reach our destination before sunrise."

It was clear to Katrina that Morning Hawk was not going to turn back and she couldn't allow her to go on alone. "Will you, at least, tell me where we are going?" she asked.

Morning Hawk pointed toward a tall, cylindrical rock outcropping ahead of them. "We are going to that mesa."

At least she knew their destination, Katrina mused and that made her feel a little better.

A while later, when they finally reached the mesa, Morning Hawk continued around the base for a short distance, then coming to a halt, said, "I will need your help for the climb."

Katrina bent her head back and looked toward the summit. It looked like an impossible climb. The mesa had to be at least seventy feet high, maybe more, and seemingly straight up. "Shouldn't we wait until there is more light?" she suggested, playing for time, hoping someone would notice their absence and come find them soon.

"It is a very small, low mesa," Morning Hawk said snappishly. "And there is an easy path to the top."

"I've never done much climbing. I'd feel much more at ease if we waited until sunrise."

"I wish to see the sunrise from the mesa." The old woman's voice took on a determined tone. "I will make the climb alone."

Maybe this is some kind of pilgrimage she feels she has to make. Her reasons really didn't matter. She'd said she needed help to reach the top. Katrina couldn't allow her to go alone. She would never be able to forgive herself if something happened to the elderly woman and she could have prevented it. "You win again, I'll come with you."

Morning Hawk grinned triumphantly. "The path begins here."

Katrina saw a ledge about a foot and a half wide winding its way up the mesa. "This is what you call an *easy* path? I've seen jumpers on ledges wider than this."

Ignoring her remarks, Morning Hawk said, "Shift the sling of wood to the front. Then take the lead and give me your hand. Walk sideways with your back against the rock wall."

Heights had never bothered Katrina but making her way along a narrow ledge, with a heavy sack of wood slung in front of her and aiding an elderly woman, made her uneasy. The wood caused her to feel unbalanced and Morning Hawk had such a firm grip on her hand, she knew that if she fell she would take the elderly woman with her. *How did I get into this mess?* she chided herself as she eased her way along. *Because, while I'm city smart, I'm country stupid,* came the answer.

To her relief, at about halfway up, the path cut into the mesa. It remained narrow, winding its way upward but there was a rock wall on either side preventing a fall to the base.

Once they reached this section, Morning Hawk began to rely on her more and more. "Do you want to stop and rest?" Katrina asked, worried that the elderly woman had reached her limit of endurance. And, she admitted she would welcome a short rest as well. The sack of wood felt as if it had doubled in weight.

"No, we must continue," Morning Hawk replied, urgency behind her voice.

Clearly this is some sort of ritual or pilgrimage the rest of the family discourages the elderly woman from performing so she suckered me in on it, Katrina reasoned. Well, as long as they'd come this far, she should let the old woman see it through if it was that important to her.

Reaching the summit, Katrina breathed a sigh of relief. Standing for a moment to rest, she looked around at their surroundings. The top was surprisingly flat and, she noted, free of any large creatures that could harm them. Her gaze turned to the view beyond. It was spectacular.

Morning Hawk had released Katrina's hand and continued on to a circle of rocks with old ashes in the center. Joining her, Katrina freed herself of the sling and, following Morning Hawk's instructions, built a fire.

"And now sit with me," the old woman instructed.

"Is the path we took the only one up to the top?" Katrina asked before choosing her spot.

Morning Hawk nodded. "Yes."

Katrina chose a position where she could see the entrance to the path and seated herself.

Morning Hawk grinned. "You have a good instinct for survival."

"Caution has kept me alive on more than one occasion," Katrina replied, wishing she'd exercised more before allowing the old woman to get her outside of the house.

From the sack she was carrying, Morning Hawk produced a thermos of coffee and two tin cups. Next came two peanut butter and jelly sandwiches. "They are my favorite," she said with a girlish laugh.

"I like them, too," Katrina admitted accepting hers gratefully. She also admitted that even hardtack would taste good at this moment.

They ate in silence watching the flames dancing and the smoke spiralling to the heavens. When they had finished with the sandwiches, Morning Hawk continued to remain silent. Finally, hoping to coax the old woman into telling her why they were here, Katrina said, "It is beautiful here. Sort of eerie but beautiful."

Morning Hawk merely nodded, but said nothing. Clearly the old woman was determined to choose when they would talk and now was not the time. Katrina let her gaze travel slowly over their surroundings and then to the sky. She hadn't lied when she said it was beautiful there. She felt as if she could reach up and almost touch the stars. She'd never seen so many.

They sat for a long time that way, with only the sounds of the night and the crackling fire breaking the stillness.

Finally, wondering if Morning Hawk had fallen asleep, Katrina glanced at her to find the old woman staring into the flames. As if she sensed Katrina's attention, Morning Hawk said, "We are taught to honor our ancestors—to learn from them." She looked to Katrina. "But there are some lineages, such as your father and those who sired him, when it is better to break with the past and begin anew. Have you made any effort to learn of your mother's people?"

"I know who they were. They were honest, law-abiding citizens."

"But they refused to have anything to do with you even after you went out on your own." Morning Hawk shook her head disapprovingly.

"Vince Garduchi is a man to fear," Katrina said in her grandparent's defense, hiding the hurt their rejection had caused.

Morning Hawk nodded. "Only the stupid do not fear evil. But you denounced it and have made your own path. Your mother's people are very unlucky to not have gotten to know you. It takes courage and a good heart to venture out into an unknown wilderness with no guide but your belief in what is right.'' Amusement suddenly entered her voice. ''Or with an old woman you fear is several eagle feathers short of a full wing.'' Taking Katrina's hands in hers, she smiled. ''My great-grandson needs a strong woman. You will suit him well.''

That Morning Hawk approved of her caused her to wish that the woman's words were true. Quickly, she squelched it. ''No, I will not. He will be shaded by the same shadow of distrust that hangs over me.''

''You are wrong. Both my family and the Logans are known as people of honor. Boyd has chosen you and he would never choose a woman he did not trust. And others will honor his choice.''

Katrina stared wistfully into the fire. ''I have too much experience to believe that is possible. But even if it was, I have vowed to bring Vince Garduchi down and I won't endanger Boyd's life for my own revenge.''

''You must have more faith in others. As for not endangering Boyd, he will not let you go after Garduchi alone. You will either have to give up that quest or get used to him being at your side.'' Morning Hawk gave Katrina's hands a squeeze. ''Look. The rays of a new day are dawning.''

Looking to the east, Katrina saw the first light of sunrise coming over the horizon. It was as if the whole earth was being born anew. *That is a fantasy,* she mocked herself. When she descended from this mesa, she would be returning to the real world. Garduchi was a part of that world and she would never be free to forget him or the taint of her family's association with him until justice was done...and she would find a way to convince Boyd that she had to do that on her own.

The sound of approaching horses' hooves reached them.

"I think we have been discovered," Morning Hawk said.

Katrina rose and saw three riders coming their way with two empty mounts in tow. Looking back toward Morning Hawk, she saw the elderly Indian woman throwing dirt on the fire to smother it. Quickly, she moved to help her. They had doused the fire and were on their way down when the riders reached the mesa.

"Katrina, Morning Hawk, are you up there?" Boyd's angry tones sounded from below.

"We're on our way down," Katrina called back.

"He obviously hasn't had his first cup of coffee yet," Morning Hawk observed with a grin.

Katrina didn't grin back. Boyd, she could tell, was furious. As they left the walled part of the trail and made their way along the narrow ledge, a wave of fear washed over her. In the dark, she had not been able to see the drop below. Now, she marveled that they had not fallen and been seriously injured or even killed.

All the way out here, Boyd had pictured Katrina lying at the base of the mesa, bloodied and broken. That she was unharmed brought relief but his lingering fright fed his anger. "I cannot believe the two of you came out here in the dark," he growled when they reached the bottom.

"I could not sleep. I wanted to go for a walk and Katrina was kind enough to accompany me," Morning Hawk said spritely, clearly unaffected by her great-grandson's tone.

Boyd directed the full force of his fury at his great-grandmother. "You could have gotten both you and Katrina injured, even killed." He parroted what Katrina had been thinking.

Morning Hawk smiled patronizingly. "Nonsense. I come here often before dawn to watch the sunrise. And if Katrina had shown the least bit of clumsiness, I would have stopped the climb." She turned toward Katrina and her smile warmed. "But she is surefooted and proceeded with just the right amount of caution...not too much and not too little."

Katrina again looked toward the open portion of the path and a chill worked its way up her spine.

Turning back to the men she saw Slade shaking his head at his great-grandmother. "You had Boyd scared half out of his mind."

"Looks like we're going to have to post a guard on any female we bring home to meet the folks," Jess said.

Morning Hawk frowned at the three men. "I don't know why two women can't go for a walk without causing an uproar."

Boyd's gaze shifted to Katrina. "You should have woken me. It's not safe for a greenhorn to go wandering around on their own."

"She wasn't on her own," Morning Hawk reminded him curtly, before Katrina could respond.

His gaze swung back to her. "She does not know what to look for to avoid the dangers out here."

"But I do. She was as safe as she would have been anywhere," Morning Hawk retorted. "Life is never guaranteed. It was necessary for me to spend some time alone with her. I would not want my great-grandson making a mistake in the choice of a wife."

"You could have sat on the porch," Boyd growled.

"It doesn't offer the view of the sunrise you can get from the mesa. Nor would it test a person's spirit." Morning Hawk walked to the gray mare. "Katrina and I are hungry after our morning's exertion. It's time to go back to the ranch for breakfast."

Boyd shook his head in frustration and again turned to Katrina. His anger had cooled but the fear he'd felt for her continued to linger. "Slade is right. I was scared half out of my mind when I found out you were gone. I still can't believe you came with her. Surely you realized how dangerous it was to go wandering around in the dark."

Again before Katrina could respond, Morning Hawk spoke. "She had no choice. I threatened to disappear into the night if she woke any of you." The elderly woman smiled at Katrina. "She has courage and a good heart. You both have my blessing." She turned to Jess. "Now, give an old woman a hand into the saddle."

This whole excursion had been a test, Katrina realized. That she'd passed gave her no pleasure. It didn't change anything.

Mentally, Boyd cursed. By putting Katrina to this test, his great-grandmother had given her more reason than ever to believe she would always be mistrusted until she proved herself. As the others headed back to the ranch house ahead of them, he said, "She shouldn't have done that, but it's her way. It's part of her culture. She would have done it to anyone I brought home."

Tears burned at the back of Katrina's eyes. "If walking through hot coals would prove to the world that I'm an honest woman, I'd do it for you. But passing your great-grandmother's test isn't going to make any difference. I doubt her approval will carry much weight in the world beyond this ranch." Recalling the cautious glances cast at the old woman by her daughter and granddaughter and Boyd's brothers, she added, "Or even here."

He caught her by the shoulders. "I've told you, I don't give a damn what the rest of the world thinks."

"Someday you will and you'll regret ever meeting me." She could no longer bear the strain of fighting him. For his good, she had to get away from him as quickly as possible. "I'm flying back to St. Louis today and I don't want you coming along."

Maybe he was making a fool of himself. Maybe she didn't love him as much as she professed. "Nobody's family tree is without a few rotten apples. I love you and I want to marry you, but I'm not asking again."

Tears welled in her eyes. "I can't."

"Won't," he corrected curtly. He motioned toward their horses. "Do you know how to ride?"

"A little." She saw the anger and the hurt in his eyes. *Better his pride is wounded than his life ruined.*

Back at the ranch, she accepted the apologies from the rest of the family with quiet reserve. Unable to eat, she went to her room to pack.

A knock sounded on the door as she zipped her bag shut. Before she could respond, White Moon entered and closed the door behind her. "My son loves you. The same argument you are using to refuse him is very like the one I used with his father. I was certain marrying an Indian would cause him grief. There are still many who are not willing to accept mixed marriages. But he convinced me I was wrong. And when I recall the life we had together and I look at my sons I have proof he was right."

Katrina walked to the window. Boyd was in one of the corrals helping Slade rope a horse. "The truth is, I'm afraid. I love him so much. I couldn't bear to see him wishing he had not chosen me. Besides, I have unfinished business with Garduchi and I won't put Boyd's life in danger for my own personal vendetta."

"My husband was a one-woman man. Once his heart was given, it belonged to me forever. My sons are cut from the same cloth. As for putting his life in danger, it is always in danger. That is the nature of the work he has chosen."

Outside, the men had roped the horse. It was rearing,

trying to break free. The hooves came down very near Boyd and panic raced through her. "What are they doing?"

White Moon joined her at the window. "That's a wild stallion Jess brought in a couple of days ago. He wants to tame him and breed him."

"You mean they're going to try to ride him?" Katrina didn't wait for an answer. Dashing through the house, she ran out the back door and all the way to the corral. "Boyd Logan!" she yelled, climbing the railing. "Don't you dare get on that horse."

Slade cocked an eyebrow. "I thought you said she'd refused to marry you. She sure sounds like a wife."

Boyd looked over his shoulder. Seeing the panic on her face, he knew she loved him as deeply as he loved her. His expression hardened. "Only the woman I'm going to marry can tell me what to do and what not to do."

The horse reared again. Terror swept through her. She couldn't bear the thought of him getting injured if there was any way she could prevent it. "I'll marry you. Now get out of that corral!"

"Slade, you hear that?" Boyd asked, as they again fought to get the horse under control.

"Yeah. Sounds like you got yourself a woman."

"I heard it, too," White Moon said, smiling widely as she approached the corral.

Jess came out of the barn. "Now that that's settled, you two think you can hold that horse steady enough for me to check that gash on his leg?"

"Anytime, little brother," Slade replied.

The panic on Katrina's face turned to anger. "You weren't planning to ride that horse at all?"

"Only a fool would try to ride a wild horse without working him a while and getting him used to having a harness," Slade said in an easy drawl. "And Boyd's no fool. He's got right good taste in women, too."

Katrina considering calling "foul" and taking back her agreement to marry him, but the words refused to come. She wanted to be with him. And his family approved. It had been a long time since she'd been surrounded by people who wanted her there.

As soon as Jess had finished doctoring the horse, Slade and Boyd freed him, then quickly exited the corral. Drawing Katrina into his embrace, Boyd said gruffly, "I hope you're not considering reneging on your agreement."

Looking up into the face she saw nightly in her dreams, she shook her head. "No. I love you too much. I just hope you never regret this."

His lips found hers for a hungry possessive kiss. In the background she heard Slade and Jess laugh and White Moon reprimand them and shoo them on their way. Then everything but Boyd was forgotten.

Fire blazed inside of her and happiness spread through her.

"I hope you don't believe in long engagements," he said, deserting her mouth to nibble on her ear.

"No, not long." She forced herself to think. There were things she had to accomplish before she could marry him. "But I do want to get moved out of St. Louis first. I want Vince to believe he has me running scared."

Releasing her, he slipped his arm around her waist. "Then let's go call moving companies. I hope you like Texas."

She froze. "Texas?"

"I'm going to follow family tradition and join the rangers."

Her chin tightened. "I knew it. You feel you have to quit

your job with the FBI because of me. Already, I'm creating problems.''

"You have nothing to do with this. Before your aunt suddenly decided to cut her ties with Garduchi, I'd put in my resignation. I wanted to fight the bad guys closer to home. I'd spent my vacation going through the testing necessary to become a Texas Ranger. I'm to report to duty in a week and a half.''

She wasn't convinced. "Are you certain you're not doing this because of me?''

"Do you have any idea how difficult it is to become a ranger? It's not something you accomplish with a phone call.''

"I had heard it was rough," she conceded.

"And they did put my little brother through the paces," Slade said, coming out of the barn grinning broadly. "No one wanted to be accused of letting him in because of his family name.''

Boyd eyed him suspiciously. "I was right. That three-day survival in the desert was your little added touch, wasn't it? I'd never known anyone else who had to do that and none of the other applicants mentioned having done t.''

"I just wanted to make certain sitting around on your luff all day in the big city hadn't softened you," Slade ossed back.

Boyd gave him an "I'll get you for that one" look, then urned his attention back to Katrina. "So how do you feel bout living in Texas?''

Katrina had seen the amusement in both men's eyes during their dry exchange. Despite any disputes they might ave, the members of this family loved each other and ould stick by each other. Of that she was certain. And ey had the kind of values she cherished. They were the family she'd always wanted to be a part of and she loved Boyd with all her heart. "Texas is good."

Grinning happily he lifted her in his arms and kissed her soundly.

As he lowered her to the ground and she, Slade and Boyd headed to the house, she promised herself that for both Boyd's and her aunt's sake, she would still honor her vow to bring Garduchi down. When she went back to St. Louis to move her things, she would send a note along with her belongings to Boyd telling him that when she had accomplished her goal, she would marry him. Then she would disappear so that he could not find her until her quest was complete.

Chapter 17

Katrina didn't think she'd ever enjoyed a meal more. They were at lunch. Boyd's mother, grandmother and great-grandmother were planning the wedding while his brothers exchanged mock comments of sympathy for Boyd. She knew that they would be disappointed when they discovered the ceremony would have to be delayed, but she put that thought out of her mind and concentrated on enjoying the moment. It could be a long time before she would be among them again.

"Do you want a large or small wedding?" White Moon asked Katrina.

"I have no one to invite," Katrina replied. But she felt no hurt. She was not alone any longer. Boyd's family had drawn her into their circle and made her feel like a wanted member.

"Small, just family and very close friends," Boyd stiplated and the women nodded in agreement.

"Would you prefer to have it here or at a church?"

White Moon asked, her question directed pointedly to Katrina letting Boyd know that this was to be Katrina's choice.

"Here would be nice if it wouldn't be too much of an inconvenience," Katrina replied and the looks of approval on everyone's faces told her that she'd made the right choice.

Morning Hawk's gaze suddenly swung to Slade and her expression became stern. "It's time you put the past behind you and went looking for a wife, as well."

"Ain't going through that again," he drawled in a voice that threatened anyone at the table to continue with that subject.

Katrina glanced at Boyd questioningly.

Leaning close, he whispered in her ear. "Slade married his high school sweetheart. A couple of years after they were married, when she was pregnant with their first child, she and the unborn baby were killed by a drunk driver. Tore Slade up real bad."

Katrina looked back at the tall Texan. His relaxed expression was gone, replaced by a taunt jawline and eyes darkened by stormy shadows.

White Moon changed the subject back to Boyd and Katrina's wedding, but Katrina noticed that Slade didn't enter the jesting like before.

The ringing of the phone suddenly interrupted. Slade slid his chair back before anyone else could react. "I'll get it," he said, looking relieved to have an excuse to leave the table.

The moment he was gone, Katrina noticed the others turn accusing faces at Morning Hawk.

The elderly woman scowled back. "He needs to get on with his life."

"We would all like to see that, but now wasn't the time to bring it up," Evening Flower reprimanded her mother. She smiled apologetically at Katrina. "Right now w should be happy for Katrina and Boyd. It is not the time to open old wounds.''

"It has been ten years. He should have a scar. But a festering wound is not healthy.''

Evening Flower cast her mother a warning look that ordered her to drop the subject as the sound of bootfalls coming back toward the kitchen caught her attention.

Slade's expression was grim as he entered. His gaze leveled on Boyd and Katrina. "That was the Senior Ranger Captain. He's flying out here by helicopter to see the two of you this afternoon. He should be here around four.''

Katrina felt a sinking in her stomach. "He asked for me?''

Slade nodded. "I asked him how he knew about you. Said he'd been contacted by some guy by the name of Gerald Eldridge from the FBI.''

Katrina's joy vanished. "Eldridge probably wanted to warn your superior that I might have underworld connections.'' Her gaze traveled around the table coming to rest on Boyd. "You see, I was right. I'll be a taint on all of you. I can't marry you.'' The words hurt as if someone had driven a knife into her and was twisting it, but she knew this was what she had to do. "The sooner I'm gone, the better for all of you.''

She started to rise, but Slade, who was still standing, reached her chair in one long stride and placed a restraining hand on her shoulder. "Not so fast, little lady. You promised my brother here that you'd marry him. That makes you one of us and it ain't easy to shake us off. I'll stand with you and Boyd when the captain has his say this afternoon. I want him to know that giving you and my brother any trouble means asking for trouble from me.''

"From all of us,'' Morning Hawk declared.

The others all nodded in agreement.

"I've lived with suspicious glances all my life. You really don't want to take that on," Katrina said tersely, again trying to rise.

Slade retained his grip on her shoulder, keeping her seated. "Anyone here want Katrina to leave?"

"She stays," Morning Hawk stated with the authority of a sage.

The others nodded.

Boyd grinned at Katrina. "You see. Once you're accepted by my family, you're a member for life."

Katrina stopped fighting Slade's hold as her gaze traveled around the assembly. "I just hope you don't find yourselves regretting this," she said warningly.

Standing amidst Boyd and his brothers, as the helicopter landed on the front lawn, Katrina considered the bitter irony of the situation. Under any other conditions, being protected by these three hulking men would have made her feel safe and secure. But in this instance, she wasn't the one who needed protection. They were the ones who needed protection from her and the damage she could cause their reputations. Silently, she vowed that she would bring no harm to them.

As the helicopter landed and its blades slowed, two men climbed out. One wore the uniform of a ranger. The other she recognized. It was Gerald Eldridge. Preparing herself for their suspicious looks, she was surprised to see the one in uniform smiling broadly as he approached.

"I'm Hank Randle, Senior Ranger Captain. Pleased to meet you Miss Polenari," he said, holding out his hand to her.

"I'm pleased to meet you too, sir," she replied, continuing to be amazed by his friendly demeanor, as she accepted his handshake.

"Looks like you've caught yourself a right pretty, spirited woman." The captain addressed Boyd as he released Katrina's hand and shook Boyd's.

"He sure has," Slade answered for Boyd.

Eldridge had been standing silently by. Now he took a step forward and extended his hand toward her. "It's good to see you looking so well. I want to apologize for what Agent Hamond put you through."

To her shock, as she accepted his handshake she noted that his words rang with sincerity. "Apology accepted."

Boyd introduced Slade and Jess to Eldridge. Knowing Eldridge's suspicious nature and recalling that the last time he'd talked to the man, Eldridge had warned him not to let himself get too involved with Katrina, he too was surprised by the man's attitude. It was also clear that Eldridge had not told the captain that he was worried Katrina could be one of Garduchi's people. Wondering just what Eldridge was up to, he slipped a protective arm around Katrina's waist. "So you want to tell us what's going on?"

"We could use a little privacy," Eldridge said.

Remembering his manners, Boyd motioned them toward the house. "Come inside."

Inside, Boyd led the two visitors into the study. Slade and Jess entered as well. When Morning Hawk, Evening Flower and White Moon also started to join the men, Hank Randle held up his hand. "This is official police business."

"We want you to know that we know Katrina is a trustworthy and decent person and she has our full support," White Moon said, standing her ground.

"I appreciate your opinion," the captain replied, adding to Katrina's surprise, "I've always had the greatest respect for any Logan's opinion. I'm sure you've judged her correctly."

I have to be hallucinating, Katrina thought.

Morning Hawk nodded, then the women left.

"No offense, but you'll have to leave, too, Jess," the captain said apologetically.

"No offense taken," Jess replied and with a touch of his hand to his hat, he followed the women out, closing the door behind him.

"Now, how about if we all make ourselves comfortable," the captain said, indicating that he'd like for everyone to sit. It was an order.

Boyd and Slade eased onto the couch on either side of Katrina, letting the two other men in the room know that they considered her under their protection.

A hint of a smile played at the corner of the captain's mouth, then his expression became businesslike as he said, "Mr. Eldridge, you have the floor."

Gerald's manner became official. "Yesterday, I received a package. It was from Leona Serrenito and postmarked on the day we figure she died. It contained two letters and a box of tapes. The letter addressed to me explained that she figured if she testified against Vince concerning his books, she was sure to be killed. So, she'd played her little game to spend some time with her niece because she knew she'd never be able to contact Katrina again. Then she did her disappearing act. She said, she wasn't certain about sending the tapes, but after being with Katrina, felt she had to for her niece's sake. She wanted us all to know Katrina was on the level. She said she was keeping the ledgers for her own protection. Didn't do her much good, though."

He paused and directed his full attention to Katrina. "I'm sorry we doubted you. But in our line of work, being cautious is the way we stay alive."

"I understand. But I don't have to like it," she replied honestly.

"So what was on the tapes?" Boyd asked.

"They were ones Leona recorded secretly in Vince Garduchi's office. One had him talking to a man by the name of Burt Simmons. Seems this Simmons owed Vince a favor and Vince had decided to collect. He told Simmons to take care of a certain contractor. The day after the conversation, the contractor disappeared. We were pretty certain Vince had something to do with the man's disappearance, but we had no body and no evidence to link him to it…until now."

Katrina smiled wryly. "So Aunt Leona did get her revenge on Vince after all."

Eldridge nodded. "She also included a tape made just before she disappeared in which Vince is mentioning his concern that Simmons might need to be watched. He says he's not sure he can trust the man to keep his mouth shut. When we played that tape for Simmons, he got the picture real fast. When Vince gets worried, he usually buries his problem six feet under. Simmons sang like a bird."

Eldridge extended a letter toward Katrina. "This is for you."

Katrina opened it and began to read. Pausing, she turned to Boyd. "She apologizes for drugging us." Reading further, she said, "She says she hopes the tapes will vindicate me in your eyes and will make me remember her with some kindness." Tears welled in her eyes. "I know she was selfish and self-serving, but she was the only relative I had besides my mother who ever cared about me."

Eldridge rose and extended his hand to Katrina. "Again, I can only say I hope you will accept my apology."

She knew his regret was genuine and could not hold a grudge. "Accepted," she said, shaking his hand. A tear trickled down her cheek. "I'm just sorry my aunt didn't stick with us. She would be alive now."

Eldridge's gaze took in all those present. "Those of you in this room are the only ones who know where these tapes came from. And I'd like to keep it that way. I want Garduchi to worry about having a mole in his organization."

Katrina wiped away the tear and smiled at this ironic twist of fate. "I like the idea of making him nervous about who he can trust."

The rest all nodded their agreement.

"Thanks," Eldridge said, then turned his attention to Boyd. "Sure you won't change your mind and come back to the bureau? We need men like you."

Boyd shook his head. "I'm where I belong."

Disappointment showed on Eldridge's face. "Too bad," he said, then added to the captain, "We'd better get going or I'll miss my plane back to Washington." As he said goodbye to Katrina, he added, "It would probably be wise if you put some distance between Garduchi and yourself. I understand he doesn't like you being anywhere in his vicinity."

"She's moving to Texas," Boyd replied. "And changing her name." A sudden thought came to him. "You should keep an eye on a St. Louis cop by the name of Russ Miller. He might be on Garduchi's payroll."

"Will do." Eldridge grinned. "Good luck, you two."

Katrina's hand tightened around her aunt's letter. Again her fears of her past ruining Boyd's future and bringing a taint to the Logan name were taunting her. "Maybe it would be best if we called off the wedding," she said, the words costing her dearly. Looking to the captain and Eldridge for support, she continued stiffly, "Those who know about the letters and the tapes know I have been vindicated but no one else will." She looked to Boyd. "Your fellow rangers will always be suspicious of me." She turned to Slade. "And you could fall under my shadow as well."

"No way are you backing out on me," Boyd declared.

Slade placed a hand on her shoulder. "As far as I'm concerned, you're a Logan already."

"And as far as the rangers are concerned, if I tell them you're all right and Slade and Boyd vouch for you, that should be good enough for them," Hank Randle said.

Slade released his hold on her as Boyd took her hand. The heat of his touch spread through her and with all her heart she wanted to be with him. "Then I guess I'll be staying here and changing my name to Logan," she said.

All the men smiled their approval.

Two weeks later, Katrina was polishing the living room furniture at the ranch. The wedding would be taking place there on Saturday. Meanwhile, Boyd had reported for duty with the rangers. He'd been assigned to Company "C" with Slade and they were both currently stationed in Lubbock.

The day after the meeting with Hank Randle and Gerald Eldridge, she'd returned to St. Louis for a couple of days to turn the house over to a real estate agent for sale and to make certain the movers didn't forget anything when they packed up her things. Now some of her belongings were in storage in Lubbock. The rest had been used to furnish the apartment Boyd had found for them. As soon as her home in St. Louis was sold, she would go house hunting.

She smiled to herself as she recalled the trip to Missouri. Boyd had wanted to accompany her, but she'd insisted she would be safe. She'd told him that her moving out of town was, in Garduchi's eyes, a feather in his cap. He'd not only gotten rid of Leona but he'd run her cop niece out of town. Besides, he had more important matters to worry about. He'd been arrested for conspiracy to commit murder.

But her arguments had fallen on deaf ears. In the end all

three brothers had accompanied her. She'd never felt so protected in her life.

Her smile quirked up at the corners. And yesterday Vince Garduchi had finally gotten his just reward. The FBI had been tipped anonymously that the judge assigned to Vince's bail hearing was on Garduchi's payroll and they had arranged to have a different judge preside. When Vince had been denied bail, he'd gotten so enraged that he'd had a heart attack and died.

She drew a deep soothing breath and her smile softened. With the captain, Boyd and Slade on her side and with Garduchi gone, she felt as if her past was finally behind her.

A knock on the front door interrupted her thoughts. Answering the summons she found a delivery man holding a long flower box.

"I've got a delivery for Miss Katrina Polenari," he said.

"I'm her," she replied, thinking Boyd was even more romantic than she'd thought.

He grinned. "I hope you enjoy these. We had to special order the orchids, but the sender said that price was no object." Still grinning, he headed back to his truck.

White Moon came down the hall to join her. "Who was at the door?"

"A delivery man," Katrina replied absently, staring through the cellophane portion of the box at the array of pink roses and white orchids. "He had some flowers for me."

"Who are they from?" White Moon asked.

Hearing the concern in her future mother-in-law's voice, Katrina looked up to discover White Moon studying her worriedly. Realizing she was letting her shock show, she schooled her face into a softer expression. *The choice of flowers had to be a coincidence,* she assured herself. Aloud she said, "I don't know, I haven't looked at the card. But they must be from Boyd. I don't know of anyone else who would have sent me flowers."

"Well, don't just stand there," Evening Flower said, joining them. "We need to get them into some water."

She was overreacting to a mere coincidence, Katrina assured herself as the three headed into the kitchen to find a vase and arrange the flowers. As soon as the box was open, she grabbed up the envelope holding the card and took out the message inside. It read:

> Congratulations on your upcoming marriage.
> May the wings of angels enfold and protect you.

M times CCL hugs.

Katrina felt the color drain from her face.

"Are you all right?" White Moon demanded anxiously.

Katrina looked to her, unable to speak. The choice of flowers had not been a coincidence. Even though the card was unsigned, there was no doubt in her mind as to who the sender was.

"You're white as a sheet. Sit down." White Moon pulled out a chair and slid it behind Katrina.

Katrina took a calming breath. "I'm fine. I was just surprised."

Morning Hawk had been looking around Katrina's arm at the card. "There's no signature."

"I know who it's from," Katrina said.

"Nice sentiment," Morning Hawk commented, studying Katrina narrowly.

"Yes, it is." Katrina forced a smile.

White Moon frowned. "I think we should call Boyd. Something about these flowers has obviously upset you.

Are they from one of those gangsters? A threat or a warning, perhaps?"

"No. Nothing like that." Katrina laid a restraining hand on White Moon's arm. "The sentiment is meant sincerely. Really, I was just shocked to get something from this particular person. But it's all right. I should have suspected. She was always full of surprises." She again looked down at the array. "They are beautiful," she said, her color returning.

In spite of the outward calm Katrina forced herself to display for the rest of the day, her stomach remained knotted. She had thought her past was wiped clean. She'd been wrong.

In bed that night, sleep eluded her. She had to tell Boyd…give him a last chance to call off the wedding. Finally, in the early morning hours, she surrendered to her inability to sleep and rose and dressed. Leaving a note in the kitchen for White Moon saying that she'd gone to the mesa to watch the sun come up, she left the house. Pausing on the porch, she filled the burlap sling with wood, then began her trek. Morning Hawk had told her that if she ever needed to think, she was welcome to go there.

She didn't really need to think. She needed to build up her resolve. She knew Boyd would vow to stand beside her. That was the kind of man he was. But she was determined to do the right thing and free him if she saw any hint of disquiet in his eyes. And freeing him was going to be the hardest thing she'd ever done.

Reaching the mesa, she climbed to the top. The first rays of dawn were coming over the horizon. Choosing not to build a fire, she laid the wood aside, then sat down to watch the sun rise. A tear trickled down her cheek. She wanted so much to stay, but then nothing in her life had ever gone the way she wanted it to. She brushed at the tear. No sense in putting off what had to be done. Boyd was currently on assignment with Slade but they were scheduled to be back in Lubbock sometime this night. As soon as she returned to the ranch, she would call him and arrange to meet with him today.

Taking the note that had come with the flowers, she re-read it, then shoved it back in her pocket and scowled at the pink-and-purple sky. "So I get the vote for number-one patsy of the year."

The sound of horses' hooves caught her attention. Rising and looking out in the direction of the ranch, she saw a rider coming her way with a riderless horse in tow. He was approaching at a gallop. Assuming it was Jess, she wondered if something had happened at the ranch. Fear swept through her...or maybe Boyd had been hurt. Quickly making her way downward, she was on the open ledge when the rider reached the mesa and reined his horse in. It was Boyd. The relief and joy at seeing him was abruptly overshadowed by the thought that this might be their last meeting.

Dismounting, he stood looking up at her. "You want to tell me what you're doing out here all alone at this hour of the morning?"

"Building my courage to tell you what I have to tell you," she replied, continuing her descent.

Boyd scowled. "Don't think I like the sound of that."

"You're going to like what I have to tell you even less," she returned.

Boyd's scowl deepened. "There was a message from my mother on my answering machine when I got back to the apartment tonight. She said you'd received some flowers that had upset you. She said the sender hadn't signed the card but you'd said you knew who they were from. She also said you'd told her that the sender meant no harm but you'd turned white as a sheet.''

Katrina had reached ground level. Boyd took a step toward her. Backing against the rock face, she held a hand out in a stopping signal letting him know that she didn't want him to approach any closer. Maintaining her resolve to do right by him was going to be hard enough. If he touched her, it was sure to crumble. "I love you so much. I don't know if I can bear to lose you, but my conscience wouldn't allow me to marry you until you know everything you might be getting into if you go through with this marriage.''

Grudgingly, Boyd respected her unspoken command for him to remain at a distance. "That sounds ominous. But whatever is bothering you, we'll see it through together.''

"The flowers were from my Aunt Leona,'' she replied stiffly.

Boyd frowned in disbelief. "Leona is dead.''

Katrina shook her head. "No. They had to be from her. My mother loved white orchids. They were her flowers. She had a small greenhouse where she grew them and there was always an orchid in a vase in her room. In the garden out back, she grew roses. From an early age, I showed a particular fondness for the pink ones and she designated them as my flower. From as early as I can remember, there was always one of those in my room even in the winter. When hers weren't in bloom she would purchase them from the florist. And on my birthday there would be a vase holding one pink rose for each year of my life. After my mother died, my father had the greenhouse torn down. There were no more orchids or roses. Leona is the only one who would remember the flowers.''

Boyd remained skeptical. "You're sure?''

"If I had any doubt, there was the message. 'Let the

wings of angels enfold and protect you.' My mother used to say that to me when she tucked me in at night. Leona knew that. When I left to go out on my own, those were the last words she said to me.''

"I guess that settles it, then. Leona is alive," he conceded.

Katrina drew a shaky breath. "There is something else."

Boyd smiled dryly. "And why am I not surprised?"

"The Roman numerals in front of the hugs at the end of the message.''

"My mother mentioned that there were some sort of gibberish in front of the word 'hugs.'"

"Not gibberish. M stands for one thousand. CCL is two hundred and fifty. One thousand times two hundred and fifty equals a quarter of a million." Katrina met his gaze levelly. "A hug for every dollar. She staged her own death. It must have really hurt her to have to give up her ring, but collecting the reward from Garduchi was more than adequate compensation.''

"Staged her own death and collected the reward herself." A hint of admiration showed on Boyd's face. "That does sound like Leona."

Katrina forced herself to continue. "That the flowers arrived here...that she sent them at all...means that she's been keeping an eye on me. Someday, for some selfish reason of her own, she could come back into my life. Marrying me will be the same as putting out a welcome mat inviting trouble to your doorstep."

"I'm a lawman. Trouble is always at my doorstep." Approaching her in a long stride, he drew her into his arms. 'If Leona shows up, we'll deal with her together. I need you in my life, Katrina. I'm not letting you go just because you're worried about what the future might hold. No one's future is ever guaranteed to run smoothly."

She looked into his face and saw no evidence of uncertainty. Still… "Are you really sure of that? I want you to have the best life possible. I don't want to be a source of misery for you."

"I'm a one-woman man. If I can't have you, I'll have to live out my life alone." He wrinkled his features into a boyishly pleading expression. "You wouldn't want me to grow into a cantankerous, lonely old coot, pining over a lost love. Wouldn't you rather envision me in a rocking chair surrounded by our children and grandchildren with you by my side?"

Tears welled in her eyes. "More than anything in this world," she admitted, grinning at the playfully pitiful face he was making.

"Good. I'm glad that's settled," he said, finding her lips for a long, possessive kiss.

Joy filled Katrina. Adding her strength to the kiss, all was forgotten but their love.

*   *   *   *   *

*Don't miss Elizabeth August's heartwarming love
story,* TRULY, MADLY, DEEPLY, *coming to
Silhouette Romance in November 1999.*

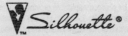

If you enjoyed what you just read,
then we've got an offer you can't resist!

Take 2 bestselling love stories FREE!

Plus get a FREE surprise gift!

**Coming this September 1999
from SILHOUETTE BOOKS
and bestselling author**

RACHEL LEE

CONARD COUNTY:

Boots & Badges

Alicia Dreyfus—a desperate woman on the run—
is about to discover that she *can* come home
again…to Conard County. Along the way she
meets the man of her dreams—and brings together
three other couples, whose love blossoms beneath
the bold Wyoming sky.

Enjoy four complete, **brand-new** stories in one
extraordinary volume.

Available at your favorite retail outlet.

Silhouette®

™

PSCCBB

SILHOUETTE BOOKS
is proud to announce the arrival of

THE BABY OF THE MONTH CLUB:

the latest installment of author
Marie Ferrarella's
popular miniseries.

When pregnant Juliette St. Claire met Gabriel Saldana than she discovered he wasn't the struggling artist he claimed to be. An undercover agent, Gabriel had been sent to Juliette's gallery to nab his prime suspect: Juliette herself. But when he discovered her innocence, would he win back Juliette's heart and convince her that he was the daddy her baby needed?

Don't miss Juliette's induction into
THE BABY OF THE MONTH CLUB
in September 1999.
Available at your favorite retail outlet.

Membership in this family has its privileges
...and its price.
But what a fortune can't buy,
a true-bred Texas love is sure to bring!

Coming in October 1999...

The Baby Pursuit

by

LAURIE PAIGE

When the newest Fortune heir was kidnapped, the
prominent family turned to Devin Kincaid to find the
missing baby. The dedicated FBI agent never expected
his investigation might lead him to the altar with
society princess Vanessa Fortune....

THE FORTUNES OF TEXAS continues with
Expecting... In Texas by **Marie Ferrarella**,
available in November 1999 from
Silhouette Books.

Available at your favorite retail outlet.

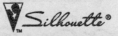